The Challenge

From the moment Arabella stepped into the ballroom, she knew the night would be out of the ordinary. There was a level of excitement she had never encountered before. And then she recognized its source: Jake Deverell. And within minutes she realized the gossips hadn't done him justice.

He was a man with a powerful, thrilling way of making her feel, and at the same time capable of threatening her in ways she couldn't even begin to imagine. And she now knew with a bone-deep certainty that while she didn't fear him, Jake Deverell was a man of whom she should definitely be wary.

Before she could act on that insight, however, Jake put his mouth to her ear and whispered, "I'll be in your bed by morning."

Originally published as The Destiny

The SWANSEA DESTINY

Fayrene Preston

FANFARE™

BANTAM BOOKS

NEW YORK • TORONTO • LONDON • SYDNEY • AUCKLAND

This edition contains the complete text of the original hardcover edition. Not one word has been omitted.

THE SWANSEA DESTINY
A Bantam Fanfare Book

PRINTING HISTORY
Originally published as The Destiny
Doubleday edition published July 1991
Bantam edition / October 1991

FANFARE and the portrayal of a boxed "ff" are trademarks of Bantam Books, a division of Bantam Doubleday Dell Publishing Group, Inc.

For information address:
Doubleday, 666 Fifth Avenue, New York, NY 10103.

ISBN 0-553-29332-X

Published simultaneously in the United States and Canada

Bantam Books are published by Bantam Books, a division of Bantam Doubleday Dell Publishing Group, Inc. Its trademark, consisting of the words "Bantam Books" and the portrayal of a rooster, is Registered in U.S. Patent and Trademark Office and in other countries. Marca Registrada. Bantam Books, 666 Fifth Avenue, New York, New York 10103.

Printed in the United States of America

OPM 0 9 8 7 6 5 4 3 2 1

To my sweet, beautiful cousin
Laura Lind,
for all the love and support
throughout the years

The
SWANSEA DESTINY

PROLOGUE

Boston 1918

Jake Conall glared through the pale morning sunlight that filtered through the small window of the kitchen at an older man standing on the opposite side of a chipped table.

"You're one lousy sonofabitch!" Jake said, his voice low, but redolent with anger.

Not so much as a flicker of emotion showed on Edward Deverell's face as he viewed the son whom he'd rarely thought of until recently. "I'm sure it gives you a sense of satisfaction to say so, Jacob, but I'm sorry to have to inform you that your opinion of me is not one I haven't heard before."

"Only my mother calls me Jacob."

"Very well . . . Jake. Have you considered my offer?"

"I've considered it." In fact, he'd thought of little else since he'd come home the previous week on the afternoon of his eighteenth birthday and found a stranger in the tiny, dingy apartment he had lived in all his life. The stranger had introduced himself as Edward Deverell, a name that had rung a bell with even a tenement kid like himself. Then Deverell had informed him that he was his father and had gone on to make him an offer that would change his whole life—if he accepted. A week had passed, but Jake still hadn't made a decision.

"I want to know something. You've gone to a lot of trouble to find me. You hired detectives, and then you had lawyers draw up papers for this agreement you want me to sign. And I want to know why! Dammit, why did you decide to do this after all these years? You wanted me killed before I was ever born, and when Mother told you she was going to have me anyway, you turned your back on her and had nothing more to do with her."

A flicker of displeasure marred Edward Deverell's impassive expression as he recalled that time. "Gwendolyn was a stubborn woman. She could have had a comfortable life if she had done as I asked."

"If she had done as you asked, I wouldn't be here for you to make your damned offer to."

"Then things turned out well."

"Well?" Jake took a step closer to him, his lips curled, his teeth bared. "She couldn't afford good medical care and she nearly died giving birth to me.

Then, to keep a roof over our heads and put food on the table, she had to take in sewing. Today she's close to blind because of the long hours she spent hunched over a piece of cloth."

"That is regrettable."

"Regrettable?" Jake swung a closed fist toward Edward, but at the last minute whirled away and braced his hands against the edge of the sink, his shoulder and back muscles bunching beneath his ill-fitting jacket.

Edward watched him with cold calculation. Even after reading the detective's reports, he hadn't been at all sure what his son might be like. The reports had mentioned a Lucas Moran, Jake's best friend. The two had been involved in running numbers, street fights, petty thefts, but no serious brushes with the law. All in all Edward was relieved; it could have been much worse given the circumstances under which his son had been raised.

Jake reminded him of himself at the same age—a sleek young animal, powerful, hungry, and bloodthirsty. He squelched the thought. In truth, he resented Jake's youth and physical strength—two things his money and power could not return to him. And he loathed the fact that his beloved son, John, had been killed half a world away in the war, thus forcing him to seek out his bastard. Fate had indeed played him a cruel trick.

Jake suddenly turned. "You have a hell of a way with words, old man." He saw Deverell flinch and realized "old man" had pricked. He almost grinned. "Regrettable. That's really good. My mother's eyesight has been ruined, and it's regrettable. Does a Harvard education teach you to use words like that?"

"I did not have the advantage of a Harvard education."

"Maybe not, but you had the means to see to it that Mother's life was made easier, damn you."

"She disobeyed me."

Jake swallowed back the bile that rose in his throat. His mother had always refused to speak of his father—who he was, if he was alive or dead. But when Jake was five he overheard a quiet, stilted conversation his mother had with a friend. She'd talked about a man who had walked away from her because she wouldn't end her baby's life before it was born. From that moment on, Jake had found it easy to hate the unknown man.

And now Deverell had come to him, twice, as a matter of fact, driven by a uniformed chauffeur and wearing fancy clothes. But Deverell had made a bad mistake. Because now Jake not only knew he was his father but also could focus his hatred.

Edward shifted his weight from one leg to the other, the oppressive heaviness of Jake's deep, raging anger unsettling him. "We're getting off the point."

"No, we're not. The point is and has always been your refusal to admit that I'm your son. Even now." He jabbed a finger toward the papers Edward had laid out on an oilskin-covered table. "You're only willing to say you're adopting me."

Edward cleared his throat. "I have thought the matter through, and I feel it's better that society think I have made an altruistic gesture to an underprivileged boy than know I fathered an illegitimate son."

Jake's black eyes narrowed. "Better for who?"

"It is the way I wish it."

"Then why the hell even bother if you're so damned ashamed of me?"

"I shouldn't have to explain this to you, Jake. It seems so clear. I want an heir, someone to carry on what I've started."

"Heirs are a dime a dozen at the orphanage. You'll find plenty of kids there who would fight each other for the right to sign your agreement and take everything you're offering."

Irritation crept into Edward's tone. "I don't want someone from the orphanage. I want to adopt *you.*"

"Right, adopt, but not acknowledge, because you don't want your rich friends to know you had a bastard. But guess what? I don't give a damn what your society friends think. In fact, I think they should know, and I don't see a thing keeping me from going to the newspapers and telling everything."

He would have been disappointed, Edward thought, if Jake hadn't realized the potent threat public exposure would make. "Do that," he said quietly, "and you'll be cutting your own throat."

"I'm tough. My throat doesn't cut so easily."

"But what about your mother, Jake? Accept my offer and you'll be in a position to give her everything she's ever wanted."

"I've been bringing home money for years. I'll do even better next year, now that I'm finally through with school."

"I said *everything* she's ever wanted, Jake."

"I can give her those things without your help. I have plans."

"Really? And how long will these plans take you? How much prison time will be involved? How much more sewing will your mother have to do?" He had him now, Edward thought, and gave a nonchalant shrug. "I can't see what there is to object to here. I'm offering you my name, a first-rate education, a prominent social standing, and a fortune."

Jake forced himself to calm down, to think, to get himself back on track. "On the surface it's a great offer."

"Above and below the surface too."

"Then tell me why you want to adopt *me*. Not someone from the orphanage. *Me*."

The reason was apparent, and Edward saw no choice but to make the admission. "Because you're the only one left with my blood in your veins."

Some of Jake's tension eased. He had needed to hear Deverell say those words. "Exactly. The way I figure it, old man, you need me more than I need you. So I guess it comes down to how *much* you need me."

"I honestly don't know what more you could want, Jake. I've asked—and this is all in the agreement—that you attend Harvard for four years and obtain a degree in business. During that time I expect you to acquire the polish and social contacts that you will need later on to conduct business and move in the society in which the Deverell name will carry you. Upon graduation you will have a job waiting for you in my company. Eventually you will inherit everything. And you'll have sons of your own to carry on. Through you, the Deverell blood and tradition will continue. What more could you want?"

"Damned good question." Jake grinned, but his dark eyes did not lighten with humor. "I spent an afternoon in the library reading old newspaper clippings about you, and I found out some interesting things. That house of yours, for instance. *SwanSea.* From everything I read, you're damned proud of it. You moved into the house and married about the same time. There was an interview from back then. Said how you saw the house as the seat of some sort of dynasty, and how you wanted sons and daughters to fill it."

"The article did not say that."

"Between the lines it did."

Edward stared back at his son, wondering if he had underestimated him. And then he heard Jake's voice lower, harden, until each word he spoke was like stone striking stone.

"You walk into my life from out of the blue and

make me an offer that will change my life forever. It seems like such a grand thing for you to do, such a generous gesture, but the truth is, I'm your last chance for immortality and you damned well know it."

A charged silence filled the small room, and Gwendolyn Conall, standing in the kitchen doorway, thought she could actually feel the force of their energies and wills colliding, thickening the atmosphere with tension until she didn't know how they could breathe.

She wished the oil lamp were lit. The room was illuminated by a narrow shaft of sunlight, but their figures were still dim to her. She adjusted her glasses, trying better to see the two men, the one, a man who had once been everything to her, the other, the boy who had never really had a chance to be a boy and who was her heart.

She wondered if they knew how much alike they were, father and son, both with the same coal-black hair, both with the same prideful stance and stubborn arrogance. Age had lined Edward's face and had added silver at his temples, but he still stood ramrod straight.

Jacob was a tougher, bigger version of Edward—handsome, smart, and cunning. She wanted the world for him, but life had made her a realist and she knew the only way he could have it was to take Edward's offer. *Dear Lord, please don't let his pride get in his way.* She offered the quick, silent prayer, knowing it was all she could do. It was between the two of them.

"Go to hell, old man!" Jake hurled the epithet toward Deverell. Then a feeling more than a sound drew his glance to the door, and he saw his mother walking away. Damn, he hoped she wasn't upset by what she'd heard. His impulse was to throw Deverell's offer in his face, then kill him. But staring after his mother as she went into her room, he suddenly realized Deverell was right about at least one thing. If he accepted him, he could give her all the things he'd always wanted to give her, starting almost immediately. She'd never have to sew another stitch. He'd never have to see her squint, or her fingers bleed, or her face look drawn and tired.

Besides, even at eighteen he'd learned there were more ways to kill a person than with a knife or a gun. To refuse the offer would dent Deverell's ego and spoil his plans for the future. But in the long run, Jake thought, if he accepted the offer just right, he could inflict more damage than by plunging a knife straight through the old man's heart. Yeah, Deverell would pay for what he had done.

"All right," Jake finally said, "but get your lawyers, because I have some terms of my own and I want them spelled out in that agreement. I'll take your name, the education, the money, and the social standing and prestige you talked about. Given time, I'll run your business better than you've ever thought of doing. But that's where what you get out of this deal stops. I want it understood that I'm going to be my own man. No one calls the shots on what I do and don't do, especially you. If I do what you want, it'll be because it's what I think best."

Edward permitted a small smile of victory to show on his face. The boy was full of himself and remarkably self-possessed for one so young. Jake would eventually come around to his way of thinking when he understood better the world into which he would be moving. "Of course."

"And I want SwanSea."

Edward's body jerked, but he quickly masked his alarm. "Naturally, as my adopted son, people will expect you to spend time there."

"No. I mean I want it to be mine."

"And you'll have it. You'll inherit it when I die." He tasted bitterness even as he said the words. Somehow he had supposed he and SwanSea would go on together until the end of time.

"No, you don't understand. If we make this agreement, I want the deed to SwanSea in my name right away, and I want you to walk out of the house and leave it forever."

"You can't be serious. It's my home and has been for twenty-three years."

"It will be my home now." Cruelty shaped his smile. "I'm going to make a mockery of your dreams, old man, and that includes SwanSea."

Edward sank into the chair. "I need time to think about this."

"You have two minutes."

Edward was alarmed to feel his hand tremble as he

rubbed his brow. How could he acquiesce to these demands? How could he leave SwanSea? He had watched the house built stone by stone. It was the only romantic dream he had ever allowed himself; it was a part of him and represented all he had accomplished. If he wasn't so appalled and furious, he might admire this bastard son of his who had temporarily bested him. But he *was* appalled. SwanSea was like his life's blood, and even now he could feel a pain growing in his gut at the thought of giving it up. But what was his alternative?

He was sixty-four years old, too old to father another child and wait for it to grow up, too old to start over. If he hadn't made the mistake of allowing John to go off on that damned grand tour, then he wouldn't have become involved in the war and been killed. He couldn't afford to make another mistake. His name and all he had accomplished had to be perpetuated—even if it meant acceding to this hoodlum's wishes. Besides, he had a trump card and he intended to use it. "All right, Jake. On the day you graduate from Harvard, SwanSea will be yours."

Jake's head came up and his eyes widened, like a wary animal sensing a trap. Waiting until he graduated wasn't what he'd had in mind, but now that he thought about it, he figured he would be pretty busy for the next four years. He planned to beat those Harvard people at their own game, whatever it was. "Okay, it's a deal."

Edward nodded. "Fine. I'll be in touch after my lawyers have redrafted the agreement."

He'd won. The knowledge rushed through Jake with a force that was dizzying.

Edward rose and started to leave, but then he stopped and looked back at Jake. "No matter what you say now, you will come to care for SwanSea. You won't be able to help yourself. You're a Deverell, and SwanSea stands for what we're all about. It is in your blood to accomplish great things and to carry on where I leave off. It's your destiny."

Jake smiled. "We'll see, old man. We'll see."

1

SwanSea
Maine
December 31, 1928

A young beauty stood atop a huge table, its base three nude crystal nymphs. Her most recent claim to fame resulted from being hoisted on the trunk of an elephant in a jungle number for the Ziegfeld Follies. But now, waiters poured jeroboams of the finest French bootlegged champagne into a towering pyramid of crystal glasses on the table, and the girl bent to dispense them, offering the guests enticing views of her scantily clad bosom.

At the other end of the ballroom, a flapper danced atop a gleaming mahogany grand piano, twirling and slapping her derriere in time to "The Black Bottom." As she danced, an admirer grabbed a shapely ankle and she tumbled gaily into his arms.

Jacob Deverell stood to one side of the glittering ballroom and lazily surveyed the chaotic merriment.

It was not yet midnight, but the party was in full swing. All in all, this gathering differed in only two respects from the hundreds of other parties he had given here at SwanSea since he had graduated from Harvard seven years before: It was New Year's Eve, and it was snowing outside.

A fire roared in the mammoth marble fireplace at one end of the room, but no one Jake saw looked as if they needed the warmth of its flames. The fuel of the night was champagne, and it was flowing like Niagara Falls.

Lucas Moran ambled up, an amused expression on his good-looking, intelligent face. "You've got one hell of a volatile mix here tonight, Jake old boy. The corrupt, the powerful, the glamorous, the dangerous, even a damned reporter to cover it all. I think the only groups not represented are nuns and orphans."

"A diverse mix is what gives a party its energy."

Lucas nodded casually. "Energy's nice. Explosive is bad, very bad."

Jake grinned, appreciating both his friend's wit and company. Lucas stood shoulder to shoulder with him and always had, even before they had started school. But where he was powerfully built, Lucas had a wiry grace. And they were different in coloring and temperament. Lucas was light where he was dark. Lucas's eyes were colored like the day, clear and sky-blue. Jake's eyes were like the night sky, black and opaque. Lucas was more cautious, yet at the same time more easygoing. Jake was headstrong and driven, and he freely admitted it.

When they were kids, their mothers called them night and day because, they said, it was sometimes hard to tell where one left off and the other began.

"What in particular is bothering you tonight, Lucas?"

"Two of Wade Scalia's men are here."

"Ram and Barton. I saw them."

"Then why in the hell haven't you thrown them out yet?"

"They're not causing any trouble. I thought I'd let them enjoy the party for a while. They even wore their spats. Elegant, don't you think?"

Lucas chuckled. "Look at them. They're over there flirting with two of last year's debutantes."

Jake's gaze followed Lucas's, then narrowed with cynicism when he saw them. The two girls were having the time of their lives, taking full advantage of the opportunity to have a relatively safe encounter with known gangsters. They were out for a thrill, and they were getting it.

Lucas pulled a slim silver case from the pocket of his tuxedo jacket, extracted a cigarillo, and lit it. "And what about Noah Calloway?" he asked after exhaling a stream of smoke.

Viewing Scalia's men as harmless, Jake had lost track of them after their arrival. But at any given moment of the evening he had known where the Treasury agent was. Noah Calloway was a man of medium height and build and had the ability to blend in with any crowd. Right now he was standing beside the entrance to the ballroom, his hands in the pockets of his conservatively cut tuxedo, watching without expression the ebb and flow of the party. A waiter approached and offered him a glass of champagne. Calloway waved him and the bootlegged wine away. Jake smiled. Calloway was obviously out for something bigger than a private cache, however large, of illegal hooch. "I assume he'll let me know what he wants when he's ready."

Lucas nodded. "He's a good guy. Too bad he's a T-man."

Jake laid his hand on his friend's back. "That's an interesting kind of prejudice you have there. Besides, admit it, not everyone can make the wise career decisions you and I have made."

Lucas threw back his head and laughed, a booming sound that mixed perfectly into the happy, high-spirited jazz being played.

Jake laughed too, then heard the volume of noise in the large room drop a level. Surprised, he glanced around to see what had attracted everyone's attention and saw a young woman standing in the doorway. She was wearing a short, sleeveless evening dress that was embroidered in silver and matte gold and drenched in gold sequins along with thousands of tiny silver beads and paillettes. Circling her softly waved white-gold hair was a wide band of the same brilliants that drizzled onto her forehead and sparkled against her ivory skin.

She looked like light.

And in front of her stood two magnificent snow-white peacocks wearing diamond collars. She held their golden leashes in her left hand.

Within moments she was surrounded by admiring men.

"Nice entrance," Lucas murmured.

Jake stared at the group, wondering at the sudden tightening in his gut. "That's Arabella Linden, isn't it?"

"Yeah, she's Kenneth's sister. I was with you when he phoned and asked if a room could be made available for her. Don't you remember?"

"Yeah, I remember." Jake swiveled to face Lucas. "I saw her arrive this afternoon and thought I recognized her from pictures in the society sections of the papers. She had two maids and fifteen suitcases in tow, but there wasn't a peacock in sight."

"Interesting. Offhand I'd say she's worked a small miracle."

"Why? Because she managed to produce two albino peacocks out of those suitcases?"

"No, because she managed to attract your attention."

Jake shrugged dismissively. "She's just another spoiled little rich girl."

"Yeah, sure. You're probably right." Lucas put two fingers to his forehead in a salute. "See you later. I'm going to go rescue the two guys standing over there with Vanessa. From here it looks as if they're arguing over her and she's had about enough."

"Better hurry," Jake advised in a wry drawl, "or she'll deck them right where they stand."

Arabella smiled and laughed at the men who circled her, all the time taking in what was happening all over the ballroom. She saw a man throw a giggling woman over his shoulder and carry her out the door. And there was a woman wearing a low-backed dress, lying stomach down on a sideboard with several men taking turns sipping champagne from the valley formed by her spine. In Boston, she went out four or five nights of the week, but the sheer opulence, glitter, and near-the-edge-of-control wildness of *this* party was beyond her experience.

As was Jake Deverell. He stood to one side, yet it was clear *he* was the center of the party. He was at least six feet tall, she judged, and heavily muscled beneath his finely tailored black evening suit. His jaw was square and hard, his hair and eyes were black, and his gaze held enough intensity to cut a diamond.

There were stories about him. Some said he was the new financial genius behind the Deverell business, yet they also said he was out to ruin the Deverell name. They said he was involved in a myriad of illegal activities. They said he had a new woman every week. They said he was dangerous. Only one thing was certain: He was the master of this great house. It was time, Arabella thought, to meet the master.

As the orchestra swung into "Lady, Be Good," Jake glanced back at Arabella's group, just in time to see people clearing a path for her as she walked toward him, the peacocks stately and exotic before her.

"Mr. Deverell, I'm Arabella Linden."

Her voice was more musical than the music being played, he thought. "Yes, I know. And I'm Jake."

She fluttered her fingers at the peacocks. "I hope you don't mind me bringing my little friends into your home."

"Not at all."

"I decided they'd be appropriate because of the peacock design of SwanSea's grand staircase. The staircase is as famous as your parties." She sent a cool glance around the ballroom, then looked squarely at Jake. "I know several people who publicly declared they would die if they weren't invited to one of your parties before the last year of the decade began."

"Is that right?"

She nodded solemnly. "Yes, indeed."

The sparkle of amusement he saw secreted in the depths of her golden eyes took him by surprise. "And are they here, these people?"

"I don't see them. I may have a lot of funerals to attend when I return to Boston."

He reached out and briefly encircled her throat with his hand, resting his thumb on the pulse at the base of her neck. "If that's the case, I'm glad *you* came, because I'd hate like hell to see you cold and in a grave."

The rhythm of her breathing was momentarily disrupted. Without much thought, she'd thrown out one of her outrageous "party" statements, and just as casually he'd returned a touch that somehow hadn't seemed casual at all.

"I didn't say *I'd* die."

"No," he said thoughtfully. "You didn't. Tell me, Arabella, is there anything you'd die for?"

It had been a long time since a man had challenged her with anything unexpected. Jake Deverell was everything she had ever heard and more, and the fact pleased her on some impersonal level. Her laugh came lightly and easily. "Let's see . . . I'd die for a sea of snow-white orchids and a crystal goblet of moonstones."

"What else?"

"A gleaming mountain of pearls and white-chocolate ice cream with diamond sauce."

"What else?"

One smooth, powdered shoulder rose and fell. "I'm not sure there really is anything else."

He gazed steadfastly at her, then looked down at her dress and flicked one of the silver beads that lay over her breast. "You have unusual tastes."

"Judging by this party," she said, careful to keep her voice even, "so do you."

"Yes, I do like to taste the unusual and rare."

He was looking at her, she reflected, as if he wanted to take a bite out of her. For a split second she considered the possibility that the experience might be worth the pain, then, slightly shocked at herself, dismissed the thought.

"And how do wild, exotic white peacocks fit into your life, Arabella?"

"Beautifully. They fit beautifully." She drew a waiter to her just by looking at him and took a glass of champagne with her free right hand.

He was no longer touching her, but his slow smile burned its way through her silver- and gold-beaded dress to her skin.

"I should have guessed that answer."

"You would have if you'd given yourself a little more time."

The thread of laughter that ran beneath her reassuring tone further intrigued him. Unlike most women, she wasn't showing a trace of sexual interest in him. As a matter of fact, she appeared completely natural and was obviously having a great deal of fun. But he was too experienced, too knowledgeable about women and society to believe her flirtation was all innocent.

She was watching someone, and Jake glanced over his shoulder to see who had taken her attention away from him. It was Kenneth Linden flirting with a pretty young thing while she propped her leg on a chair and adjusted her garter. He looked back at Arabella with speculation. "I can't imagine your having to rely on your brother to escort you to a New Year's Eve party."

She replaced the scarcely touched glass of champagne on a waiter's tray and sent him on his way with a smile. "Really? And do you have a good imagination?"

Irritation prickled at him. Her effortless replies didn't seem to be intended to charm him, yet were doing just that. "No one has ever complained about my imagination."

She smiled sweetly. "I'm sure they haven't."

"So answer my question. Why are you with your brother?"

She gave him a look that said the answer was obvious and she was astonished he would even ask. "I always choose with whom I want to be, and for tonight and for the next few days, I chose my brother. And, of course, the peacocks."

There were so many things he could say or ask, but he decided it would be more interesting to follow her lead and see where she took him. "The peacocks . . . do you often take them to parties?"

"Hardly ever, actually, but this is a special occasion."

"How's that?"

With a grace and graciousness that could only be inborn, she extended her bare arm and handed him the golden leashes. "Because I brought the peacocks for you. To thank you for saying I could come tonight and stay for the house party."

He stared thoughtfully down at the leashes in his hand. "You know, grand staircase or no grand staircase, most people bring wine to their host."

The spark of amusement in her eyes became more pronounced. "Haven't you heard of Prohibition?"

The idea that rumors about his bootlegging had reached her caused him neither amazement nor disturbance. His gaze dropped to the soft curve of her lips. "So, Arabella, you brought me a pair of peacocks for saying you could come to my New Year's Eve party. I wonder what you'd give me if I really put myself out and did something truly extraordinary for you."

"Could you? Do something extraordinary for me, I mean?"

Suddenly his expression seemed sharper, more dangerous. He didn't answer, but merely looked at her. She wasn't slow. She knew that flirting with Jake Deverell was an entirely different matter than flirting with the young men in her crowd. But she saw no reason to be intimidated by him or to change her ways, even temporarily. And she was curious. He had let her get away with the Prohibition remark. He might decide not to let her get by with her flirtatious question. She waited.

"I'll work on it," he said softly, and at the same time made a motion with his hands that drew a silver-haired, exceedingly dignified man to him. "How are things going, Marlon?"

"Reasonably well, I'd say, sir."

"Splendid. Well, it seems, Marlon, that we have two new pets. Would you mind taking them to Bernardo?" He handed him the peacocks' golden leashes. "Thank you." Marlon nodded and turned away. The peacocks followed, their tails spread into snow-white fans. "Marlon is my majordomo," he said to her by way of explanation, "and Bernardo is my head groundskeeper."

"I know."

He stared at her and after a moment nodded. "Of course you do."

"Both men were of great help."

"I'm glad to hear it." His mouth twisted wryly. "Most of the staff has been here since SwanSea was built. They don't really approve of me, but for SwanSea's sake they tolerate me."

"Tolerate?" The idea of the man before her passively accepting anything startled her. "I'm surprised you haven't replaced them."

"If a man has a job that he likes and he's reasonably good at it, he should be able to keep it."

"That's a rather marvelous way of thinking."

He shrugged away her praise. "It's only practical. I like to be comfortable, and I have no wish to spend days interviewing a new household staff." Wade Scalia's men were returning to the ballroom from the bar that was set up outside in the hallway, he noticed. Each of them had a highball glass in hand. Scotch, undoubtedly, Jake thought. It was not only their favorite beverage but also their source of support.

"Who is that woman who keeps watching us?" Arabella asked suddenly. "The one sitting on top of the sideboard over there."

Jake threw a glance over his shoulder, quickly spotting the woman to whom Arabella referred. Her shingled hair was hennaed and her cheeks and lips were rouged. And the fringe that formed the skirt on the short red chemise she wore was coming off, strand by strand, as she gave it to the three men standing in a semi-circle before her. One shapely thigh was already exposed. "That's Marian Talbot," Jake said, his gaze returning to Arabella. "She's my date for the holiday."

"Date?" Arabella was shocked. Or was she disappointed? No, she told herself, she couldn't be feeling either of those emotions. If she had given the matter any thought at all, she would have known he wouldn't be alone. But he'd been paying such close attention to her, she had simply assumed there was no one at the party who was special to him.

"Date." He flicked at one of the brilliants that dripped from her headband onto her forehead and watched the play of light over her skin.

"She's ruining her dress," she said, all at once finding it difficult to breathe. No man on such short acquaintance had ever dared touch her as Jake was doing.

"It doesn't matter. She has dozens of others upstairs."

She took a step back from him, an automatic action, almost as though it might help her see him better. But his expression remained enigmatic and she had no clue as to what, if anything, he might feel for the girl. "She's trying to make you jealous, you know."

"Then she's wasting her time," he said flatly, "because I don't get jealous."

"Never?"

"Never." Ram and Barton, he noted, were idle at the moment. And Noah Calloway had moved from his position by the door and had come deeper into the ballroom. He mentally cursed. He supposed it was time to do a little housecleaning. Jake reached for Arabella's hand and raised it to his lips. "Enjoy the party."

She saw Jake motion to a tall, sandy-haired man and then he disappeared into the crowd. Without being aware of what she was doing, Arabella put one hand over the other, covering the spot where his lips had been.

Jake dropped his elegantly shod feet onto the rich, exotic citron wood surface of the big desk in the study, leaned back in his chair, and viewed Ram and Barton with what appeared to be mild interest. "Scalia has all bootlegging sewed up from Boston south to New York and beyond. What does he want with our operation?"

"You don't have to turn over the entire thing to him, Jake," Ram said. He was a thickset man with thinning hair and narrow eyes, and he was smart enough to be Wade's right-hand man. "He'll accept a percentage of your net."

"But it has to be the percentage he says," Barton added, "and he has a hefty number in mind." Barton was tall and broad-shouldered, with a small scar on his cheek and a nose that showed signs of being broken more than once.

Jake grinned at Lucas, who was leaning against a bookcase. "I think Wade's been drinking too much of his product."

"I think Wade's just flat out lost his mind," Lucas said in a drawl that didn't disguise the steely determination underlying his words.

Ram shifted uncomfortably in his chair. "Look, gents, we're only delivering the message, but if I was you two, I'd pay attention. Wade Scalia is a big cheese, and he don't take it too kindly when things don't go his way."

"That's right," Barton chimed in. "And he feels you're making too much money out of your territory. You don't need it, he says, being as how you got all the Deverell money you want."

Jake spread his hands out, a gesture implying that he was puzzled. "You know, it's funny. I don't remember ever giving a damn about what Wade thinks or feels, but let me consult my partner on this. What do you say, Lucas? Do you remember ever giving a damn about what Wade thinks?"

"Can't say as I do."

Jake suddenly dropped his feet to the floor and stood. "Sorry, boys, but I think you made a trip for nothing. I'll have one of the butlers find your coats. Have a nice drive back to Boston."

"Coats?" Ram looked at Barton with disbelief.

"You ain't sending us out on a night like this, are you?" Barton asked, glancing from Jake to Lucas and back again.

"There's a snowstorm out there!"

"No, really?" Lucas pushed away from the bookcase and followed Jake to the door. "Gee, that's too bad. But you see, guys, you came here uninvited, and we don't have any room for gate-crashers."

"We'll sleep in the kitchen," Ram offered.

"Sorry," Jake said at the door. "That's where my dogs sleep. Good-bye, gentlemen."

2

"HORSEFEATHERS, Bella, I saw the way you were flirting with Jake." Kenneth Linden shook his head with exasperation, his feelings decidedly mixed about his sister being at SwanSea. He was a tall man with a receding hairline made more pronounced because he combed it straight back. But he had attractive masculine features and golden-brown eyes that women couldn't seem to resist. "The trouble with you is you began flirting in the cradle and you never stopped."

Just then the band started an exuberant rendition of "Runnin' Wild." A girl wearing a pink sequined dress and a headband that sported a lush pink feather took to the dance floor. Doing the shimmy, her arms outstretched, she was delectable with her thighs flashing and her bottom swiveling. The sight sent a passing waiter stumbling, but Kenneth rescued the last glass of champagne from the man's silver tray and took a deep drink.

Arabella viewed her brother from beneath her lashes and wondered with concern how many glasses of wine he had had so far. It wasn't even midnight yet. "Really, Kenneth, you're exaggerating. Jake Deverell is our host. I was merely thanking him for having me. By the way, I think he liked the peacocks."

"More than likely he'll have the cook make peacock stew tomorrow. Now, listen to me. Mother and Dad wouldn't be too keen if they knew you were here—"

"How are they going to find out unless you take it upon yourself to cable them in Europe? Besides, Papa brought me here himself once when he had business with Edward Deverell."

"That's different. You were a little girl then. And in case you hadn't noticed, Jake runs an entirely different house from Edward Deverell's."

She had noticed. "Oh, applesauce, Kenneth. Isn't it a little late to suddenly begin playing the overprotective brother?"

With a frown he took out a handkerchief square and patted his damp forehead. "You're my baby sister, and I'm responsible for bringing you here."

A negligent wave of her hand told him what she thought of his reasoning. "I insisted. Anyway, SwanSea is one of the most famous houses in the country, not some terrible den of iniquity." She darted a quick glance around the room and told herself she wasn't looking for Jake. But she did happen to note that he was nowhere to be seen.

"It's all in the perspective, kiddo. At any rate, I want you to pay attention to me because I know what I'm talking about. Jake Deverell is not a man to trifle with."

An emotion showed on his face, and just for a moment she thought it might be fear. She was well aware she was overly sensitive where he was concerned these days, but it had almost sounded as if his warning had been meant for himself as well as her. "Kenneth? What's wrong?"

"What? Nothing. What could be wrong? All I'm saying is be polite to him, but save your flirting for someone else. When Jake and I were at Harvard together . . ." His voice trailed off.

"What, Kenneth?"

"Never mind. It's not important." He had been about to tell her about the Wellesley girls who had been wild over Jake and gone to great lengths to gain his attention, but then he had remembered the older woman with whom Jake had been involved the entire four years they had been at Cambridge. He was sure Arabella would be fascinated to hear about that woman, but she wasn't going to hear it from him. *Lord,* his head felt as if it were swimming. He shouldn't have skipped the buffet table, he supposed, but his nerves had been jumping and he'd gone straight for the hooch.

Arabella hooked her arm in his with a deliberate

casualness. "You know what I'd really like? A cup of coffee. I'll bet you a nickel we can find some coffee if we really look. What do you say?"

He patted her hand. "Sounds like a swell idea. In fact, I think I'll go sit down in a corner somewhere and have a rest. Bring me back a cup of coffee, and I'll give you a dime."

"Big spender," she teased, but she was worried as she watched him make his way across the dance floor, weaving around the wildly gyrating couples dancing to a jazzy number. She had the real and unhappy feeling he needed more than a cup of coffee or a plate of food. He was her big brother, four years older than she, and she had idolized him from the time she was old enough to toddle after him. But now at twenty-five she felt much older. She knew something was bothering him—and had been for some time. That was why she had finagled an invitation to accompany him to SwanSea. She had hoped that spending time together away from Boston might ease his tension and make it easier for him to tell her what was wrong. She fervently prayed he wasn't gambling again.

The band segued into a slower pace with "I'll See You in My Dreams," and Jasper Wellington, the handsome young scion of a prominent Boston family, a man she had known for years, swept her onto the dance floor.

"You're holding me too tightly, Jas," Arabella said, laughing.

"I can't help myself! You're sooo bea-u-ti-fuuul. I'm *overcome*!"

She patted him on the shoulder, reflecting wryly that the alcohol content of the hooch must be pretty high tonight. "I don't think it's me that's overcome you, Jas."

"Yes, yes, you have! And you'd make me the happiest man alive if you would say you'd be my wife."

Arabella sighed. "I can't marry you, Jas. Remember? I've already told you several times. I can't marry you because I'm not in love with you."

"Oh, that's right."

"But I'm dancing with you, Jas. Doesn't that make you happy?"

He brightened. "Yes, you're right! It does."

"Excuse me, but I'm cutting in."

Jas turned to the dark-complected man who had tapped him on the shoulder. "Jake! Nice to see you, old boy! And great timing. You'll never guess what's happened. Arabella won't marry me, but she has consented to make me happy by dancing with me."

"That's nice, Jas," he said without once taking his eyes off Arabella, "but now she's going to make me happy by dancing with me. Isn't that right, Arabella?"

"I'm not sure," she said with a feigned indifference made difficult to maintain by her racing pulse. "I did promise to make Jas happy."

The corners of his mouth lifted. "He looks happy to me. Jas? You're happy, aren't you?"

"Jake's right, Arabella. I'm really happy."

"Then that's settled."

With a suddenness that left her dizzy, Jake drew her out of Jasper's arms into his, and danced away with her just as the band switched to the slowest version she had ever heard of "It Had to Be You."

"You look surprised," he said after a moment. "Did you really think I wouldn't come back to you?"

"I never gave it a thought," she lied with perfect equanimity.

"Jas didn't seem too cut up about your turning down his marriage proposal."

"He's used to my rejections. Besides, when he's drunk, he's like a child, easily diverted."

"I'm cold sober and you're going to have a hell of a time diverting me."

"From what?" she asked, quite sure no girl with a modicum of sense would have done so, much less follow up with the next question. "Are you going to ask me to marry you?"

Her silver and gold dress had a low back, as most of her evening frocks did, but her dance partners always kept their hands at her waist. Jake's hand rested flat on her bare back, the tips of his fingers in the valley of her spine. And when he moved his fingers, as he did occasionally, it sent a burning shiver through her.

He smiled down at her, his lips full and sensual. "I wouldn't be able to stand the rejection when you said no."

"That's a very gallant answer."

"Enjoy it. It may be the last gallant thing I ever say to you."

She swallowed, wondering why they seemed to be dancing even slower than the song called for. The hard, steel-corded muscles in his thighs, stomach, and chest pressed against her as they moved to the music, making her wildly sensitive to the amazing extent of his masculinity and strength. "I hope your date doesn't mind you dancing with me."

A dark brow quirked over amused black eyes. "Do you really care what she thinks?"

"Are you really so hard that you don't?"

He didn't answer, and that bothered her more than anything he might have said.

"Where is she?" She tried to look around the ballroom, but at that moment he drew her even more firmly against him and whirled the two of them in a different direction to avoid a collision with another couple. The beads of her dress clicked together and created a blinding blur of light as the short skirt flew outward, wrapped high on her legs, then settled again.

"She's not here. She's on her way back to Boston."

She drew in a sharp breath. "Tonight? In the snow?"

"The snow has died down considerably. She'll be all right. My chauffeur is driving her. Besides, I'm sure they won't be the only ones out on the road tonight."

His scent drifted around her, compellingly primal

and singularly masculine. Surely he wasn't holding her any more tightly than Jas had, yet she couldn't remember this particular sweet sensation she was feeling as her breasts brushed against the hard wall of his chest. She drew a ragged breath, unintentionally increasing the sensation. "Was it her idea to leave?"

Jake's hand clasped hers tighter, turned it, and drew it inward. The back of his hand was pressing into her breast. This whole dance, she thought shakily, was too intimate.

His dark, glittering gaze held hers. "You don't need me to answer that, do you?"

She heard the bandleader say, "Ten seconds to midnight."

"You asked her to leave," she said.

"Yes."

People were counting. There was a roaring in her ears. "Because of me."

"Yes."

Horns blew. People shouted. Glittering confetti and multicolored streamers came tumbling down from the frescoed ceiling painted and inlaid with silver, gold, and mother-of-pearl swans and peacocks.

"Happy New Year, Arabella," Jake said right before he bent his head and took possession of her mouth.

And it *was* a possession. In that split second, as a fiery shock raced through her, every kiss she had ever received faded from her memory. And reality as she knew it was suspended as his lips commanded, demanded a response.

She sensed grave danger. She could feel him pulling her into a shimmering web of sensuality so strong that if she gave in and went, she wasn't sure she would ever be able to break free. But, at least for this small moment out of time, she couldn't seem to help herself.

Her hand clenched and unclenched on the fine material of his tuxedo jacket. She stood on tiptoe, wanting more of his kiss, only peripherally aware of the celebration around them, the madness within obliterating the madness all around. Heat was curling down into her lower body, threatening to catch her on fire. Uncharacteristically, she felt an urgent need for that fire, and she went in search of it, opening her lips beneath his, thrilling to the feel of his tongue as it thrust deep into her mouth.

Time had no meaning; neither did sound. The ecstasy was new to her, and she wanted it to go on and on. When he finally did pull away, Arabella thought an eternity had passed and was astonished that the band was still playing "Auld Lang Syne." His eyes were black velvet, mesmerizing, drawing her in as if they would absorb her as they did light.

"We're going to have to do something about this," he said huskily.

He was talking about the fire they had created, but she didn't feel capable of a coherent answer.

"You have glitter in your hair." He brushed a hand

across the blond strands, showering glitter this way and that. Then he pulled at tangled streamers that had somehow wound themselves around her until she was free, at least from the streamers. And all the while she stood still, like a little girl getting tidied up for a party. Except she felt nothing like a child. Her senses were reeling, her lips were pulsing, and her breasts were aching strangely. The clock had struck twelve, a new year had begun, and her world had turned upside down.

"Miss Linden's wrap, sir," Marlon said from behind her.

Arabella turned, bewildered to find Marlon holding out her ermine cape.

"Thank you." Jake took it from him and draped it around her.

"Are we going someplace?" she asked, dazed.

"Just outside."

He took her hand in his and drew her across the room to tall French doors. He opened one and led her out onto the darkened terrace, then closed the door behind them. The snow and cold swirled around them. Then Jake was pushing her against the wall, shielding her with his big body.

Her senses ignited once more, though he had scarcely touched her. "What are we doing out here?" she managed to ask.

"You'll see." His voice was a seductive rasp. "Put your arms around me. I'll keep you warm."

Without fully understanding why, she did as he

said, sliding her arms around his neck, letting her fingers lightly touch the ends of his hair. "You don't have an overcoat on," she whispered.

He slipped his arms beneath the ermine and around her so that his hands were on her bare back. "You're all the heat I need. Give it to me, Arabella. Give me your heat."

With desperation she tried to impose at least a modicum of sanity on the situation. "Jake, I don't think we should be out here."

A laugh rumbled low in his chest. "Oh, Arabella. Don't lose your courage now."

"I'm not. It's just that your guests—"

"Can all go to hell."

And then he was kissing her again, boldly plunging his tongue into her mouth, rubbing it against hers in a way that sent waves of incredible pleasure through her. Somewhere in the far reaches of her mind she was embarrassed and shocked that she couldn't find the strength to resist him. But they were isolated together, and his body was giving off a fire that was melting her. He wrapped his arms tighter around her, deepening the embrace, sliding his hands beneath her dress until his long, lean fingers were touching the sides of her breasts.

"Which room did they put you in?" he asked, his mouth against her ear, his voice a low growl.

"I—I don't know." She cried out with soft delight as his tongue dipped into her ear and she felt a burning need shoot to the insides of her upper thighs. "It's on the third floor."

"But which room?"

"I—"

"Never mind."

His mouth went back to her lips, this time opening them wider, plunging his tongue deeper, and pushing sheer raw passion through her bloodstream. She clung to him, soft and pliable, and helpless against his iron strength.

He broke off the kiss with a groan of suppressed violence. "We'll go to my room."

"What? No, I—"

His hand closed on her jaw, and he tilted her face up. In the light from the ballroom she could see the harshness of his expression, the intent in his eyes. "I want you, Arabella."

Her heart leapt. She was half excited, half afraid, and her emotions were threatening to run away with her. She knew she had to say something, do something, make some sort of decision. But she was stunned by the sheer enormity of her feelings and the events and emotions that had put her into his arms.

"Arabella?"

Self-preservation was a powerful force. Her tongue swept moisture over her suddenly dry lips. "I—I don't think so."

"Why not, for God's sake?"

With his arms still around her, his excitingly blatant arousal pressing against her lower body, she couldn't think of a single clever thing to say. She blurted out the truth. "I've never had a lover before."

Her golden eyes glistened in the pale light, full of desire, but also of uncertainty, and for a moment he almost believed her. But she played the game too well to be an innocent. "Then," he said with a softness that was a persuasion in itself, "it's a good thing we've finally met."

A sudden series of explosions was followed by the lighting up of the sky. Colors flared in the night. He straightened away from her and pulled the edges of her cape together, swathing her once more in ermine but leaving her skin imprinted with the feel of his hands. "Fireworks," he said, "more or less on time."

The doors burst open and people began to spill from the ballroom out onto the long terrace, oohing and aahing at the brilliant colors exploding among the falling flakes of snow.

Arabella watched the bursts of light and pattern that lingered like frozen stars. And all the while she felt Jake's gaze on her. He could make her melt with passion on a dance floor in the middle of a crowd. He could make her cry out with need on a cold, snowy terrace. He could make a fireworks display happen in a snowstorm.

In all her life she'd found little that frightened her. She had been raised within the security of a loving family, and rarely had been told she couldn't do anything. In the years after her debut, there had been too much to see, to do, to allow herself to be tied down. And luckily there had been no man who threatened her resolve.

She had seen this holiday at SwanSea as an opportunity to be with her brother, with the added advantage of being able to enjoy again the great house that had made such an impression on her as a young girl. She hadn't come to charm her enigmatic host. Her entrance with the peacocks was quite typical party behavior. She used her creativity and innate sense of drama, along with her good looks, to create a stir at most of the lavish affairs she attended.

But from the moment she had stepped into the ballroom, she had known the night would be out of the ordinary. There was a level of excitement she had never encountered before. And then she had met its source: Jake Deverell. And within minutes she had realized the gossips hadn't done him justice. He was a man with a powerful, thrilling way of making her feel, and at the same time capable of threatening her in ways she couldn't even begin to imagine. And she now knew with a bone-deep certainty that while she didn't fear him, Jake Deverell was a man of whom she should definitely be wary.

Before she could act on that insight, Jake put his mouth to her ear and whispered, "I'll be in your bed by morning."

With a heart that seemed to be beating louder than the fireworks, Kenneth closed the door to Jake's study and said a brief prayer that the elaborate display outside would last long enough to give him the time he needed. At the big golden desk he began to open drawers and rifle through the papers. Some minutes later he found what he sought, and he reached for the telephone.

"Operator, I'd like to make a long distance call, and I want it billed to my home telephone number."

Far out over the ocean, the top half of the sun had just cleared the horizon when Lucas came to Jake's suite of rooms, barefoot and wearing only a robe over a pair of trousers.

Jake was slouched in a big armchair that faced the east windows, but he glanced around as Lucas walked in. "What are you doing still up?"

"One of our men telephoned," Lucas said succinctly. "Our shipment from Canada has been hijacked."

"Sonofabitch!" Jake straightened and raked his fingers through his hair. "Anyone hurt?"

"No, thank God."

A muscle flexed in his jaw. "Wade."

"Who else? Ram and Barton probably stopped at the first telephone they could find when they left here last night and let him know we wouldn't go for the percentage deal."

Jake drummed his fingers on the arm of the chair, then surged to his feet. "This is only a minor setback. We'll be behind on our delivery schedule for a few days, but we should be able to catch up pretty fast."

"Do you have any idea how he knew which route this shipment would take?"

"No, but I think it'd be worth our while to turn over a few stones and see what crawls out."

Lucas nodded. "You bet, but in the meantime what are we going to do about Wade?"

"I don't think we need to do much of anything. Once he sees these tactics haven't worked, he'll stop harassing us."

"I hope you're right."

Jake watched his friend as he paced over to the fireplace, then abruptly walked to the window. He could never stay still when he was bothered by something. "It's only Wade, Lucas. He's always liked to play games."

"Right. And he's always liked to win."

Jake held up a finger. "But he rarely did." Lucas turned and paced to the dresser. Jake sighed. "Okay, if it'll make you feel any better, I'll telephone him and have a chat."

Lucas stopped. "I think that would be a good idea. It's your attention he wants, Jake."

"Then he'll get it, at least for a few minutes. And our next shipment *will* take a different route. There's nothing to worry about. Go back to Vanessa and get some rest."

"Yeah, I will." He put a hand on Jake's shoulder and squeezed. "And when are you going to get to bed?"

"Soon. Soon."

With a knowing grin Lucas nodded. "Yeah, sure. I'll see you later this afternoon."

After Lucas had left, Jake returned to the chair, leaned his head back and closed his eyes. The energy pulsing through his veins assured him it would be a while yet before he was ready to sleep. He was always like this when he got wound up about something.

Wade. He smiled to himself. If Wade was trying to impress him, it wasn't working. Wade should know he didn't impress easily. . . .

A vision of Arabella Linden came unbidden into his head. She had been a blaze of light in her silver and gold dress. She had been a blaze of heat in his arms. And the taste and feel of her had nearly had him in flames.

Arabella . . .

3

THE sound of someone throwing a log into the fireplace tugged at Arabella, pulling her into wakefulness. She stirred beneath the white silk sheets, then frowned. That light—Lord, where was it coming from? Had some misguided maid opened the drapes without her permission? With a muffled moan she rolled over and buried her face in the pillow. She had an inner clock that was very good at telling her when it was time to wake up, and her body was practically screaming at her that it would be hours yet before she was completely rested. She drifted back toward sleep. . . .

The mattress sagged as a heavy weight came down on it.

"Arabella."

Her eyes opened, and suddenly her sleep-shrouded mind was forced to consider the amazingly good possibility that Jake Deverell might actually be sitting on her bed. Slowly she rolled over.

He was dressed as she had last seen him, in formal attire, except he had discarded his jacket, opened his vest and shirt, and undone his black tie. Outlined by the brilliant white light of morning, he looked dynamic and dangerous beyond words. She wasn't sure whether it was the light or the sight of him that hurt her eyes.

"Good morning," he said.

"Is it?" she asked in a thick, scratchy voice.

"Is it what?"

"Morning."

"It's eight o'clock."

"Eight o'clock in the morning?"

"That's right."

"Not evening."

"No."

With a groan she placed her hands over her eyes to try to block out the light, *him*. It didn't help. She could still see him in her mind, dark and perilously compelling. Normally she preferred to ease herself into the idea of a new day, taking a good hour before she demanded anything strenuous of her brain. Obviously this morning would be an exception. Already her heartbeat was accelerating. She let her hands drop from her eyes and congratulated herself on maintaining a calm expression. "What are you doing up?"

"I haven't been to bed yet."

"Good heavens."

"You know, Arabella, I'm getting the distinct impression that you think eight A.M. is a little early."

"Mornings are difficult for me. I *never,* under *any* circumstances wake before noon."

He crossed his hands over his chest and nodded. "I suppose that makes sense when you dance all night."

There had been many times in the past when she had danced until dawn, but last night, as Jake knew very well, she had not. When the fireworks display was over, she had excused herself and come upstairs. She had locked the door in an attempt to keep him and his hot touches and kisses out of her thoughts, forgetting completely that Jake would have duplicates of all keys.

She brushed a wisp of hair from her eyes. "Was there something urgent you wanted to see me about, Jake? Something that couldn't wait until one or two this afternoon?"

"Get up. I want to show you something."

"Now?"

"Now." He shifted closer to her, closed his hands around her upper arms, and pulled her to a sitting position. Her scent followed her, an essence of femininity and sensuality that worked on his mind and on his body.

She was soft from sleep, her skin warm and velvety.

And her silky white-gold hair hung loose around her shoulders, longer than the popular bob—but then, if he had thought about it, he would have realized she would be a trendsetter, not a follower.

"I told you I'd be in your bed by morning."

She blinked. "Is that why you're here? To prove to me you were right."

He brushed at the cloud of her white-gold hair, clearing it away from her face. "Maybe I wanted to prove it to myself."

There was a dark growth of the night's beard on his hard jaw, and she could smell the scent of spice, musk, and masculine sexuality. After a moment's thought she shook her head. "No, I don't think so. You're too confident to have to prove anything to anyone, even to yourself."

For the first time he smiled, his amusement putting a seductive, twinkling light into his black eyes. "Then there must be another reason that I'm here. Why do you think that is, Arabella?"

The covers had fallen to her waist; her nightgown was a wisp of ivory silk and lace. But she wasn't cold in the least, she thought hazily. The fire burned high in the fireplace, and his fingers were lightly stroking the skin of her shoulders, warming her more than the fire ever could. "You said you wanted to show me something?"

"Ah, yes." His breath fanned against the side of her face. "Actually I want to give you something, a present."

"Jake, I can't accept a present from you."

"Really? How odd."

She received the distinct impression he didn't care what her answer was, that he wanted only to prolong this time with her on the bed. He hadn't kissed her, hadn't touched her with any great degree of intimacy, yet she was aware of the possibilities. . . . At any moment he could take her into his arms and try to make love to her. And she had already taken the measure of the man—what he tried, he accomplished.

He skimmed his fingers across her lips, then down her neck. "You must accept presents from men all the time."

"It depends."

"On what?"

"On the gift. On the man."

"And on your mood?"

"Sometimes," she admitted. Her chest was tight, she noticed idly, and she felt strangely short of breath.

"What kind of mood are you in now?"

"Lousy."

"How can anyone who looks like an angel feel lousy?"

He was still smiling, and she wished she knew what he was thinking. "Mornings . . ."

"Oh, of course."

He was playing with her, she thought, like a tiger with a kitten, creating a languorous warmth within her until she was at the point where she wished he would do something, anything. "Jake . . ."

Slowly, leisurely, he lowered his head toward her, giving her plenty of time to duck away from him. But for the moment at least, her muscles were frozen. She wanted his lips on hers, she realized with astonishment; she wanted his tongue in her mouth. . . . And so she waited for his kiss with an eagerness too strong to suppress.

He took her lower lip between his teeth and gently nibbled, then tugged. Nothing more, but it was enough to send heat skimming along now-wide-awake nerve endings.

And then, startlingly, she was sitting alone on the bed, and he was across the room, opening the door to the armoire. He pulled her ermine cape out and took it off its white satin hanger as he walked back to her. Beside the bed he reached down for her hand and drew her to her feet.

"Where are your slippers?" he asked, draping the ermine around her shoulders.

"I don't know." At that moment if he'd asked her name, she wasn't certain she would have been able to tell him. His abrupt withdrawal from her had left her to cope with a strong, annoying sense of deprivation.

"Here they are. Under the bed."

She stepped into the fur-trimmed, heeled slippers, and then he was leading her to the French doors which he opened wide.

Arabella's breath caught in her throat at the sight

that greeted her. The cold air was still and quiet. All signs of the previous night's inclement weather was gone. The sky was vividly blue and unmarked by a single cloud. A pristine layer of brilliant white snow covered the grounds and layered the branches of the trees. And here and there ice crystals glinted in the sun.

"There is my gift to you," he said softly. "A bright, fresh day with which to start the new year, 1929."

She should have known his gift wouldn't be banal. Awed, she clapped her hands with delight. "It's *beautiful,* Jake. Truly. It's as if during the night God created a new shade of white and a brand-new smell of clean."

He laughed, pleased with her response, and guided her out onto the terrace. "And if I had let you sleep, you would have missed it. By this afternoon there would have been tracks and footprints everywhere. It wouldn't be the same."

The scene was a wonderland, enchanted and exquisite, and the tough, hard, mysterious Jake Deverell had showed it to her. She was amazed. She glanced at him. "You're right, and it's the most original gift I've ever received. Thank you."

He pulled her back against him and folded his arms across her upper chest, giving her his warmth and support.

"No one understands why I like to come to SwanSea in the winter but this is one of the reasons. Maybe you see a lot of sights like this on Beacon Hill, but in the North End, where I grew up, snow turned dirty the minute it hit the streets."

"You grew up in the North End?" That might explain some things, she thought. He was an extremely sophisticated, assured man who controlled great wealth and power, yet she sensed a raw, uncivilized layer in his makeup and a coiled tension that at any moment could turn lethal. "Do you ever go back?"

"I don't have to." His lips thinned. He carried the neighborhood with him. In fact, he never wanted to forget the crowded, airless tenements where he, Lucas, and Vanessa grew up. His hands on her shoulders, he turned her around to face him. She looked beautiful, fresh from sleep, her mouth curved with a soft smile, her golden eyes filled with the wonder he had just shown her. Her pale hair shimmered against the ermine, tone against tone. He took a handful and let it sift through his fingers. Then abruptly he stepped back into the bedroom. "Get some sleep. I'll see you later."

She followed, closing the doors behind her. "What about you? Are you going to sleep?"

Already across the room, his hand on the doorknob, he glanced back at her, a sardonic twist to his lips. "Are you asking me to come to bed with you?"

Her stomach fluttered, but she met his direct gaze with one of her own, her chin high, her voice calm. "No. I believe the question was, are you going to get any *sleep*."

He smiled. "I may catch a nap later."

She waited until he had left, then threw her cape across the foot of the bed and slid beneath the covers. But sleep didn't come immediately. One thought kept going through her mind: Jake Deverell had made her his prey.

She was used to being pursued, but the men who pursued her knew the rules of the game: Flirt, dance, and be merry, and take nothing seriously. She had known Jake for less than twenty-four hours, but already she knew that he acknowledged no rules and would be very serious about the chase.

Like a diamond, Jake had many facets. He was a man hard enough to send another woman out into a cold night to be driven home because he had found someone who interested him more. Yet he was also a man who could see the value in something as simple as a still, clear morning when the landscape was painted with snow. He had grown up poor, yet he was now rich and helped to run one of the largest and most profitable firms in the nation. And beneath all the layers was a burning drive . . . along with something else. When she knew what that something was, along with what he burned for, she might know him.

Her lids grew heavy, and she wondered if truly knowing Jake Deverell was possible and if it would even be in her best interest to try. And she fell asleep wondering if he was capable of learning rules.

"Jake, nice of you to call," Wade said on the other end of the telephone line, confident, amiable.

Jake smiled. Wade had kept him waiting five minutes before he had come to the telephone, a tactic, Jake was sure, meant to rattle him.

"I understand you got a problem."

"You understand wrong."

"Oh? I was sure I had heard you had a problem with a shipment. I figured that was why you were calling me."

"I'm telling you, I don't have a problem in the world."

"Then why are you calling?"

Jake's smile broadened as he heard the impatience in Wade's tone. He had changed very little. "To tell you a few things, the first being that your stiff-arm tactics won't work with me. They never did."

"Someone been trying to muscle you, Jake? Damn, that's a shame. Anything I can do to help?"

"The second thing I want to tell you is, there is nothing I have that I will give you, and there is nothing that I have you can take. Got that?"

"I hear what you're saying. I'm just wondering why you're wasting your time telling me, that's all."

"And the third thing is, use what few brains you have, Wade. This isn't one of those games of craps we used to play in the alleys of the North End. The stakes are high. Keep your head and you'll get your share."

There was silence, then, "You know, I used to beat you at craps, Jake."

"Only when you cheated, Wade. Only when you cheated. Good-bye."

As soon as Jake hung up the phone, he banished Wade from his thoughts and conjured up Arabella. He stared out at the fresh, clean day and remembered. Last night she had been the clever sophisticate, all light and beauty. This morning she had been warm, silky, and sensually pliable. It was a combination guaranteed to make men lose their heads. No wonder she was one of the leading "belles" of Boston. And he was willing to wager she would be as fascinating in bed as she was out. Desire knotted his stomach at the thought. He waited a moment, willing the painful wanting to ease. Then a new thought entered his mind: Arabella came from wealth and privilege, a Brahmin straight from Beacon Hill. *Edward would be so pleased.*

Jake threw back his head and laughed.

On a specially built platform at one end of the frozen pond crowded with skaters, a small band played "Do, Do, Do." Arabella glided across the ice in rhythm to the charming Gershwin tune. The afternoon coat she wore and its matching muff were of white velvet trimmed with white fox. The roses that were embroidered on the back of the coat were one of the signatures of the ensemble's designer, Paul Poiret, but in her honor the roses were white instead of the usual red.

Beside her, Kenneth, in a beaver coat was wobbling. "Kenneth, watch out!" She jerked him out of the path of another skating couple, almost overbalancing them both.

She sighed and once more scanned the crowded pond. The seal, sable, chinchilla, and fox furs that the men and women on the pond wore had been dyed a myriad of fashionable colors and made her feel as if she were in a giant kaleidoscope. The crowd was gay and laughing. The scene would have been perfect if Jake were there. She *wanted* him to be there. She liked sparring with him. And Lord help her, she liked kissing him, flirting with the danger, knowing she had no intention of going further. The problem was, Jake had no intention of stopping with a little petting.

Rubbing his hand over his face, Kenneth groaned. "Lord, I shouldn't even be here. I had trouble getting out of bed. What am I doing trying to ice-skate?"

"You're out here to keep me company and fill your lungs with some of this marvelous fresh air," she said, frowning at the shadows beneath his eyes. How could she ever talk with him if, when he wasn't swoozled, he was so hung over he couldn't speak? "You're as pale as a ghost. The air will put color in your cheeks."

"I could have opened a window."

"But you wouldn't have been able to keep me company if you'd stayed in your bedroom. Quit complaining. Besides, it's your own fault you're feeling so bad. If you hadn't been so heavily into the hooch last night, you'd be full of pep."

"Quit being a shrew, Bella. I laid off the giggle water after you brought me the coffee."

She turned and skated backward in front of him, her brow pleated with concern. "Then why do you look like the wreck of the *Hesperus*? What's wrong, Kenneth?"

"I say, is that hot buttered rum they're serving over there?"

Her gaze followed his to the tables covered in crisp white linen that had been set up at the edge of the pond. Marlon was overseeing rows of silver chafing dishes and huge silver bowls of steaming liquid. Sheepskin-covered chairs and park benches rimmed the pond for guests to lounge in while they ate and rested. SwanSea's owner and staff certainly knew how to pamper people, Arabella thought.

In the distance she could see the house basking in the sun, its shape a mammoth art-nouveau fan-shaped seashell. Where, she wondered, was SwanSea's master? Still sleeping? It hadn't been that many hours ago that he'd come to her room. . . . "I'm sure they also have hot chocolate."

He took her hand. "Let's go see."

Jas was there, the tuxedo he had worn the night before showing beneath his overcoat. He was huddled in one of the chairs, sipping from a steaming bowl of soup. He brightened when he saw them. "Hello, Lindens." He placed the bowl aside, stood, and took Arabella's hand and kissed it. "My darling, you look entrancing this morning. Tell me, did I ask you to marry me last night?"

"Yes, Jas, you did."

"Good, I was hoping I did. Did you accept?"

She smiled. "No."

"As it turns out, that's terribly convenient. I have a date later to play tennis, and I'd hate to have to break it. But"—he held up a warning finger—"I'll ask you again."

"I'll be waiting."

He fixed his bloodshot eyes on her brother. "Kenneth old boy, you look like hell. What are you doing up so early?"

Kenneth checked the watch on his wrist. "It's two o'clock in the afternoon, Jas."

"Imagine that!" As if amazed, he glanced back at his soup. "I thought I was having breakfast. I must have lost track of time along the way. Poker game. You should have been there, Kenneth."

Inside her fur muff Arabella unconsciously gripped her hands together.

"I don't play cards for money anymore," Kenneth said easily, "but maybe later I'll be up for a game of bridge."

Arabella's hands relaxed.

Jas shook his head. "Count me out. I promised Julia Turngate a game of tennis. Jake has a swell indoor tennis court. Oh, look, that's Vanessa Martin standing over there with Jake. She's a real Sheba, isn't she? *Great* gams."

At the mention of Jake's name, Arabella's head snapped around and she saw Jake, standing in almost the exact center of the pond. How could she have missed him? she wondered. The sunlight glinted off the snow and highlighted the healthy shine of his coal-black hair that was smoothed back from his forehead. He was wearing a sealskin overcoat with a sable collar dyed black, and he looked big, sleek, and excitingly mysterious. Draped over one arm he held a mink coat that obviously belonged to the breathtakingly lovely, raven-haired woman who slowly skated backward in a circle around him. She had a doll's face and a woman's body, and he was smiling at her in a way that spoke of long-time intimacy.

Arabella felt a stab of pain, and it took no great mental calculation on her part to identify the pain as jealousy, though she couldn't remember experiencing the emotion before. Jake's attention span was definitely lousy, she thought sourly. Last night he had sent his date out the door so he could be with her. And now he was with yet a third woman.

"You know, I think I've seen her in a couple of movies," Kenneth was saying to Jas.

"Yeah, she's under contract with MGM. She started out in silents and made the switch to the talkies."

Kenneth nodded. "Now I remember. She's really good."

"She's getting bigger with each movie. Everyone says she's on the verge of becoming a full-fledged star."

Kenneth and Jas had completely forgotten she was standing there, Arabella thought with an amusement greatly tempered by the sight of how at ease Jake and

Vanessa seemed to be with each other. As she watched, he pulled her to a standstill and wrapped the mink around her. She remembered him wrapping a fur around her, then drawing her out onto the dark balcony and kissing her until . . . A shudder of heat raced through her, and she turned her back on Jake, Vanessa, and the still-chatting Kenneth and Jas. With determined cheerfulness she made her way to the refreshment table.

"Marlon, tell me about the hot chocolate. Was it bootlegged in from abroad or is it the potent, local bathtub variety?"

He permitted a small smile to touch his stern lips. "It's definitely local, Miss Linden, and one of our better choices today."

"And the marshmallows? Would you recommend them also?"

"I would say they would add exactly the right touch to your chocolate."

"Well, in that case, I think I'll have a cup."

He bowed slightly. "I will pour it for you myself, Miss Linden."

She smiled at him, then in spite of herself let her gaze return to where she had last seen Jake. He was no longer there. But Vanessa had skated to a stop at the table a few feet from her.

"Everything looks tops, Marlon," Vanessa said.

"I'm glad you're pleased, Miss Martin."

The familiarity and fondness in Marlon's voice as he spoke to Vanessa irritated Arabella. She studied

Vanessa while Vanessa in turn studied the tables laden with food and drink. She hadn't seen any of the woman's movies, but she saw so few. Real life had always appealed to her much more than made-up stories about life.

"Here is your chocolate, Miss Linden."

She tore her gaze from the lovely Vanessa and accepted the chocolate from Marlon. "Thank you," she murmured.

"I think I'll have some of everything," Vanessa suddenly said, her gaze still on the table. "I'm starving."

Marlon bowed. "I'll be glad to prepare a plate for you. Shall I make up one for Mr. Deverell too?"

Vanessa gave a careless shrug of her mink-clad shoulders. "It wouldn't do any good. You know he won't eat. Now, let's see. I'll have some of the prime rib and the corn pudding. And the lobster. It looks wonderful. Add just a little of the crab. And the potatoes Anna. Marlon, you're the absolute berries."

"Thank you, Miss Martin."

"What's that cream sauce? I should probably have some of that too."

Admiring Vanessa's unrestrained appetite, Arabella took a seat on one of the benches, then grimaced when she saw Randolph Bruce approaching. A man of medium height and build, his brown hair was parted in the middle and its natural waves combed back on either side of his large oval face. He was the society reporter for one of Boston's leading newspapers, and Arabella had learned to tolerate him over the years. She braced herself for one of his quizzes and then was surprised and relieved to discover she wasn't the object of his attention.

"Playing hooky from the studio, Vanessa?"

Vanessa sighed as she turned. "Hello, Randolph."

"Happy New Year. I didn't get a chance to tell you last night."

"Yes, it was a bit hectic." She sent Marlon a smile as she took a full plate from him, then glanced around and saw Arabella. "Do you mind if I sit here?" she asked her, indicating the opposite end of the bench with a motion of her hand.

"Not at all. I'm Arabella Linden."

Vanessa's hand jerked and her gaze turned cool. "Of course. I saw you come into the ballroom last night, but I didn't recognize you without your peacocks." She dropped down beside her. "I'm Vanessa Martin."

She was even more beautiful close up, Arabella thought. Her raven hair was bobbed, her skin was like porcelain, and her eyes were the darkest of blues and held an expression that bespoke many years of living. They were old eyes, she realized. Vanessa Martin, who couldn't be any older than she, had *old* eyes.

"Happy New Year, Arabella," Randolph said, having trailed Vanessa. "I saw your entrance last night. Congratulations. It was your best yet. I plan to give it a nice write-up."

"I'm sorry to hear that."

"Arabella, one of these days you're going to hurt my feelings. All your friends court me so I'll write about them. Everyone does except you. Lord, you wouldn't believe the things I've been promised."

"I'm sorry, but I can't seem to do what other people do."

"Ah-ha! And that's exactly what makes you so newsworthy. You're just like Jake." His gaze drifted to the opposite side of the pond, where Jake was standing.

Arabella looked, too, and saw him with the man he'd been talking with the night before. They made interesting foils for each other, Jake with the tension that was so much a part of him, the other man more at ease with himself and his surroundings.

"Jake is *the*, bar none, most colorful and fascinating person I've ever encountered," Randolph said admiringly. "Lucas tries to keep out of the limelight, but he's nothing short of the cat's meow himself. Right, Vanessa?"

She forked a bite-size piece of lobster into her mouth and ignored him.

Randolph let out a belly laugh. "But Jake—he makes even better print than you, Arabella. What are you doing here, by the way?"

"I decided to take a break from skating and have some hot chocolate." She held up her cup. "You should get some. It's delicious."

He rolled his eyes at her deliberate misinterpretation of his question. "Finding you on a bench isn't unexpected. Finding you on a bench at *SwanSea* is. Unless, of course"—his tone turned speculative—"you're Jake's newest girl."

"I met him for the first time last night."

"That doesn't mean a thing."

Desperate to pull herself from a trap she could see closing around her, she nevertheless kept her head. "Really, Randolph, I don't know why you should be so surprised to find me out of Boston. I might live there, but I've never restricted myself to the city limits."

He snapped his fingers. "Now I have it. Kenneth went to Harvard the same time as Jake, didn't he? Jake invited Kenneth and Kenneth invited you."

She bent her head for a sip of hot chocolate, feeling relief that she and Jake wouldn't be sharing the headline of Randolph's next column. Up until this moment she had accepted her frequent presence in his column with a calm because she understood the part Randolph played in the life of society—sometimes greatly annoying, sometimes fun, columns like Randolph's were in essence an adulation and, generally speaking, harmless. And because nothing he had ever printed about her, whether it was true or untrue, had really been important to her, she'd never minded. But now the idea of having thousands of strangers read something that wasn't true about her and Jake made her shudder.

Satisfied with his own explanation, Randolph turned back to Vanessa, who had been steadily eating.

"You never answered my question. Are you playing hooky?"

"You're screwy, Randolph. The studio knows exactly where I am."

The wind ruffled his hair, picking up thick chunks on either side of his part and making it look as if his head had sprouted wings. "Oh? And if I telephoned them and mentioned I had seen you here, they wouldn't get upset?"

The stare she gave him was without any visible emotion. "Do whatever you like, Randolph."

He laughed. "Don't worry. I'm not going to call them. Why should I? I *want* you to become a star. You'll make much better print. At any rate, I've told you before, I think you ought to have Jake and Lucas buy you your own studio and then you wouldn't have to dance to Louis B. Mayer's tune." He tucked the ends of his silk muffler more neatly into his chesterfield. "Ladies, I'm sure I'll see you tonight at dinner."

Vanessa returned to her plate of food and Arabella was left to deal with the questions careening through her mind. Vanessa had visibly cooled when she had told her who she was. Even now she was ignoring her. She glanced down at her nearly empty cup of hot chocolate. Maybe she should get up and leave, she thought. But why should she? There was nothing wrong with a good, healthy curiosity. "Are you a friend of Jake's, Vanessa?"

Vanessa nodded and kept eating.

"How long have you known him?"

"A long time."

"Where did you meet?"

Vanessa set down her fork and turned her head to gaze at Arabella with the same expression she had given Randolph, one that gave away nothing of what she was thinking or feeling. It was an expression common to Jake, Arabella realized.

"What exactly is it you want to know?" Vanessa asked.

Why, Arabella wondered, was this woman so hostile toward her? "I'm curious about your relationship with Jake."

"You said it yourself. We're friends."

"Randolph mentioned a man named Lucas. Who is he?"

"Another friend of Jake's."

She was telling her nothing, Arabella thought, frustrated but still curious. "Have I done something to offend you, Vanessa?"

"Nothing you could help."

"I beg your pardon?"

"It's *who* you are—a rich and spoiled girl. I have trouble with your kind." She shrugged. "Nothing personal."

"Vanessa, you're judging me without knowing me."

"Is your family rich?"

"Yes.

"Do you only have to ask to get what you want, no matter what it might be?"

Arabella paused, getting her first glimpse of herself as someone else might see her. "I gather your background is different."

"I grew up in the North End. My name is not Martin. It's Martignetti."

"Did you know Jake there?"

"Oh, yes. He and Lucas both. Usually Irish didn't mix with Italians, but they made no distinction." Vanessa handed her empty plate to a passing footman. "Don't worry about what I think about you. Jake has had a lot of girlfriends over the years that I didn't like."

As Vanessa had intended, the remark hurt Arabella. It wasn't her way to give hurt for hurt, but in this case she felt it would be a mistake to allow Vanessa to see her wither beneath her remark. "You know," she said, her tone thoughtful, "I'm sure I've seen some of the movies you were in. I just can't remember you. Silly of me, isn't it? But then, it's so difficult to keep track of all the bit players."

One perfectly arched brow rose slightly, a salute to the well-executed parry. Then with a smile Vanessa rose and skated away, passing Jake on his way to Arabella.

"Sleep well?" he asked, gracefully sliding to a stop in front of her.

Did he do everything gracefully? she wondered. Even seduction? "Yes. Did you get any sleep?"

"A few hours. Skate?" he asked, taking her hand.

She grinned, feeling unaccountably happier now

that he was by her side. "You have a unique way of inviting a girl to skate."

"I have a unique way with quite a few things, Arabella."

"No doubt," she said, prudently deciding not to pursue his remark.

He put his arm around her waist and took her hand in his, and they glided off. To her surprise, they skated well together, Jake pacing himself so that their rhythm and strokes matched. Out of the blue the thought came to her: They would make love wonderfully together. Shaken, she groped for a subject to get her mind off such a dangerous idea. "Who is that blond-haired man over there? The one with Vanessa."

"Lucas Moran. Vanessa is his girl."

The wave of relief that swept through her surprised her, and she realized that despite Vanessa saying she and Jake were just friends, the germ of jealousy had remained. Well, nerts! She had to overcome these new and strange emotions. They were confusing her, and she was finding that being confused wasn't a pleasant experience. "I wondered. Randolph Bruce mentioned him and so did Vanessa. She said the three of you had grown up together."

"What did Randolph say?"

"He said Lucas made good print but not as good as you. Apparently you outdo even me in that department."

He laughed. "And how does that make you feel?"

"Unfazed. My mother was raised with the precept 'A lady's name appears in print only twice in her lifetime: when she marries and when she dies.' To a point, Mother's opinion has relaxed with the times, but if I were to do anything truly scandalous and it were to be printed in the columns, she would be horrified."

"Scandalous? Such as?"

She looked up at him through the thickness of her golden lashes. "Such as the item that appeared last year about you. I believe it concerned you, a certain young married woman, and a hotel in Atlantic City where you bought out an entire floor of rooms to give yourself and your guest privacy."

He laughed again, remembering how enraged Edward had been when he had read that particular item.

"Or," she said, continuing, "anything that might be illegal, such as, oh . . . bootlegging, for instance."

Damn, but she entertained him. "You know, don't you, Randolph will write that you attended my New Year's Eve party?"

"Yes. In fact, he's already told me so. But Mother's in Europe with my father on an extended tour. Besides, I didn't say the idea of my name appearing in print would prevent me from doing something I truly wanted to do."

"A thoroughly modern young woman." His black eyes glinted.

In truth, she felt anything but, and for a brief

moment that betrayed everything she believed in, she longed for the days when young couples were chaperoned and a girl was protected—from scandal, yes, but also from herself. "Does Lucas work for you?"

"No. We're partners in a couple of things, but he has other business interests."

"Did you leave the North End together?"

His expression took on a sardonic cast. "Not exactly. I went to Harvard, and Lucas went into the army. But we got together afterward, and about three years ago he was out on the West Coast on some business for himself and accidentally ran into Vanessa. Only their work separates them now, and only when there's no other alternative."

"That's nice. I suppose they'll be married soon."

"You'll have to ask them."

He fell silent, guiding them both around the pond, leaving her to ponder what he had said.

Arabella liked him for remaining friends with another man through many stages of life, from childhood to adulthood. And, she mused, the friendship was strong enough to allow a third person into their circle, another old friend, a girl for Lucas. Surely that spoke of a certain steadiness in Jake. But what was she trying to convince herself of anyway? That a man who could maintain a long-term relationship with a man could also have one with a woman, a loving one? Inside her muff her hand fisted. Jake had a history with women that proved otherwise. And what did it matter? She wasn't seriously interested in him. She would forget him as soon as she returned home. For now she should have fun. The issue resolved, she forced herself from her introspection and heard the music. "What is that song the band is playing? I don't think I've ever heard it before."

"It's called, 'I've Got a Crush on You.' It's by George Gershwin."

"I wonder why I've never heard it."

"I'm not surprised. It was a featured song in George's musical, *Strike Up the Band,* that closed out of town a couple of years ago. He gave me the sheet music so the musicians I hired could play the tune here."

She blinked. "He must be a very good friend of yours."

He grinned. "George is reworking the musical and hopes to bring it back next year. But there are lots of other great shows on Broadway now. Why don't we go?"

She stopped herself before she could blink again. "To New York?"

"Why not? Broadway should appeal to you."

It probably would, she thought. And Jake appealed to her even more, but she wasn't ready to become another in a long line of Jake's girls. The excitement would be incendiary . . . and in the end leave her in ashes. She shook her head. "Thank you, but no thank you."

"Oh, come on. We can drive down, say on the thirteenth, and stay at the Waldorf."

She lied without a qualm. "I already have an engagement for that date."

He tightened his hold on her waist and angled his blades against the ice, bringing both of them to a sliding stop. Then he circled to in front of her. "With whom?"

She feigned an air of nonchalance. "Someone interesting."

He frowned. "Doing what?"

She glanced at the nails of one hand. "Something fascinating."

She looked so pure, so untouched, he thought, dressed in her white velvet-and-fur coat. Sweet baby curls of white gold escaped her white cloche and lay against flawless ivory skin. She looked like an ice princess, pure and chaste. But her wit was quick and sophisticated and her eyes were wickedly golden, and no virgin had ever heated his blood the way Arabella did. He laid his hands on her shoulders and placed his thumbs beneath her jawline, tilting her face closer to his. "Fight me," he said softly. "Run from me. It won't do any good. You will be in my bed soon, and I'm going to make you forget every lover you've ever had."

A traitorous thrill raced through her, but she had to correct him. "I've never—"

He laid a finger over her lips and gently moved them back and forth. "Shhh. Sooner or later it's going to happen. And if I have my way, it's going to be sooner."

"Sir." Marlon's dignified drawl cut through the charged air.

Irritated by the interruption, Jake jerked around to see his majordomo standing on the ice in his shoes. "What is it, Marlon?"

"Mr. Calloway is preparing to leave, but he would like to have a moment with you in your study before he does, if it would be convenient, of course."

Jake smiled thoughtfully. At last he would find out what was on the government agent's mind. It should be interesting. "Have you told Lucas?"

"Yes, sir."

"Very well. Wait right there and I'll help you off the ice."

"That's not necessary, sir."

"*Wait.*" He looked back at Arabella. "Will you be at dinner tonight?"

She nodded. "Unless Kenneth decides he wants to return home early."

"He won't."

His confidence sent a chill down her spine. "Jake?"

He pushed off, gliding toward Marlon, but he stopped and looked back. "Yes?"

She opened her mouth to ask him not to get Kenneth involved in any poker games, but then closed her mouth again. Kenneth would never forgive her if he found out she had mentioned such a thing to anyone, much less Jake. "Nothing. Never mind."

His brows drew together. "You look worried. What is it?"

She shook her head. "Nothing. Go on. I—I'll see you at dinner."

He hesitated, started away again, then stopped and skated back to her. And right there in the center of the frozen pond he kissed her until her cold lips were warm and the chill she felt had vanished.

4

"MARLON tells me you're leaving," Jake said, walking into his study and addressing Noah Calloway, who was sitting in one of the two leather chairs in front of the big desk. Lucas followed on Jake's heels and chose the second of the chairs.

Noah nodded. "The roads are clear now." He paused. "Although I understand there were several guests who left last night in spite of the weather, I prefer safer driving conditions."

Jake's lips slanted with an appreciative grin. He dropped down into the chair behind the desk and leaned back. Noah had an intelligent face, and brown eyes that spoke of knowledge he would never tell. It was Noah's job to put him in jail. It definitely made for an interesting relationship. "You know, Noah, you're too smart to work for the government forever. You should quit and work where you'll make decent money."

Noah grinned. "I appreciate your concern over my employment, Jake, but it suits me. Besides, I meet a lot of interesting people in my work."

"I have to give you that. Didn't I see you talking with Sheila Howard last night?"

"Yes." Noah smiled. "I'll probably be seeing her again."

"Congratulations," Lucas said.

Noah cleared his throat. "Yes, well . . . Jake, I want to thank you for allowing me to be here. When I called, I wasn't sure you would."

Jake gestured, moving his hands outward. "Why wouldn't I?"

"I think we both know the answer to that."

"Well, since we do, perhaps you wouldn't mind telling me *why* you wanted to come."

Noah studied the crease in his trousers, his forehead ridged with thought. Finally he looked up, first at Lucas, then at Jake. "I wanted to try to get a complete picture of you. I've heard of SwanSea, of course, but I wanted to see for myself how you lived. I wanted to see you away from your work, at ease and among friends."

Jake's voice went toneless. "Like I was an insect under a microscope."

"I'm sorry. It's my job."

"I believe I mentioned that you should change jobs."

"And I told you, it suits me."

Jake stared at him for a moment, then glanced at Lucas. "So, Noah, what did you learn from this study of yours?"

"Primarily that you never let your guard down. You have a strange assortment of friends and acquaintances. You have a fabulous house that you treat as if it were a shanty. In short, Jake, I learned that nothing about you adds up."

Lucas took out a cigarillo and lit it. "What sum are you trying to reach?"

"The sum of Jake. And you too. You're almost as much as an enigma as he is. I need to know which way the two of you will jump in a given circumstance."

"Why?"

"Because I'm about to present you with a proposition, and I need to be able to trust you. My career could go down the drain if you failed me."

"I'm intrigued," Jake said, idly toying with a pen.

"I'm scared," Lucas drawled.

"No you're not. I don't know why, but you two don't scare."

Jake flung the pen onto the desk. "That's enough of trying to dissect us. Just tell us what the proposition is."

"All right. You are as aware as I am that we have absolutely no evidence linking either of you to anything illegal. I know you're running a highly successful bootlegging operation. But what I know and what I can prove are two different things. Now, word is you two grew up with Wade Scalia. The word is also out that he's rekindling a rivalry with you, only this time it's not a kid's game. And, fellahs, I have to tell you, the last thing I want or need on my hands is a gang war."

"As far as I'm aware," Jake said, toying with the pen again, "you've got nothing to worry about."

"What exactly is it you want from us?" Lucas asked.

"I want to use you to put Scalia away."

Jake exchanged a look with Lucas and saw an answering flash in his clear blue eyes.

Unable to read the look that had passed between the two men, Noah went on. "Scalia's deep into the rackets. If we could put him away, it would be a major coup. Now, you know him—"

"We knew the kid," Lucas said. "We don't know the man."

Noah waved an impatient hand. "Still, he feels a definite rivalry with you two, particularly, I understand, with Jake."

Lucas chuckled. "He never got over the fact that Jake wouldn't let him win at King of the Mountain."

"The point is, I don't want blood from here to New York because—whatever his reasons are—he wants your territory."

Lucas sent Jake a puzzled look. "What territory is he talking about?"

Jake pushed back from the desk and stood. "It

doesn't matter. The answer is no. I'm sorry, Noah, but I'm not interested."

Noah stared at him for a long, speculative moment, then at Lucas. "What about you?"

"I'm with Jake."

He levered himself up from his chair. "Then I guess it's time I was on my way. Jake, thank you again for your hospitality."

"You're welcome anytime."

Noah gazed around him, a wry expression on his face as he took in the opulent furnishings and the rows of citron wood shelves packed with leather-bound books stamped with fourteen-karat lettering. "Somehow I don't think I'll be back. But, Jake, Lucas, if you change your minds, call me."

"Good-bye, Noah."

"Have a safe trip."

Lucas waited until Noah had gone, then asked, "Are you sure about turning down his offer, Jake?"

"What are you talking about? Do you really want to stop? You brought me the whole idea of our operation in the first place, and you're making money faster than they can print it."

Lucas blew out a final stream of smoke, then ground the cigarillo out. "Yeah, that's true. I've made a lot of money, more than enough for what I want. And I've made some good investments, including choice parcels of land out in California. I can quit right now. I'm set for life."

Jake sat back down and studied his old friend.

"You're getting tired of being away from Vanessa, aren't you? I don't blame you. I know you two want to make your home out there. Look, you can quit anytime you want, you know."

Lucas shrugged. "Yeah, I know. And even though we've never talked about it, I also know why you won't quit. Your old man is practically apoplectic over your participation in the little sideline we have going, and it would make him too happy if you stopped."

Jake grinned. Lucas knew him better than anyone on earth. "But my reasons shouldn't affect you. You can quit today if you want, and I'll continue paying you your percentage."

Lucas shook his head. "We've been through too much together. I would never bail out on you. Besides, I wouldn't feel good about leaving you with this, Jake. You enjoy the knife's edge too much. Every now and then you need me to pull you off before the blade slices into you."

Jake's grin faded. "You're closer to me than any brother ever could be, and I'm damned glad you're staying. But, Lucas . . . there's no way I'll get hurt."

Candles lined the center of the long mahogany table, their flames reflected in the gleam of the silver and the brilliant shine of the crystal. A score of footmen in gold-buttoned black uniforms hovered discreetly, ready to spring into action. Arabella viewed the scene, thankful and relieved that the lengthy dinner was drawing to a conclusion. Much to her dismay, she had been placed at the foot of the table with Jake at its head. This placement, she knew, would mark her in the eyes of the other guests as Jake's new girl. She had tried to get Marlon to switch her place, but he had been adamant in an extremely polite, unyielding way. It was Mr. Deverell's wish she be placed at the opposite end of the table from him, and therefore that was where she would sit. In the end, she had decided to brazen out the situation, and count her blessings that Randolph Bruce had left for Boston in the early afternoon.

By evening the number of guests had dwindled to about forty, with only twenty-six coming down to dinner. The others had chosen to dine in their rooms, requiring a small break in their merrymaking.

Arabella sipped her wine and eyed Jake. He was lounging in the big chair, lazily smiling at the marcel-waved beauty next to him who was leaning toward him, her hand on his arm, speaking softly. An untouched plate of food and glass of wine sat in front of him.

He seemed relaxed, but Arabella could sense the tension in him. His command of the dinner table and everything happening around him, even when he didn't seem to be paying attention, seemed so obvious to her. Suddenly, as if he knew she was watching him, Jake turned his head and gazed at her. One dark brow arched and his smile deepened, then he returned his attention to his dinner companion.

Vexed, Arabella angled her body toward the

United States senator on her right. "I'd be most interested to know your opinion of President-elect Hoover. He has said he will carry out 'the ideas of the American people,' but I can't help thinking that sounds a trifle vague. I know you're from the same party as he, and that very probably you are a confidant of our new president. Perhaps you could explain his plans to me more in depth."

The rotund man with bushy eyebrows beamed at the opportunity to take center stage. "My dear, I'd be glad to. Herbert and I have had extensive conversations on this very subject. . . ."

From the other end of the table, Jake smiled to himself. It had been a whim to have her seated opposite him, but now he was very glad he had. She had risen to the occasion and had presided from her place of honor with an elegance and beauty and grace that amazed him.

Her hair was unadorned and drawn back in gentle waves to her neck, where it was softly rolled. A wide collar of pearls circled her long, lovely neck. The bodice of her dress was a transparent shell of white silk chiffon that fell from the shoulder to the dropped waist without a side seam. He'd marveled at the dress before dinner. Brilliants of some sort were scattered over the sheer shoulders and patterned around the hips. The skirt was made out of a heavier white silk and thickly embroidered in pearls. Beneath this astonishing dress she wore a deeply cut, simple white silk underslip. A Poiret, he imagined, and one of the most tantalizing yet completely ladylike dresses he'd ever seen. His palms tingled from his need to slide his hand between the transparent shell and the slip to her breast.

He stood and all eyes went to him. "When everyone is ready, I believe Marlon has coffee and spirits waiting for us in the drawing room." He strode the length of the table to her and held out his hand.

Because everyone was watching, she accepted, rose, and as she had intended, everyone else followed her example, rising and, most important to her, resuming their conversations.

Jake started toward the door, still holding her hand, but she pulled away. "I'd like to speak with Kenneth before I go into the drawing room. She'd observed her brother closely during dinner, gratified to see him drink only water. Now might be the last opportunity she'd have to talk with him before returning to Boston.

"Here he comes now," Jake said. "I'll wait for you."

"I'd like to speak to him privately."

"About leaving early?"

"We'll be leaving tomorrow as planned."

"I doubt it. Not you, at any rate." He brushed his thumb across her lips. "I'll meet you in the drawing room in a few moments."

Her lips were still tingling from Jake's touch when Kenneth walked up, his expression brooding. "It seems that despite my warning, you are involved with Jake. You always were a headstrong girl."

"I'm not involved with Jake or anyone."

"That's not what it looks like."

It wasn't what it felt like either, but she couldn't say so to her brother. Her feelings for Jake were something she was going to have to work out alone. She hooked her arm in his, and they began to stroll toward the door. "We're still leaving in the morning, aren't we?"

"Yes. I really don't want to stay any longer, although most of the others will be staying on. Jake virtually runs an open house here."

"But you enjoyed our stay, didn't you?"

"Well enough. Why do you ask?"

She shrugged with what she hoped was an appropriate insouciance. "I had hoped to spend more time with you while we were here."

He frowned at her. "We *live* in the same house, Arabella. What's with you?"

They were in the great entry hall now with its forty-foot ceiling and Louis Comfort Tiffany–designed staircase that climbed a story then branched in opposite directions to climb another story. At the top of the stairs there was a twenty-foot stained-glass window crafted in vibrant green, purple, gold, and blue, and representing a peacock's head and body. Then the breathtaking jeweled colors were brought into a marble mosaic that swept down the staircase and onto part of the hall below, portraying the vivid plumage of the peacock's tail. The staircase, she remembered, was the reason she had chosen to bring Jake the peacocks.

She glanced around to make sure no one was near, then pulled Kenneth to the side. Above her she noticed a large rectangle of faded color where a picture once had hung. The difference in the color was so faint, she didn't think she would have seen it if she hadn't been standing beneath it. Her distraction was only momentary. "Kenneth, I've been worried about you."

His laugh was surprisingly hollow. "Whatever for? It's not *I* who's got Jake Deverell panting."

She jerked on his arm. "Stop that! I think you know exactly what I mean. I've heard you pacing at night, unable to sleep. I've seen those worried expressions on your face when you think no one is looking. Now, just tell me. Are you gambling again?" Over Kenneth's shoulder she saw Jake leaning against the balustrade of the grand stairway, watching them. Determinedly, she ignored him. "Are you?"

"No," he whispered, bending closer to her. "I'm *not,* and I wish you'd just leave me the hell alone. I don't care for your little-mother-hen act one bit."

Kenneth rarely spoke harshly to her; she was somewhat surprised, but not deterred. "So I'm supposed to accept the fact that you're worried about Jake's pursuit of me, but I'm not supposed to say a word when I'm worried about you. Is that it?"

"Yes, that's it exactly." With a curse he drew her into his arms for a quick hug, but then he pushed her backward until she was an arm's length away and held her there with his hands on her shoulders. "Listen, Bella, I love you for being concerned about me, but I'm going to be fine, just fine. Trust me on this. I can take care of myself."

"Can you? Can you really? Should we call Papa?"

He started. "Lord, no! You know as well as I do that when he covered my gambling debts last summer, he said it would be the last time. He said from that point on I would have to get myself out of my own messes, and that's what I'm trying to do."

"Then there is something wrong. Is it more gambling debts? Kenneth, I can help you. I haven't run through my trust fund as you have. And in addition there's my salary from the foundation. I can give you—"

"Stop it! I'm not taking money from you, and I don't want to hear any more about this."

"I'm not a little girl, Kenneth. I'm a woman, and I can help you if you'll give me a chance."

His lips twisted. "I'm all too aware that you're no longer my little sister. You've grown into a fascinating woman. Why do you think Jake's so interested in you?"

"The subject here is *you,* Kenneth, not me."

He rubbed his forehead. "All right, all right. I did have some gambling losses last month. But, Bella, I've stopped gambling flat out. I've placed my last bet, and that's a promise. What's more, I'm going to be able to pay back my debts without any trouble at all."

She crossed her arms under her breasts. "What do you mean, you're *going* to be able to? Does that mean you don't have the money right now?"

Grinning, he shook his head. "Don't you know girls as pretty as you aren't supposed to be smart too?" It was a rhetorical question. "Listen, the matter is as good as taken care of. I will be able to pay it back as soon as we return to Boston. Now, will you please ease up on me?"

A tiny pucker appeared between her brows. "Have you won some money since we've been here? Is that how you'll repay the debt?"

"*No.* I told you I haven't gambled, and I wasn't lying." He ran his hand around the back of his neck. "Good Lord, Bella, stop harping."

"I'm sorry. It's simply that I'm worried."

"I'm sorry to worry you. You're the best sister in the world." Emotion choked his voice, and he gave her another quick, hard hug, then briskly straightened. "Now, that's settled. I'm promised for bridge. Want to join me in the card room? Someone might need a fourth."

She shook her head. "I don't think so. I'll see you in the morning." She rose up on tiptoe and kissed his cheek. "I love you, and I'm very proud you're my brother."

As Kenneth turned to leave, she braced to face Jake, dark and brooding in his tuxedo. She hadn't forgotten he was there, and he certainly couldn't be overlooked. Against the exquisite backdrop of the staircase he looked very pagan.

She chose a straight course across the hall, distancing herself from him, but he was quickly beside her, matching his steps to hers as they walked to the drawing room.

"How can I help you, Arabella?"

The question so startled her, she almost missed a step. "I don't need anything."

"Are you sure? It looked to me as if you and Kenneth were having a fight."

She shook her head. "You misinterpreted the situation. We were discussing bridge strategy."

"You must take your bridge very seriously."

Actually, the game didn't appeal to her at all, and luckily Marlon saved her from having to reply.

"Sir, may I have a word with you?"

"Certainly." Jake closed long fingers around her upper arm and gently massaged the soft skin of her inner arm. "Do you mind?"

A warm excitement skittered through her. "You can do as you choose, Jake."

He smiled slowly. "Can I? That sounds promising."

"Jake—"

"I'll catch up with you in a few minutes."

She entered the drawing room, feeling as though he had left his fingerprints on her skin. She knew most of the people there, either from Boston or having met them in the past few days. A pianist was knocking out the jaunty "Ain't We Got Fun" on a baby grand in one corner of the room. A group was gathered around singing, "In the meantime, in between time, ain't we got fun." It could be her generation's anthem, she thought as she continued gazing around the room.

A jazz baby ingenue sat on the lap of an ardent admirer. Another couple danced the lindy hop. One group played Mah-Jongg, shouting, "Pung!" and "Chow!" uncaring that the condensation from their drink glasses was ringing the finish of the marquetry wood table around which they sat. She had always revered beautiful things, and she had noticed before the careless treatment of the wonderful things in the house. She simply didn't understand why Jake allowed it.

She spotted Vanessa. Her short dress was made up of red glass beads and ostrich feathers, and she was slanted back against a wall with Lucas leaning toward her, his hand propped beside her head. Vanessa glowed with love as she gazed up at Lucas, completely changed from the hard-edged woman Arabella had met in the afternoon. As she watched, Lucas raised his hand and touched Vanessa's cheek. The gesture was so loving, so tender, so full of intimately shared emotion, Arabella felt like an intruder and turned away to begin slowly strolling through the room.

Her mind was still very much on the scene she had witnessed, but here and there she heard pieces of conversation.

"My sister just came back from England before the

holidays and she bought a copy of *Lady Chatterley's Lover* there and smuggled it into the country with her. It's the *most* deliciously wicked book. You must read it."

Passing another group, she heard, "We attended the Gershwin concert in New York a few weeks ago where he conducted 'An American in Paris.' It was extraordinary, almost like a poem set to music that had both jazz and sound effects. Perhaps he'll perform it again soon."

Arabella was too preoccupied for the conversations to hold her interest long. The shared love she had seen in Lucas and Vanessa had directed her thoughts toward Jake, his intentions toward her, and what she should do about it. Young women her age were daring. The last decade had been an exciting time to be young. Much to the dismay of many a mother, foundation garments had gone out the window and what they termed barbaric music had come in. Women smoked, cut their hair, wore short skirts, drank champagne as their mothers had drank tea, took lovers, and everyone thought it was swell.

Ain't We Got Fun. Absolutely, she thought. And she had participated in nearly everything and more, in many instances had led the way. But if she'd indulged herself, she'd also made sure she did a proportionate amount of good for people not as fortunate as she. And amazingly enough, through it all she had steadfastly refused to give her heart or her body to a man.

She had always believed that somewhere there was

a man for her, someone with whom she could link her destiny, someone who would be her mate for life, the father of her children. But something essential had always been missing from the men she had dated. She hadn't known what was missing until she had met Jake. Now she thought that the missing element might have been Jake himself—and the wondrous way he made her feel when she was with him, along with the way he could heat her blood when he kissed and touched her.

Still, secret parts, important parts of her—like her heart—remained old-fashioned. And there was a belief seeded deep inside her: Love and commitment had to come before lovemaking.

But now . . . She was falling for Jake so fast, she felt as if she had vertigo. Everything seemed to whirl around her. Only he stood still, watching, waiting, tugging at her even when he was doing nothing.

Her heart was lost, but not her soul. And, she vowed, no matter the temptation, she would never make love with him knowing he didn't love her. Quite simply, the betrayal of her values and the ultimate hurt would be more than she could bear.

"Arabella," someone called from a group standing by the tall marble fireplace. "You've read Virginia Woolf's *Orlando,* haven't you? Come tell us your opinion. Don't you think it's too too strange?"

She smiled, glad to have the excuse to get her mind off Jake. But it didn't work, because even as she was explaining her favorable views of a heroine who is sometimes a hero, Jake came into the room. She tensed for his approach, but somewhat to her chagrin he went to a sophisticated-looking woman with penciled brows and hennaed hair who gestured to him. Arabella recognized her as a well-known divorcee.

When he reached the woman, she snaked a long, lovely arm around his neck. "Darling, you must give me these chairs," she said loudly enough for Arabella to hear. She indicated a pair of carved Brazilian rosewood chairs by the fireplace. "I'm mad for them."

"Then they're yours."

Arabella gasped. The rosewood of the chairs had been fashioned in elegant swirling movements to exactly match the carving in the marble fireplace.

Jake heard her exclamation and excused himself. He put a hand on Arabella's elbow and led her away from the people to whom she had been talking. "I've got something to show you."

She took his wrist and pulled it up so that she could glance at his watch. "It's midnight. It can't be another new day. Not even you could do that."

He sighed with mock exasperation that, disturbingly, she found most attractive. "Arabella, no one doubts me but you. Why is that?"

She pretended to guess. "An indispensable, well-tuned self-protective instinct?"

He chuckled. "I wouldn't harm a hair on your head."

"You're not going to get the chance."

He sighed again. "Arabella, it's very, very bad to challenge me."

Blood was singing through her veins, making her ruefully aware that he brought all her senses to life until colors seemed more vivid, sounds seemed louder, and he seemed the only man in the world. "That was really more a fact than a challenge, Jake."

"You do persist, don't you?"

He guided her from the room to Marlon, who was waiting in the entry hall with her ermine cape. Without a word she let Jake drape it around her shoulders. Her father had always chided her penchant for seeking adventure and flirting with danger, but she knew that deep down he trusted her, and she trusted herself. Tomorrow night she would be back home, away from this glorious place, away from this glorious man. She *wanted* to be with him and go wherever he was taking her.

They left the house and walked across the snow beneath a star-filled sky and a silver moon. The night was still and quiet, the air crisp and cold. When they reached an immense iron-and-glass conservatory, he ushered her inside. The lights were dimmed; the air was warm and perfumed and she could hear a fountain splashing.

"I feel like I'm in a moonlit garden on a spring night," she murmured in wonder.

"I'm glad you like it."

She didn't like it, she thought. She *loved* the special

treat he had given her, taking her away from the others to bring her to this enchanted place.

"Did you think I wouldn't like it? Everything about SwanSea is fabulous, you know that."

He shrugged, his face shadowed and moody. "It serves a purpose. It provides a place for my friends to play."

They began walking, choosing one of the paths that led through the beds that contained hundreds of varieties of exotic flowers and plants. Here and there couches and chairs were placed—comfort and luxury among the beauty.

"I don't believe those people back there in the drawing room are your friends."

Her astute observation brought a half smile to his face. "Why not?"

"Friends wouldn't treat your home so shabbily. They were dropping ashes onto the carpets, leaving rings on the wood."

"It's nothing to worry about. The staff will clean it up as soon as everyone has gone to bed."

"But the damage will have been done. Why don't you demand that your guests treat your home with more respect?"

"Because their behavior doesn't concern me." His tone was of good-humored exasperation.

They had come to a stop by a large marble fountain in the middle of the conservatory. She took off her ermine cape and swirled it over the back of a damask-covered couch. "May I ask you a question?"

His lip quirked. "Anything, Arabella."

"How could you have given those chairs away to that woman?"

"Elise?" He slipped his hands into his trouser pockets and eyed her consideringly. "She wanted them."

"But obviously they were specially made for the house. They match the fireplace."

"Elise is an old friend. She owns a furniture store in Boston, so her interest in the chairs is natural."

Old friend. More than likely, the woman was a former lover. "But what if she sells them?"

"I don't care what she does with them. They're hers now. Arabella, I don't understand why you're so caught up with this." He heard the sharpness of his voice and silently cursed. He hadn't meant to let his anger slip through to her, but before he'd joined everyone in the drawing room, there had been a telephone call from Edward. As usual, they'd argued, and "his father" wanted him back in Boston as soon as possible. "His father" could damned well wait.

She rubbed her arms. "It's just that SwanSea is your home. It seems to me you would treasure it."

"You think because I grew up in the North End I should be overwhelmed by SwanSea's magnificence?" He kept his tone light, but his words carried a bite. "I should feel lucky, right? A filthy Irish street kid having all this. My, my."

"Don't try to turn this on me, Jake. *I* grew up on

Beacon Hill, and if this were my home, I wouldn't allow *anyone* to behave in it as if he were in a barn."

"Such passion." He touched one of the brilliants at her shoulder. "And you're squandering it on something that's no more than stone and mortar."

"Did you give away the painting in the entry hall?"

He frowned. "What are you talking about?"

"There's a spot on the wall where you can tell a painting once hung. Did you give it away too?"

He sighed and pinched the bridge of his nose with his thumb and forefinger. "No, Arabella. If my instructions were carried out properly, the painting is in the attic, face to the wall. It's a portrait of Edward Deverell."

"But why would you do something like that? He built SwanSea. Great heavens, he *adopted* you and gave you all this."

"I'm one lucky guy, aren't I?"

"You sound so bitter. Why?"

He raked his hand through his hair. "Look, I didn't bring you out here to talk about either SwanSea or Edward Deverell. For God's sake, give it a rest!"

She'd been aware she was going too far even while she was doing it. But she had been driven to try to understand this man who was the cause of such tumultuous feelings within her. "All right." She looked around, then reached for her cape. "I've seen what you wanted to show me. It's lovely, but I think I'll go back to the house now."

He grabbed her arm. "Wait. I didn't mean to snap

at you. Besides, you haven't seen what I brought you to see."

"I know why you brought me out here—to make love to me."

"Arabella"—his voice was a soft chastisement—"if I had intended to make love to you, I would have taken you to my bedroom. That's for later."

"Then, why—"

"I wanted to be alone with you so I could ask you to stay here with me for a few days instead of returning to Boston tomorrow with Kenneth."

He said he was *asking,* but she heard no doubt in his voice as to her decision. And he had said, their lovemaking would be *later,* as if her consent were a given. "Why should I stay, Jake? So that in a few days you can send me back to Boston in a snowstorm after you've become bored with me? No, thank you."

"I would never do that." He touched a finger to her temple, strangely troubled by the idea of her being sent out into the night by him or anyone. "Stay with me, Arabella. Please."

His please was almost her undoing. "I—I can't."

"Can't or won't?"

"Both."

"I'm not going to accept that answer, you know."

"You'll have to by tomorrow, because I will have left."

He stared at her for a long moment, then walked to a wall and pulled a cord. One end of a silken net fell and hundreds of exquisitely colored butterflies fluttered free.

Her hands flew to her face in wonderment. "Ohhh . . . how beautiful! Where did they come from? How did they get here?"

"I had Bernardo arrange it. He breeds them as a hobby. He's found a way to break the laws of nature." He walked back to her.

"Butterflies! In January!"

"Bernardo has managed to breed them so they can break free from their chrysalises in winter."

The butterflies whispered through the air, flitting from bush to flower. "They're exquisite, Jake."

He took up the conversation with a relentlessness that belied his ability to think of such an extraordinary gesture as the butterflies. "And what if I refuse to allow you to leave?"

She swallowed and wasn't surprised to find a hard lump in her throat. Jake was a forceful, persuasive man, and he had no intention of letting her go easily. "You have nothing to say about it."

He framed her face with his hands and stared deep into her eyes. "What if I make love to you so often tonight and so well, you'll be too exhausted to leave?"

She felt as if she were swimming against a heated tide and she was about to go under. "You won't unless you plan to rape me."

"Rape is an atrocity. What I plan to do to you will be a pleasure for both of us. I'll show you . . ."

Unable to wait a moment longer, he pulled her into

his arms and did what he had wanted to do all night. He slid his hand between the chiffon shell and the silk slip and closed it around her breast. Her breast fit perfectly into his hand, her body perfectly in his arms. Emotion slammed through him, and he was shaken. Why had he waited so long? Certainly he had never done so with any other woman. He felt her nipple tighten with his caressing and groaned. At this very moment his desire for her was consuming him.

His ever-present anger with Edward had become even greater during the telephone call. Soon it would die down again to its usual simmering rage, but for now his anger and his need for Arabella seemed mixed together. There was an overwhelming urgency in him. He *hurt* with wanting her, and he hurt with his anger, but she could help him. She could release him from at least part of his torment.

Even as he was thinking this, he felt her arms slide around his neck. He laughed softly and captured her lips with his and began taking and taking. And she responded until she was practically boneless against him, all softness and fire. A hard shudder raced through him. There was something new and fresh about the way she made him feel. And she had a sweetness about her he wasn't used to . . . almost an innocence.

"Jake . . ."

The sound of her voice was nearly lost beneath the loud beating of his heart. He slipped his hands beneath the white slip and the pearl-encrusted skirt and cupped her bottom, lifting her and pulling her hard against him. "You're going to have to wear this dress for me again sometime," he said roughly, "but I think for now it's served its purpose."

Her heart jumped as his lips closed over hers. She could feel herself weakening. With every touch, with every kiss, she was falling more under his spell. She had to help herself, but the pleasure was deep, deep inside her. . . . She couldn't stop herself from moving against him, drawing another groan from him and eliciting a series of hot kisses down her throat to the collar of pearls and below them to her breast.

"Jake"—she cast about in her mind for something that would break the spell, something that would free her from his control—"you said we'd go to your bedroom."

"I've decided a couch will do very well," he muttered, guiding her toward the nearest one and lowering her onto its plush cushions.

He started to follow her down, but something made him hold back. He stared down at her, drawing ragged, painful breaths in and out of his lungs. Moonlight streamed through the glass roof, bathing her in an incandescent light, making her appear luminescent. The pearl-encrusted skirt lay high on her thighs, revealing an enticing expanse of silken skin between the top of her rolled stockings and the hem. Beneath the transparent bodice, her slip strap had fallen from her shoulder, and the slip itself gaped low on her breast. Butterflies fluttered around them, stirring the perfumed air with their delicate wings. In some ways, he realized, she reminded him of a butterfly with her elegance and beauty. And right now there seemed to be a certain fragility about her. . . .

Dammit, what was this hesitancy in him? He didn't understand it. He wanted her until he was almost blind with it. But he had never knowingly hurt anyone or anything innocent.

She wasn't an innocent. She couldn't be.

He went down to her and settled himself on top of her, fitting himself into her curves and valleys, then had to clench his jaw as heat rolled through him. He had to slow himself down, he thought ruefully, or this wouldn't last more than a minute.

But he couldn't resist putting his hand around her breast once again. "If you feel this good with your clothes on, I can't wait to take them off."

She curled her arms around his neck; he pulled back.

She made a soft sound; he heard a thundering in his brain.

This wasn't right. *Dammit, something wasn't right.*

He jerked to his feet.

Bewilderment clouded Arabella's eyes as she looked up at him. "Jake?"

"Get up." He reached down for her arm and hauled her upright. She was confused, and he didn't blame her. But, dammit, he could not tolerate one more second of looking at her on that couch without tearing her clothes off and driving into her sweet body.

Why hadn't he? What in the hell was wrong with him? He could have taken her, he thought, disgusted at himself. It would have been so easy.

His anger grew—at her, at Edward.

He was going to let her go, for now at least, and he didn't know why. "Let's get out of here."

"I—I don't understand."

He pulled her to her feet and hastily, clumsily, rearranged her clothes. "I shouldn't have left my friends. I'm the host."

"I don't believe you."

"Dammit, Arabella, would you rather stay here and have me take you on that couch? Because, sweetheart, in case you don't realize it, you are one minute away from being ravaged in about every way there is."

Tears threatened, but the sight of his dark, angry expression kept them at bay. "I don't deserve your anger, Jake Deverell. And I don't deserve to be talked to like that. And to answer your question, I can't wait to leave this place."

Arabella couldn't sleep. Her skin was too hot, her nerves too agitated, her mind too busy. She kicked the covers aside and reached for her robe. Without knowing where she was going, she left the room.

Her robe of ivory Alençon lace drifted out behind her as she walked the shadowed halls. All the doors leading off the halls were closed; everyone was asleep.

She took the stairs down to the second floor, remembering the day she had walked these same halls as a child. There had been a different kind of quiet then, the quiet of a house partially closed and suffering grief, the quiet imposed by the master of the house who had eyes that didn't smile.

The house had a new master now, a master with eyes that could glint with heat and who filled the house to bursting with people. And still there was quiet, the quiet of a house, enduring, waiting.

Except. What was the *thumping* sound?

She started down the stairs toward the landing and the Tiffany window, the sound growing louder as she went. Stopping before she reached the landing, she peered over the railing and looked down into the immense entry hall. Jake was there, stripped to the waist, hitting a small rubber ball against the wall, using all the strength that was in him. His muscles rolled and flexed with fluid power and sweat gleamed over his dark olive skin with his violent exertion. Time and again his hand connected with the ball, slamming it against the wall on the exact spot where Edward Deverell's portrait had hung. Lucas sat quietly on one of the bottom steps, his eyes following his friend's every move. Vanessa was asleep, her head in Lucas's lap.

Above them Arabella sank unseen onto a step and gazed down into the hall between two railings.

Jake was like a man obsessed, she thought. A man with furies and his own private demons inside him.

What were they? What drove him so? What caused his burning and his inability to rest? Could *she* possibly have anything to do with it? No, she quickly answered herself. He had stopped the lovemaking, not she. His anger toward her had been totally irrational, and she had been left bewildered and chagrined.

Cold seeped through the delicate lace of her robe, but she couldn't tear her gaze from the scene down in the hall.

Jake moved with agility and power, smashing the ball again and again against the wall as if he were trying to destroy something there.

What did one do about loving such a man? His longtime friend, Lucas, supported him with his presence, but when all was said and done, he could only watch. What chance did she have with only a tender, brand-new love to offer him, a love that he wouldn't even want?

Her heart ached as she watched the poignant, emotionally charged scene below. She felt an instinctive need to help him, to reach out her arms and comfort him, to ease his pain. But she didn't have to think twice to know he would never give her the chance. In truth, she didn't think he could truly love a woman, and she was more convinced than ever that she should leave in the morning.

The thing was, she had never lacked for courage in anything. And after years of remaining uninvolved, she had tumbled hard for Jake. It went against her nature to turn her back on those she loved . . . or on danger. What should she do?

Her heart, mind, and body was telling her to stay. But her self-protective instincts were telling her to run as fast as she could.

She rose and walked silently back up the stairs.

Arabella dodged a snowball as it flew across the entry hall, its target a red-cheeked girl who shrieked with delight when it missed her. Choosing a snowball from her own arsenal, the young woman aimed and tossed.

Arabella frowned. The massive carved black-walnut front doors stood wide open, admitting not only the afternoon sunlight, but the snowball fight as well. Everyone involved was having a grand time.

She saw Marlon standing impassively to one side. Where was Jake?

"Ready?" Kenneth asked, coming up beside her, pulling on his gloves.

"Yes. The maids have already left with the luggage in the second car."

"Then I guess there's nothing to do but get on the road." A snowball hit the side of his neck. With a good-natured laugh, he brushed the snow away. "Good-bye, everybody. See you soon."

"Good-bye," Arabella echoed, and waved, then followed Kenneth out. But when she reached the doorway, something made her look back. And her breath caught in her throat.

Jake was standing at the top of the landing, his

chest bare, his legs planted wide apart, his hands in the pockets of the trousers he had worn to dinner the night before, the same ones he had been wearing early this morning when he had seemed bent on destroying the wall with the ball. He hadn't been to bed, she realized.

Breathtaking jewel-colored light streamed from the stained-glass window behind him and outlined his dark, powerful shape in clear, sharp detail. The sight of him pulled at her like a gravitational force.

She lifted her chin and stared back at him, wishing with everything that was in her that she could read his expression. She wasn't sure what it was she wanted from him—a sign perhaps that he was sorry she was leaving, a softness that would tell her one day he might love her. If he had done any of these things, if he had even lifted his hand toward her, she would have gone back to him. Heaven help her, she would have.

But as she watched, her heart in her throat, he turned and walked slowly back up the stairs.

5

HIS brow furrowed with concentration, Edward studied the latest profit and loss statement that Jake had brought him.

Jake watched him, a wry half smile on his lips. The figures were excellent, but he didn't expect praise. In the past eleven years, Edward hadn't uttered one word of praise to him, no matter his accomplishments. In fact, nothing had changed between them since they had first laid eyes on each other the afternoon of Jake's eighteenth birthday in the tiny, run-down apartment he had shared with his mother. He still hated Edward for his despicable treatment of his mother all those years before when she had come to him and told him she was pregnant, and Edward still hated him for not being his legitimate son, John.

Edward's coal-black hair was generously sprinkled with silver now, and a few wrinkles had been added to his face. But his carriage was still rigidly straight and his manner arrogant and imperious. And, Jake thought, he was still every bit the cold-blooded bastard who had come to his mother's apartment so long ago. Even at seventy-five years of age, Edward didn't have a mellow bone in his body.

Eleven years earlier Jake couldn't have imagined being in a plush office on the top floor of the Deverell Building, nor could he have imagined that he would take to business as he had. To his surprise, he had discovered he had a special knack for it. He had done some brilliant and innovative work with the company since his Harvard graduation and had increased profits many times over.

His original idea had been to ruin the business gradually until all that Edward had achieved was gone—even if it had meant going against his own best interest. But once he had gotten involved, he hadn't been able to help himself. He *loved* the business and he was good at it. Besides, there were other ways to hurt the man. . . .

Edward finally looked up at him.

"Well?" Jake asked, knowing exactly what Edward would say.

"The profit is adequate."

"It's much more than adequate, and you know it."

Edward shrugged. "To say it's adequate doesn't imply criticism. On the contrary, I'm quite satisfied."

"You damned well should be."

Edward leveled a sharp gaze at him over steepled fingers. "But the figures are the only thing I'm satisfied with. Two weeks have passed since I telephoned you at SwanSea and told you to return to Boston. I expected you to come back immediately."

"I had guests. It would have been rude to leave them."

"You *always* have guests, Jake. In fact, you probably have people staying there who are left over from parties you gave two years ago."

"You think so? I'll have to check."

Edward scowled. "The point is, I needed you back here immediately."

Well aware of why Edward was so eager to see him, he crossed his legs and settled back in his chair with a nonchalant ease. "Anything serious?"

"Yes, dammit, it is."

Jake's mouth relaxed into a full smile. Edward always began their meetings with his emotions under control. By the end of their meetings, the vein on his forehead was pulsing.

"I found out that you had gone around me and stopped our policy of buying stocks on margin. I want to know why."

He might harass and irritate Edward on other things, but when it got to the bottom line of business, he was always serious. "I went around you because I knew you would never agree, and I stopped our policy of buying stocks on margin because I felt it was time to do so."

"What in the hell does that mean?"

Jake rolled his shoulders, unsure if he could explain his feeling. "Since 1924, you and your cronies have been playing fast and loose on Wall Street."

Edward stiffened. "There are no regulations or laws against our practices."

"No, but I'm beginning to think there should be. You and your friends bid up a security, get other people interested in it, bid it up some more, then sell it, and you walk away with a profit. But you've built a house of cards, and when you walk away, it comes tumbling down. I think Wall Street has become a giant house of cards, and I just don't feel people can keep up this manipulation much longer."

"Then you're a fool."

Jake pointed toward the profit and loss statement on the desk. "A fool couldn't be responsible for that, old man."

Edward sliced a hand through the air. "Bah! This country is operating on a sound foundation, and it's no time for the fainthearted. We can only get richer."

"Yeah, but not on the stock market. And that's the other half of my plan. I'm going to start selling off our stocks and securities."

"*What?*"

Jake viewed him impassively. "By August we'll be completely out of the market."

Edward's hand slapped the desk, causing the profit

and loss statement to flutter, then settle back down about an inch from where it had been. "I won't have it, damn you! I'm still the president of this company."

"You may have the title, but I have the power."

"It's power I've given you. I can take it away."

Jake grinned. "But you won't. As much as you might begrudge me my successes, Deverell comes first with you, and you would never ruin your precious company, even to spite me."

Edward coughed, brought his hand to his mouth, paused a moment, and coughed again. Then he settled back into his chair. "But I don't happen to think this course of action is in our best interest. In fact, I think it's foolish, stupid, and asinine. There's a fortune to be made—" He broke off, coughing.

Jake poured him a glass of water, handed it to him, and waited until he had drunk it. "We have several fortunes, Edward, and I'll make us several more. But not on the stock market. Not now."

"I tell you, I won't have it!"

"When you give yourself time to think about it, you're going to come to the same conclusion as I did. But you still won't admit that it's a good idea, because then you'd have to give me credit and you'd never do that, would you? You can't stand for anyone, not even your son, to put you in the shade. But then, you still won't acknowledge that I am your son, will you?"

Edward stared back at Jake, the expression in his black eyes as opaque and impenetrable as Jake's. "That's a closed subject, Jake."

Fresh anger spurted through him. "To you, maybe."

Edward sighed. "I read about your New Year's Eve party."

"Oh, I see," Jake said, rubbing his forehead. "We're going to talk about SwanSea for a while, are we? Well, let me put your mind at ease. SwanSea is still standing. It's a tough old house."

"That's because I built it to last. I wanted my children and their children to be able to live in it for generations to come. I still do." When Jake didn't say anything, he went on. "I was pleased to see that the Lindens were there."

"You know them?"

"I know their father. He's a very prominent banker. I've done business with him for years. His son and daughter are exactly the kind of people you should be associating with." He coughed again.

Jake frowned. "Are you all right?"

"Yes, yes, I'm fine. In fact, Arabella Linden would make a most appropriate wife for you."

"Appropriate." Jake mulled over the word, thinking how like Edward to use it in regard to Arabella. She had all the proper credentials, along with wealth and social position. On the other hand, Edward hadn't deemed Jake's mother an *appropriate* wife for himself because she had been only a poor young Irish widow.

He had been holding a weapon back, Jake mused, but perhaps it was time to use the one thing that would hurt Edward even more than the ruination of his business. "I've been meaning to tell you for some time now—you can forget about having any grandchildren. Because I will never marry and I will never have children."

Edward's jaw dropped and his eyes widened incredulously. "You can't mean that!"

"I mean every word."

"But you must marry. I need grandchildren to carry on the Deverell name."

"You need," he said succinctly. "I don't, and there's nothing you can do about it." But Edward would try, Jake reflected, and he looked forward to the confrontations they would have. "You won't acknowledge me as your son, Edward. Why should I be concerned about the perpetuation of the Deverell name?"

Edward jabbed a finger at him. "Because it's in your blood to do so, dammit!"

"Don't you mean my *illegitimate* blood, Edward?"

"Jake, you've always put entirely too much emphasis on the issue of whether or not I acknowledge you. It's not important. You should be grateful for what I have given you."

The expression in Jake's eyes went from cool to ice cold, but his tone was utterly casual. "I do plan to be squiring Arabella around town in the next few months. I'm sure you'll be reading about us in the papers."

Edward leaned forward, hope written on his face. "Then you do plan—"

"To have an affair with her? Yes, most definitely."

"An affair! Good God, Jake, she's a Brahmin. You can't just have one of your usual sordid little affairs and then flaunt it, not with a girl like Arabella Linden."

"Why not?"

"B-because I won't allow it."

"You can't stop me." An unpleasant smile formed on his lips. "Face it, old man. The king is dead. Long live the king."

Jake pulled his new custom-built red Cadillac Sport Phaeton to the curb in front of Arabella's house and switched off the engine. This was the first time he had tried to contact her since he had been back in Boston. What had happened between them in the conservatory her last night at SwanSea still bothered him, and he'd been trying to figure it out ever since. Backing away from a willing woman he was interested in was a first for him.

Not forgetting her as soon as she left was another first.

There was hardly an hour that had gone by that he hadn't thought of her. She'd gotten into his mind and under his skin. And perhaps most surprising was that there'd been no woman since, not because he hadn't had the opportunity but because he hadn't been interested.

His meeting with Edward had convinced him to

forget his doubts and questions and go to her. The meeting *and* the constant ache in his loins.

He vaulted up the stairs and rang the bell. A maid in a drop-waisted black uniform and wearing a white pleated headband answered. "Yes?"

"I'd like to see Miss Linden, please."

"I'm sorry, sir, but Miss Linden is preparing to leave. Perhaps you'd care to come back another time—"

"Who is it, Sylvia?" Arabella called, buttoning her figure-hugging honey-colored wool and gold-fox-trimmed coat.

"I don't know, miss—"

He pushed past the maid and stepped into the large marble entry hall. "It's me."

About to pull on her gloves, Arabella stopped. "Jake—"

With a smile he walked to her, took her hand, and kissed it. "You remembered my name. How nice."

For a moment she thought she would fall apart. Her heart was racing so fast, she feared it would burst, and she didn't seem to be breathing at all.

Lord, she couldn't allow him to see how much he affected her.

Using sheer force of will, she compelled her breathing and heart rate back to normal. "Why wouldn't I remember you? I have a remarkable memory."

"I knew there was something I liked about you."

"My memory?"

He grinned. "The fact that you're remarkable. You are, you know."

"Jake," she began, careful to keep her tone even, "what are you doing here? It's been over two weeks—"

"Did you honestly think you'd seen the last of me?"

"I didn't know what to think." Jumbled and confused, her thoughts had kept her in a constant state of turmoil. And now she realized that two weeks apart from him had not resolved one doubt or uncertainty she'd had about him, nor had it dimmed her love for him.

He stepped closer. "I'm here now."

She straightened, meeting his gaze levelly. "And why is that, Jake?"

"To ask you to join me for dinner tonight. I know a place—"

She felt as if she were standing once again in the doorway of SwanSea, gazing up at him, searching for a sign that he might care for her. "No, I'm sorry, I can't."

He put a finger beneath her chin and tilted her face upward. "Dinner, Arabella. Not lovemaking."

She'd made the wise, sensible decision to leave SwanSea and him behind. Now, seeing him again, her wise, sensible decision was fast going out the window. His presence was too forceful, too compelling. And she was too much in love. "Dinner? That's all?"

"That's all, unless, of course, you want more."

Kenneth walked briskly up, a leather folder in his hands. "Arabella, here are those papers—" The sight of Jake brought him to an abrupt halt. The color washed from his face. His first thought was that Jake had discovered what he had done, but quickly he realized he was mistaken because Jake was smiling. He drew a deep breath and extended his hand. "Jake old boy, what a nice surprise. I didn't know you were back in town."

"I haven't been very long. I've come to invite your sister out tonight. Actually, I've come to court her."

Kenneth forced a chuckle. "Get in line."

"You know better than that." He turned back to Arabella. "I'm not any good at standing in line, but I hope you appreciate the fact that I waited until the afternoon to pay you a call."

"That was very thoughtful of you." In fact, she'd been waking up earlier and earlier. She took the folder from Kenneth.

Jake frowned. "Where are you going?"

"I'm on the board of directors of the Linden Foundation. I go into the office several afternoons a week."

A black brow rose mockingly. "Our lady of good works and baskets."

Kenneth stiffened. "Arabella does much more than baskets of food for the poor. She's been responsible for many marvelous programs."

Arabella smiled at her brother, touched and a bit puzzled by his defense. Usually he didn't bother, knowing she could defend herself. "As a matter of fact, one of those programs is waiting for me now. If you two gentlemen will excuse me, I need to leave."

"I'll go check to make sure they've brought your car around," Kenneth said, striding toward the front door, leaving the two of them together. He had warned Arabella more than once about Jake and she had refused to listen. But she was on her home ground now, and if he were still a gambling man, he'd give her even odds with Jake.

"I'll excuse you," Jake said to Arabella. "And I'll be back around nine this evening."

She started to refuse. She was being a fool, and she knew it. But she would hate herself forever if she backed away from something as safe as a dinner with him. Besides, she would have her own home to go to after their evening was over—and her chaste, safe bed.

He rubbed his hand over the soft ends of the fox collar. "I'm surprised to see you in something other than white."

"I decided it was time to give colors a chance."

He threw back his head and laughed. "That's such an Arabella thing to say." He curved his hand along her jawline. "I've missed you. Tell me you've missed me."

Her heart skipped a beat. *Yes, Lord, she had missed him.* "I could tell you that, but then I would be lying."

He smiled lazily. "So lie to me, Arabella. You tell such sweet lies."

"I've missed you," she said, doing just as he asked and praying it did sound like a lie.

He chuckled softly and pressed a warm kiss to her lips. "I'll be back tonight."

A panel slid open behind an iron grille and a frowning face appeared. Jake held up a card. The face smiled, and in a moment the door opened. "Come right in, Mr. Deverell."

Jake guided Arabella into a posh speakeasy located in the basement of an old mansion.

"I didn't know this was here," she said as he slipped her elaborate wrap of white ostrich feathers from her shoulders. Beneath it she was wearing a silver lamé, sleeveless, V-neck dress that was trimmed with silver glass beads and glistened with every move.

"You'll like it. The liquor hasn't been diluted and the food is excellent. And the vestibule is equipped with four alarm buttons."

The cloakroom girl smiled at him as he handed her their coats. "Nice to see you this evening, Mr. Deverell."

"You too, Alice."

Up on a stage, an eight-piece band played the zesty and infectious "Charleston," and the two dozen or so people on the dance floor swung into the energetic, high-stepping dance.

The headwaiter seated them with a flourish in a secluded corner booth. In the center of the linen-covered table, a small lamp with a fringed shade provided intimate lighting. "I'll be your waiter this evening, Mr. Deverell. Would you care to give me your drink order now?

Arabella laid her silver-beaded evening bag on the table beside her and gave Jake a wry smile. "Why do I have the feeling you've been here more than once?"

"I have no idea. What would you like to drink?"

"Champagne." She threw an idle glance around the large, smoky room and wasn't surprised to see people she knew. She waved to a few, happy beyond belief to be with Jake once more.

"Frank, I'll have a Scotch," Jake told the waiter, "and the lady will have champagne. For dinner we'll have whatever the chef recommends."

"Right away, Mr. Deverell."

She leaned toward Jake, her tone conspiratorial and confidential. "Are the owners of this place your customers?"

He was delighted to see the sparkle of amusement in her eyes. It deepened the golden color of her eyes and was the same spark that had so attracted him the first night they had met. "Customers? Why, Arabella, I have no idea what you could mean."

"Customers. You know . . . *bootlegging.*"

His expression registered shock. "Arabella, bootlegging is *illegal.* Isn't that right, Frank?" he asked the waiter, who had lived up to his promise of "right away" and returned to deliver their drinks.

"That's what I understand, Mr. Deverell."

"See?" he asked teasingly. "Frank knows it. Why don't you? Don't you keep up with the news?"

She waited until Frank had given them their drinks and departed. "I think I have a right to know whether or not I'm out with a bootlegger tonight."

He angled his body toward her and slid his arm along the banquette behind her head. "Would you be disappointed if I told you all of my activities are completely legal?"

She gave him a deliberately flirtatious bat of her eyelashes. "Most likely I would, because it would no doubt be a lie."

"But I tolerate your lies."

She lifted her champagne glass to her lips and sipped. "That's because my lies are sweet. You said it yourself." Seeing him again and being with him had gone to her head. She might as well have drunk a magnum of champagne. But so far he was acting the perfect gentleman, and she found sparring and flirting with him a heavenly, irresistible experience.

"I should have known you'd remember that. You did tell me earlier today that you have a remarkable memory."

"Well, Jake? Are you a bootlegger?"

He shrugged. "I wouldn't want to disappoint you, so I guess I have to say yes."

Even though she'd known what his answer would be, she was shocked at his casual confirmation. "But why?"

"It keeps me busy."

"Jake, you have other things that keep you busy. Why take the risk?"

"I see no reason not to. It's easy and it's fun."

"I can't believe your father approves of this."

His expression turned perceptibly cooler. "Here's Frank with our salads. They look good, don't you think?"

Much to Arabella's irritation, she was forced to drop the subject, because after Frank served them, Randolph Bruce strolled up to their table.

"Jake, Arabella, how wonderful to see you here tonight. Can I take it that you two are becoming an item?"

Arabella picked up her fork, briefly considering the effect it would have as a weapon before she stabbed a carrot with it. "You can take it any way you like, Randolph, but to say that two people are becoming an item when you've seen them out together only once would be exceedingly stupid, not to mention inaccurate. Don't you agree?" With that she popped the carrot into her mouth.

Randolph burst out laughing. "You've given me a great quote, Arabella. Jake, is there anything you'd like to add?"

Amusement played around Jake's lips. "I think Arabella has spoken for both of us."

"Great, great." Randolph had whipped out a notebook and began scribbling away. "By the way, how is it that Vanessa's still in town? I would imagine the studio is hopping mad about now, aren't they?"

Jake took a sip of his Scotch. "You'll have to ask her that."

"I've already tried. She and Lucas are having dinner over there." He pointed across the room. "As usual, neither of them is talking."

"Vanessa believes that the public has a right to news only of her movies, and that her private life should stay private."

"Well, she's wrong! Ask Mary Pickford and Douglas Fairbanks. Ask Lillian Gish or Charlie Chaplin. Only one person's ever gotten away with a silent treatment of the press, and that's Greta Garbo, and Vanessa's a long way from being in her league."

Jake absently swirled his glass of Scotch. "That's enough, Randolph."

Jake's cool tone stole a portion of the color from Randolph's face. "Sure thing, Jake. Oh, by the way, I have a tip that this place is going to be raided at midnight."

"I know. I heard the same tip. We'll be gone by then."

As soon as Randolph sauntered away, Arabella turned to Jake. "You didn't tell me you'd brought me to a place you know is going to be raided."

"What would be the point? I intend for us to be long gone before midnight. Unless, of course, you'd like to stay."

One brow arched wickedly. "Is there a back way out of here?"

"There are several."

"Then let's stay until we hear the alarm."

He grinned. "Ah, Arabella, you do entertain me."

She made a sound of affront. "You refer to me as one would a trained seal in a circus act."

"Trust me, Arabella. It's never entered my mind to think of you as a trained seal. Perhaps, though, now that I think about it . . ." He leaned toward her and pressed a finger to her skin at the lowest point of the V of her dress.

Her breath caught. Touching her between her breasts was an erotic, outrageous thing for him to do, and she couldn't for the life of her gather the strength to brush his hand away. "What?"

"Now that I think about it, you're like one of those pretty ladies who dance along a high wire. You're fearless, and sometimes when I watch you, I feel like my heart is in my throat."

The heavy muscles of his trousered leg pressed against hers, and his voice held a caressing quality that skimmed over her skin, heating her. "Why?"

"Don't you know?" he asked huskily.

She shook her head.

Briefly, quickly, his finger dipped beneath the dress, sliding over her breasts and bringing her heart to a temporary stop. "I don't know either."

Even with the blood rushing hotly through her veins, distorting her perception, there was no way she could doubt his sincerity—his honesty was ringingly clear both in his tone and expression. Was it possible that he was as confused as she about their effect on each other? The thought gave her hope and sent her mind whirling. She wanted to pursue the subject they had inadvertently started, but found herself suddenly shy. "No?"

"No," he said softly, his gaze on her lips.

She waited to see if he would say anything more. When he didn't, she went in search of something innocuous they could talk about that would slow down her pulse and cool her blood. "You were right about the salad. It's wonderful. Why haven't you eaten anything?"

He pushed his plate away and pulled back from her. "I misjudged my appetite. I'm not really that hungry."

Missing his nearness, she curved her body toward his. "I've never seen you eat. Even when we have dinner together, I eat and you don't."

"Perhaps," he said evenly, "I've never been hungry the same time as you."

"Perhaps. But the afternoon of the skating party I heard Vanessa say to Marlon, 'You know he won't eat' in reference to you."

"Think about it, Arabella. I couldn't maintain my weight if I didn't eat."

"But—"

"I'm sure you misunderstood Vanessa. Ask her if you like."

She had a sudden image of Lucas and Vanessa on the stairs while Jake tried to purge himself of his private demons with an excessively violent game of handball. Tired as she obviously had been, it hadn't occurred to Vanessa to get up and go to bed. Instead, she had stayed where she was on the hard marble step, eventually falling asleep with her head in Lucas's lap. No, Arabella thought. Vanessa would never tell her anything Jake wouldn't want her to know. The loyalty the three shared made them close ranks fast. She shook her head. "Vanessa doesn't like me."

"Vanessa has had a hard life."

He said it as if it explained everything and as if he intended to explain no more. "If Vanessa has had a hard life, that means you have too."

He tugged at a fairylike white-gold curl. "You do have a lively mind, don't you?"

"Well? It's the truth, isn't it?"

After a brief hesitation he said, "She was a girl. It was harder on her."

"How—"

"Would you like to dance?"

Cole Porter's lovely ballad "I Concentrate on You" was being played, and Arabella knew the invitation to dance meant the end of the subject. She sighed.

He put two fingers over her lips, feeling the sweet warm breath as it escaped. "I want to hold you in my arms."

What could she do? Though he didn't know it, he held her heart, and it had reached the point where there was very little she could deny him. "All right."

"Take your purse."

The sudden light of humor in his eyes surprised her. "Why?"

"Because my tipster said this place is going to be raided at *eleven* o'clock."

6

WITH a lopsided grin for Jake, Lucas folded the newspaper he'd been reading and tossed it aside. "Randolph Bruce says that you and Arabella Linden are a hot item."

Vanessa lazily stretched, sending the sleeves of her dove-gray wrapper sliding down her lovely arms. "Randolph is a louse. I don't know why you put up with him, Jake."

The three of them had just finished dinner and were lounging in armchairs in front of the fireplace in Jake's hotel suite.

Amusement tugged at the corners of Jake's mouth. "He serves a purpose, you know that."

"Sure, I know. You make certain Randolph sees and hears what you want him to, he prints it, and

Edward Deverell reads it. But Randolph is still a louse."

"And in this instance Randolph may also be right." Lucas took a moment to light a cigarillo. "You've been out with Arabella almost every night for the past two weeks. And knowing you as well as I do, I'd say you've either fallen hard for her or you have some other plan in mind. I think it's both."

Vanessa moved down in the chair and lay her head against its back. "I almost feel sorry for the girl."

Jake looked at Vanessa in surprise. "She said she didn't think you liked her."

"I don't have to like her to feel sorry for her. She's mad for you, Jake."

Was Arabella really in love with him? he wondered. The thought staggered him. He had never considered the possibility before, and he wasn't sure how he felt about it. Other women had been in love with him, but they were different from Arabella. . . .

Being in love with a woman was a foreign idea to him. Desire, on the other hand, was an idea with which he could deal very easily. Or it had been . . . until he had met Arabella. He was still troubled by that night in the conservatory. Since they had been going out in Boston, he had deliberately kept things light between them, giving himself time to try to figure out what it was that had stopped him from taking her.

And the status quo obviously suited her. She seemed completely at ease with him, flirting and bantering, glittering with beauty and life. No, she couldn't be in love with him. And his contentment to allow their situation to remain the same was rapidly coming to an end. The continual and growing ache in his body reminded him constantly that he was going to have to have her soon.

"She's going to get hurt, Jake."

"Arabella? No, no. She's too sophisticated not to know the score." The knowledge made him feel better. "Besides, what is all this? Except for a few extremely sarcastic and extremely pointed remarks, you two have never shown much interest in who I've taken out or how often."

Lucas exhaled a heavy stream of smoke. "Arabella seems different."

"And you seem different with her," Vanessa added.

Jake lifted his hand in a gesture of concession. "I couldn't say how I act with her, but I will say she's not like any other woman I've ever been involved with."

Lucas studied the end of his cigarillo. "I guess that's what we're trying to figure out—just what your involvement is with her."

"Why? Look, this is nothing for you two to worry about."

Vanessa reached over and touched his arm. "We're not worried. Just interested and concerned. For you. Besides," she said, her voice turning light, "I'm going to have to be leaving soon, and I won't be around to give you the benefit of my sage advice."

Jake's brows shot up. "Is MGM giving you problems?"

She nodded. "It seems this year for the very first time there's going to be some kind of awards ceremony at the Roosevelt Hotel. It's to be called the Academy Awards. And the whole idea was Louis B. Mayer's. Seems he feels films need a more dignified image."

Lucas chuckled. "I can't imagine that."

Vanessa sent him a playfully fierce look. "Anyway, since Mr. Mayer is my boss, I've got to go back. The ceremony isn't going to be held until the middle of May, but the studio wants me back in California as soon as possible for promotion and a new film. I'm going to try to put it off for another couple of weeks though."

"Why? Sounds like something that would be good for your career." Jake glanced at Lucas. "You're going with her, aren't you?"

Lucas shook his head. "I don't think I'd better. There's been another message from Wade through Ram. He's really serious, Jake. And the eighth customer in about four weeks has gotten in touch. Wade's men are trying strong-arm tactics, trying to get them to change suppliers. I've got everyone on the alert. I've also beefed up the guard on our best customers."

Jake uttered a mild expletive. "You'd think Wade's own rackets would keep him too busy to worry about our little operation."

"Well, obviously that's not the case."

"Maybe not, but I don't understand what Wade Scalia has to do with your staying here. You can't be *that* worried about him."

"Dammit, Jake. Is it going to take a Howitzer blowing up next to you to make you understand he's out to get you? He's waited for years to be in the position where he can finally one-up you."

Jake spread out his hands. "He's hijacked one shipment. No one got hurt. What do you want me to do? Retaliate in some way? That would only up the ante, and you know as well as I do that he would come at us again. Then we'd have to retaliate for his retaliation, and then we'd be smack in the middle of the war that Noah Calloway is so eager to avoid." He paused. "On the other hand, I know you're against giving him a percentage of our business." Grim-faced, Lucas nodded and Jake went on. "The only alternative I can think of is to ignore him and hope he'll eventually realize we are not going to budge from our position."

Lucas sighed and ground his cigarillo out in the ashtray. "You're right, you're right. I guess I just keep thinking there's a fourth alternative, one we haven't thought of yet."

"If you come up with something, let me know. In the meantime, dammit, go to California with Vanessa."

"No, I wouldn't feel good about it."

"Well, I know you're not going to feel good about

watching her train pull out of the station without you."

Vanessa spoke up. "It's all right, Jake. I understand. Lucas would be miserable out there worrying about you." She smiled. "Besides, I'm going to expect daily telephone calls keeping me updated on you and Arabella."

Jake groaned. "You two aren't going to let up on this, are you?"

"The thing is," Lucas said with a grin, "I believe you started out with one thing in mind and it's changed into something else. Only I don't think you realize it yet. I don't have to tell you that anything you do is fine with us. We just want to make certain you know what you're doing."

"I do," Jake said. "Of course I do."

The next evening Jake's words returned to him. He had taken Arabella to the same speakeasy they had gone to on their first date, and they were in the same dimly lit, secluded corner booth. She was wearing a gold sequined and beaded dress with tiny, narrow straps. Her hair was hidden by a small, close-fitting evening cap that dripped identical golden beads onto her forehead and around her face. And every time she moved, light played over her skin and heat skidded through him.

He could barely keep his eyes off her, much less his hands. Lucas had been right. He had a plan in which Randolph Bruce played a prominent part, but his plan and his desires were getting all mixed up. It had been hell holding himself back these last couple of weeks, being close to her but never allowing himself to go past a certain point. He had never been so careful with a woman before, and he didn't know how much longer he would last. She was so vibrant, so alive, so beautiful. Every time he looked at her, he felt a primitive urge to possess her, to make her his own, no matter the cost to him or his plan.

Being with her without making love to her was wearing on nerves he hadn't known he had. And he didn't think he could continue escorting her out every evening, making sure they were seen when what he really wanted to do was to keep her home with him, undress her slowly, and make love to her all night long.

Arabella smiled at the waiter as he whisked her empty plate away along with Jake's full plate. "I don't know why you bother ordering dinner, Jake. You don't even take one bite."

"Maybe I'm hungry when I order, but by the time the order arrives, I'm so engrossed with you, I forget all about food."

"Applesauce."

"You talk so prettily, Arabella."

"Horsefeathers."

He chuckled, and Arabella smiled back at him, feeling a distinct tug in the region of her heart. She was falling deeper and deeper in love with him, until it had reached the point she wasn't sure she would be able to walk away from him again as she had at SwanSea.

Sadly, she was no closer to understanding him. They had spent a lot of time together over the past couple of weeks, though hardly ever alone. He made no declarations of love as so many of the men she'd dated over the years had. And although he touched her and kissed her often, it was usually when they were out at one night spot or another. In addition, though he made no secret of the fact that he wanted her, he hadn't tried to seduce her. Her senses were in a constant state of upheaval, her mind in a continuous state of confusion.

And she remembered the day he had come to her home to invite her out and said that it would only be dinner, unless she wanted more. . . .

"Oh, there's Myriah," she said, pointing toward the dance floor, where a young woman was doing a sedate fox trot with her partner. "Heavens, look at all those strands of beads she's wearing. She takes pride in adding one more strand for every new boyfriend. But if those beads ever begin to twirl in the wrong way and tangle together while she's doing the Charleston, it's my opinion she's likely to strangle herself." She shrugged. "Oh, well, at least she'll die knowing she was well loved."

Jake grinned. "Or at least frequently."

Arabella chuckled.

He reached out and encircled her throat with his

long fingers. "Your laugh plays me as if I were a musical instrument."

A thick strand of desire curled through her, and she stared at him, not sure what to think or say. He had just admitted that she affected him. And after all, she knew he couldn't be dating any other woman, not as much as they went out. If only he could come to love her. . . .

He pulled his hand away, leaving her skin feeling cold and deprived. She smiled at Jas, who was across the room, then made a sound of dismay. "Randolph's here again. Why is it that he's always around?"

Jake shrugged. "He goes where the people he writes about go."

She toyed with her champagne glass. "Do you read his column?"

"Occasionally." He grinned. "Usually Edward keeps me informed of its contents, at least when my name appears."

"You and I have been in there quite a bit lately," she said carefully.

He took a drink of his Scotch. "Yes, I know."

"Don't you mind?"

"Not particularly." He glanced at her and saw that she was frowning. "Is Randolph printing untruths?"

"Actually I don't know."

He set down his glass and shifted around to her. "What do you mean? What's bothering you, Arabella?"

"Yesterday's column stated that we were a hot item. The problem is, I don't know if we are or not."

The simple, direct statement affected him as no amount of coyness would have been able to do. "I would say it's fairly accurate," he said carefully. "After all, we're out together practically every night."

"But not alone. Never alone."

"I thought that was the way you wanted it. If it's not, I'll be happy to change it."

"What I'd like is to know how you feel about me."

"It's not obvious?"

"You shower me with attention, Jake, but it's all very . . . very lighthearted. You treat me as if I'm a—a doll."

"You want me to treat you like a woman?" He slipped his hand beneath her skirt and ran his hand upward until he passed the top of her rolled stockings and found the expanse of soft, silken thigh.

She gasped. "Jake!"

"I thought you knew. I've been wanting to do much more to you and with you ever since we started seeing each other again here in town. But I've been holding myself back, waiting for some sign that you were ready for more."

She tried to deal with the excitement and shock washing through her as he skimmed his hand back and forth over her skin, drawing closer and closer to the edge of her panties. "Jake, for heaven's sake, there are people around us."

"No one can see. We're back in this corner. Besides, the tablecloth is a shield."

"But you can't—"

He hadn't intended to do this, he thought, and felt himself hardening. His long fingers glided even closer to his ultimate objective until at last he was able to stroke and probe her sweet tenderness.

He heard her give a soft gasp, and he saw her eyelids drop with a sensual languor. Every muscle in his body clenched. Her reaction, he thought, was a mere hint of how responsive she would be to him when he finally had her all to himself, naked, and beneath him. Suddenly he was impatient with her clothes, the people around them, *everything*. He slid his fingers into her, and the little cry she gave went straight to his loins, making him hurt with need. "I want to feel all of you, without your clothes," he murmured huskily, stroking her. "I want to be inside you in a different way, a better way. Tell me you want the same thing. Lord, you're burning and damp and ready. You want me, I know you do. I can feel how much. Say it, Arabella, please, say you want me. I need to hear it."

There was an obstruction in her throat. There was heat running through her veins. There was a wonderfully strange kind of pressure building inside her, making her want to move her hips against his hand. Through a haze she could see people moving about and dancing, she could hear the band playing some peppy tune. But, heaven help her, Jake was right.

Desire was pounding through her with the force of thunder, and she *was* burning, burning with need for him. Helplessly she reached out for him and touched his face, not knowing what she would say until she heard herself say it. "Jake—"

"Let's leave," he said roughly. "Let's go back to my hotel."

"Well, well, the lovebirds," Randolph Bruce said.

The restless motion of Jake's hand stopped, and slowly he eased his hand away from her.

"Can I tell my readers that we'll be hearing wedding bells soon?"

With every nerve and cell in his body shrieking for Arabella, Jake took a long drink of Scotch. This was the moment he had been waiting for. Just for an instant he wondered if he was doing the right thing. But he wanted this damned "courtship" to end. He wanted to get her out of there and back to his hotel. "You can tell them anything you like, but there won't be any wedding bells." Then he turned and kissed her fully and passionately on the lips.

He heard Randolph chuckle. "I'll tell them that. See you later."

Jake broke off the kiss. "Let's get the hell out of here." The stricken look in Arabella's eyes hit him in the solar plexus. She was hurt, and strangely enough he could feel her pain. *What had he done?* "Arabella—"

She was stunned. In her world, the correct order of a man and woman's relationship was flirtation, then if they cared to carry it further, courtship, and then if they fell in love, marriage. She had hoped . . . "Jake, exactly what have you and I been doing these last couple of weeks?"

"Nothing yet."

"Yet?" She couldn't seem to stop her voice from quivering, and she felt sick to her stomach.

Dammit. Impatiently, he thrust a hand through his hair. For some really stupid reason, he hadn't foreseen this moment when she would question him. "I've made no secret that I want you, Arabella. Badly. But I'll never marry you. I'll never marry anyone. My decision not to marry shouldn't affect us though. I won't let it, and I won't let you let it."

At the moment she couldn't decide if she was more angry, astounded, or hurt. In actuality, she was feeling *all* those emotions to the point that she could barely think. "But *why*?"

His mouth tightened, and he realized he could still taste her. "Let's get out of here. We'll go back to my hotel."

Arabella sat there for a moment longer, simply looking at him. His face was hard and shadowed, his eyes opaque. She had given her heart to him, and unaware, he had handed it back to her in pieces. She reached for her purse. "I'm leaving, but I will be taking a taxi."

What two lovebirds, whose names have the initials JD and AL and who are seen billing and cooing nightly at nightclubs all over town, like their love affair just as it is—without marriage? It is official, babies. There will be no wedding bells for these two modern kids.

Kenneth hurled the paper across the room. "That bastard!"

In an ivory crepe georgine and satin dressing gown, Arabella sat composedly at the opposite end of the breakfast table. "Yes," she said in agreement.

"Jake's been squiring you around town all this time and making people believe you're having an affair." His balled hand came down on the table, rattling the china. "Lord, this is all my fault."

Trying to maintain an air of normalcy, she took a bite of toast. In truth, she was fighting against exhaustion, having been unable to sleep a wink all night. "Don't be silly, Kenneth. You didn't go out with him. I did."

"Yes, but I gave up warning you about him after making only a couple of stabs at it. I should have kept trying to get through that thick skull of yours."

"You pay me the most delightful compliments, Kenneth."

Kenneth didn't respond to her listless attempt at teasing. "Dammit, Bella, I've been too caught up with myself lately, and I didn't pay attention to what was going on right beneath my nose."

Her coffee cup landed back in its saucer with a dangerous *clink,* but her tone and manner remained cool. "Kenneth, please. I'm really not up to this."

"Oh, hell, Bella, I'm sorry. But I'm so angry, I can't think."

"Well, force yourself to think. Everything that has happened between Jake and me, even that odious article in Randolph's column, is water under the bridge. I'm going to forget it and I suggest you do the same." She glanced down at her hand still on her coffee cup and saw it trembling.

"Sure, honey," he said soothingly. "Stay home for a while. Everyone will forget in time."

She tossed back her head. "I have no intention of staying home. Why should I let Jake Deverell spoil my fun?" *Because, Arabella, it's impossible to function when your heart is in pieces.*

"Have you seen the morning paper?"

Jake jerked the receiver away from his head for a moment to allow his eardrum to return to normal. "No, I haven't, Edward. What's wrong? Have we gone to war again?" Intentionally, he had not read the paper, knowing exactly what would be in it. He could still see Arabella's stricken expression, and there was a cold, empty place in the pit of his stomach because of it.

"You've gone too far this time, Jake. You've not only disgraced that poor girl, you've disgraced our family name."

"It's only my name by adoption, Edward. I don't have any particular fondness for it. And as for Arabella, I haven't disgraced her. These days everyone has love affairs. Find me someone who doesn't and I'll notify Randolph, because *that* will be news."

"Decent men don't have love affairs with decent women."

A vein began to pound in Jake's temple, his fingers clenched around the base of the handset, and he brought the mouthpiece closer to his lips. "You had an affair with my mother, you rotten bastard, and if you ever even *think* the thought that my mother wasn't a decent woman, I'll do what I should have done years ago and kill you with my own hands."

"Well—" Edward broke off with a spasm of coughing, then moments later resumed. "Well, naturally I wasn't thinking of your mother when I said that. But I would like to make one more point, and that is a decent man doesn't flaunt his affairs and then announce to the world that he will never marry."

One by one Jake's fingers unclenched from the base of the handset. "I guess that means I'm not a decent man, then. But you knew that, didn't you? I'm your bastard." He paused. "You know what I've never been able to understand? The fact that you didn't even take the time to get to know me before you told me you would never acknowledge me as your son. To me, your actions are as indecent as mine, old man. Maybe more so."

"Dammit, Jake! Why do you have to continually bring that matter up? I've explained it to you time and again. Why can't you grasp the delicacy of your situation and the proper balance you must maintain in order to be part of society?"

"The delicacy of my situation?" Jake's voice rose and hardened with each word. "The proper balance? Don't you mean why can't I understand a father who refuses to acknowledge his son?" He set the base of the phone down and pressed his finger and thumb against his lids. An ache had formed behind his eyes. And in the darkness of his mind he could see Arabella, exquisite, breathtakingly beautiful, and in pain. Even though the whole purpose of the last couple of weeks had been to hit Edward in the area where it would hurt him the most—his obsession for a great family dynasty—he wasn't enjoying this conversation as he had thought he would.

"It's obvious, Jake, that you and I will never agree on this subject. You didn't work for years to be accepted in society like I did. Your entree was handed to you—by me. So I suggest we drop it and go on to another subject that is weighing heavily on my mind. What are you going to do about the Linden girl?"

Jake opened his eyes and found he could still see Arabella. What was he going to do?

"There's nothing *to* do, Edward. Randolph printed the truth. I never plan to marry, and I've told you why. God forbid I should sire another Edward Deverell. And as for Arabella, it is my hope to continue as we've been going. She makes me happy, and there are not a lot of things or people who do."

A click sounded in his ear, then a droning buzz. So

Edward had hung up on him. The corners of his mouth turned up, and he dropped the telephone receiver onto its hook. In times past, he realized, he would have laughed out loud. In times past he wouldn't have admitted to himself the truth of what he had told Edward. Arabella *did* make him happy, *very* happy. His expression turned grim. And he was going to see her now.

"I'm sorry, sir, but Miss Linden has gone out."

Arabella's butler was pompous and balding, and Jake was having a hard time being civil to him. "What do you mean, she's gone out? It's not even noon yet!"

"That is true, sir, however, Miss Linden has definitely left."

A muscle jerked along Jake's jawline. "What is your name?" he asked as politely as he could manage.

"Perkins, sir."

"Well, Perkins, could you please tell me where Miss Linden has gone?"

"She was not specific about her destination."

"I see. Then did she say when she would return?"

"I believe she mentioned that she wouldn't be home until late."

Jake exhaled a long breath. "All right, then. Would you be kind enough to tell Miss Linden when she returns that Mr. Jake Deverell was here to see her and asked that she please telephone no matter the time." He drew a notebook from an inside pocket, scribbled two numbers on a page, then tore it out and handed it to Perkins. "One of these numbers is my office, the other is my hotel. I'll be at the office until six-thirty, after that I'll be at my hotel. Do you have that?"

"Yes, Mr. Deverell."

The expression on the butler's face told Jake that he had offended the man. But Jake couldn't be bothered with watching his words.

He was frantic to see Arabella. He should never have let her leave the nightclub in that damned taxi the night before without trying to talk to her, even though he didn't know what he would have said. Just as he didn't know what he would say when he spoke with her later this afternoon.

As the afternoon passed, however, and the evening progressed, Jake began to realize he might not get a chance to talk to her. He telephoned the Linden house and was told by Perkins that Arabella had come in and then gone out again. And, yes, he had given her Jake's message. Since there were thousands of speakeasies operating in Boston and hundreds of private parties going on, Jake had no idea where to look for Arabella. And he was forced to wait until the next day to try to see her again.

But in the morning when he presented himself at the house, Perkins informed him that Arabella had gone out of town for an unspecified length of time. And no amount of cajoling or threats could get any more information out of him.

Jake went away, angry and miserable, and the cold, empty space in his stomach grew.

7

In front of the Beacon Hill mansion of Jas's parents, Jake parked his Sport Phaeton in between a gold Packard Runabout and a cream Mercedes-Benz and switched off the ignition.

Arabella was inside.

He had spent days trying to see and talk with her, only to be frustrated at every turn. Even his letters were returned unopened. He had learned early on that the Sphinx had nothing on Perkins. Kenneth, too, had been conspicuously unavailable.

He had finally resorted to enlisting his friends. But every time someone would spot her and call him, she would be gone by the time he got there.

Finally tonight Lucas had telephoned to tell him Arabella was at Jas's, and that he and Vanessa would keep an eye on her and make certain she didn't leave before he could get there.

His heart beat loudly in his ears as he stared at the massive three-storied house with lights and music spilling from the Palladian windows and fanlights. The Lindens had an equally impressive home not far away, as did Edward. Jake's mouth quirked as he remembered that when he graduated from Harvard, he had refused to live with Edward. Instead, he had settled with grand style into an apartment in the Hotel Vendôme. Its comfort and convenience had suited him, besides putting him close to the new house he had bought his mother. Last year, though, he had moved downtown into the new Ritz-Carlton. His apartment overlooked the lovely Public Garden, and the hotel's service was high class. Even so, in the past he hadn't stayed home much.

Now he was home each evening, afraid to leave in case Arabella called. He wasn't sleeping, he was barely eating. In fact, the only thing that was going well in his life at the moment was his work. But his triumphs in the financial world had come to matter less and less to him. And all because of a woman.

An unforgettable woman.

He slammed his fist against the steering wheel. Lord help him, he was stalling.

With a curse, he opened the door and got out.

In the middle of a lively fox trot to a jazzy rendition of "When My Baby Walks Down the Street," Arabella froze.

Her dance partner, a young banker named Ed Forsyth, looked down at her with concern. "Is there anything wrong?"

Dismayed, she stared toward the back of the large room. Lucas and Vanessa were there, chatting casually with Jas. Lord, why hadn't she noticed them before? How long had they been there? Had they seen her? It didn't matter, she told herself firmly. Either way, she had to leave.

"Arabella, are you ill?"

Giving him an apologetic smile, she stepped away from him while inventing an excuse. "No, not at all. It's merely that I completely forgot I wrote Mother and Father and told them I'd be back home tonight in time to receive their transatlantic call."

"Oh? Where are they?"

She made a vague gesture with the large ostrich-feather fan she held. "On the Nile somewhere. I really enjoyed our dance, but I must leave now."

"I understand. May I ring you tomorrow?"

With another smile and a flirting move that were both purely automatic, she swept the soft, lush royal-purple plumes of her fan across his chest. "I would have been disappointed if you hadn't asked. Good-bye, Ed."

Making her way off the dance floor was fairly easy, since none of her dancing friends realized she planned to leave. As she walked into the hall, she breathed a sigh of relief.

Then Lucas stepped in front of her, blocking her escape. "You're not leaving yet, are you? It's early."

Ways to get past the handsome man briefly flew through her mind, but she dismissed them all as either silly or impractical. No, she thought, this time she was caught. But then, she had known she wouldn't be able to evade Jake forever.

With a flick of her wrist she opened her fan to its full five-foot span. Relaxing, she began to gently move the fan back and forth. "Hello, Lucas." She turned her head to Vanessa, taking in the vision she made in a glittering Chinese-blue dress and matching cap. "Hello, Vanessa."

The expression in Vanessa's extraordinary dark blue eyes was cool. "Arabella."

"You must have worked up quite an appetite out on the dance floor," Lucas said. "May I get you a plate of food?"

"No, thank you. I've eaten." She paused. "I make it a point never to miss a meal, unlike your good friend Jake."

Vanessa glanced at Lucas but remained silent.

Arabella closed the plumed fan, then opened it again. "By the way, how long are you estimating it will take Jake to get here?"

With a twinkle in his eye, Lucas slipped his hands into his trouser pockets. "Not long. That Sport Phaeton of his is new, you know, custom made to his specifications. He's really proud of it, and he drives it like the wind."

"Or like demons are pursuing him?" she asked with casual interest. "You know, the strangest thing happened my last night at SwanSea. I came downstairs in the middle of the night—I may eat, but occasionally I can't sleep—and I saw Jake in the great hall below me, hurling a ball against a wall so violently, it was as if he was trying to rid himself of demons. You two were on the stairway."

Lucas and Vanessa exchanged another glance.

"Are you sure you wouldn't like a plate?" Lucas asked again. "Perhaps a glass of champagne?"

"No, but thank you for asking."

Vanessa touched Lucas's arm. "I would love some food, darling."

Lucas gazed at her for a long moment, and the watching Arabella felt a pang of jealousy that she would never know the kind of closeness these two had, where words were unnecessary.

He nodded and smiled. "A little of everything, I suppose?"

"A lot of everything."

He bent and kissed her cheek. "I'll be right back."

"Take your time." After he left, Vanessa turned to Arabella, her expression now thoughtful. "I understand you've been having a grand time lately, out every night, quick trips out of town."

Arabella fixed a bright smile on her face. "Having fun is what life's all about, isn't it?"

"Tell that to Jake. He hasn't been having too much fun lately."

"Gee, I'm sorry to hear that."

Vanessa gazed so calmly at her that Arabella momentarily regretted her flippancy. She would love to know what had given such a young and beautiful woman eyes that looked as if they had seen the world and had found very little of it to like.

"Jake's a good guy, Arabella."

Her lips quirked. "I'll have to take your word for it."

"My word is good."

"Vanessa, why are you talking to me like this?"

"Because I'm concerned."

A genuine smile spread across Arabella's mouth. "And somehow I don't think it's me you're concerned about."

"You're right."

"Vanessa, I've never seen anyone more capable of taking care of himself than Jake."

"I thought you said you saw him at SwanSea in the great hall your last night."

For once Arabella didn't have a snappy comeback.

Lucas reappeared, waving a mounded plate. "Here you are, Vanessa. Lots of everything, as ordered."

She smiled up at him. "Thank you."

And suddenly Arabella realized that when Vanessa looked at Lucas, her eyes didn't appear old.

Jake was startled when he first saw Arabella with Lucas and Vanessa. He had never seen her in a color as dark as royal purple, but as usual her taste was exquisite. The dark, rich color made a perfect foil for her fair beauty. Her metal moiré dress was tubular, its only decoration tiny straps made of deeply purple amethysts that went over her ivory shoulders. And she was holding the ostrich-feather fan at an angle so that the plumes cascaded to the floor in a dramatic, graceful fall.

How had he gone so long without seeing her?

Vanessa, the plate in one hand, the fork in the other, delightedly regarded the food Lucas had brought her. "You really made a mistake, Arabella, when you didn't let Lucas get you a plate."

"It won't be my first mistake lately," she said, and to her surprise Vanessa ignored the pointed tone of her remark.

"You should reconsider. This is going to be wonderful."

"Tell me something, Vanessa. Why is it that your friend Jake doesn't relish food the way you do?"

Vanessa paused, her fork halfway to her mouth. And Arabella had the oddest feeling Vanessa was about to say something, but she didn't have the opportunity to find out.

"Hello, Arabella."

With wildly racing pulse, she pivoted slowly toward Jake. It must have started snowing, she thought absently as she tried to cope with her suddenly sharpened senses.

Every small detail about Jake seemed to register

with her at once. The fact that he wasn't wearing a hat, the fact that snowflakes dusted his coal-black hair and the broad shoulders of his big black wool overcoat. The fact that beneath the overcoat he was dressed casually in an open-neck white shirt, V-neck gray and black patterned sweater, and gray trousers. The fact that all his energy and vitality was concentrated solely on her. The fact that his jaw was shadowed with a faint growth of beard, making him appear even more ruggedly masculine than usual.

"Hello, Jake."

"I want to talk to you."

"Then we are at an impasse, because I don't want to talk to you. I waited for you only because it's almost become more trouble than it's worth to avoid you. And because your friends were so charmingly determined to make sure I didn't leave." She glanced over her shoulder and discovered that Lucas and Vanessa had vanished. "Well, Lucas was charming. Vanessa was"—she paused, searching for the right word—"interesting." She shrugged her shoulders, then caught the attention of a passing footman. "Would you please get my wrap for me. I'm leaving now." The servant nodded and hurried away.

Jake closed long fingers around her upper arm and drew her to the side of the staircase to give them more privacy. "I'm not letting you go until you agree to talk to me."

She wrenched her arm from his grasp as anger shot through her. And all her inner hurt and fury came screaming out in a rush of words that were even more effective because they were so quietly spoken. "All right, then, Jake, by all means let's talk and get it over with. For a couple of weeks you took me out. We dined, or rather *I* dined, we danced, we laughed, we had a great time. Poor foolish me, I thought we were in the middle of a wonderful courtship. And if you had been any other man, it would have been a courtship. But then that was where I made my mistake. You're *not* any other man, and it was a tremendous blunder on my part to believe you were even remotely like others. But I understand everything now. Where I believed, hoped we were establishing a relationship that one day might become permanent, you saw me only as someone you wanted to have an affair with." She paused to draw a breath. "Now, as I see it, this is where it gets a little tricky, because during the time you were squiring me around town, you never once tried to make love to me."

"I was trying to wait until you were ready."

"Damn you, don't you dare gloss it over and make yourself sound noble. You knew that if you pressed the issue too soon, I would refuse. No, Jake, you were trying to gain my confidence and sweeten me up so that when you finally did make your move, I would fall into your bed with the same ease as all your other girlfriends have done before me. Now, strangely enough, there's a part of me that can almost accept that. You're not the first man to use strategy on me to try to get me into bed. And I'm sure people would say you were simply an average red-blooded man doing what every other average red-blooded man does when he is attracted to a woman. Except, just as I did, they would be making a horrendous mistake to think you were like anyone else. Because, Jake"—she jabbed him in the chest with a rigid finger—"for some twisted reason I cannot fathom, you were trying to make sure everyone in Boston believed we were having an affair." She paused to draw a breath. "Now, can you tell me why that is?"

During the time she had been speaking, her anger and pain had come at him like waves, soaking into him. He could do little more than stand and listen. And after all she had said, he still wasn't going to be able to tell her what she wanted to know, what she deserved to know. The answer was a tangled, complicated mass of his own anger and pain. "No."

Arabella stared at him. He looked like a man in anguish, but she didn't believe it for a minute. He was too hard, too calculating to let things touch him. "Why did you even bother to track me down?"

"Because I want to go on seeing you."

If he had said because he planned to pull out a gun and kill her, she couldn't have been more surprised. "Why? For heaven's sake, *why*?"

"Because I still want you as much as ever, in fact more. And because I can't sleep without dreaming about you, and I can't be awake without thinking about you. I dream you with my eyes wide open, Arabella."

She swallowed, trying to ease her tightening throat. "Let me see if I understand this. You still want to have an affair with me."

"Yes."

"An affair without the possibility of marriage."

"Yes."

"No possibility at all."

"That's right."

"And you won't tell me why."

"I can't."

"Here's your cape, Miss Linden," the footman said, holding the ermine out to her.

"Thank you." She took it and swirled it over her shoulders.

Jas stuck his head over the banister of the staircase. "Arabella, you can't be leaving. It's early yet, barely midnight! Jake. You made it after all! And I'm mad for your attire. I'll have to remember—when you expect everyone will wear evening dress, come casual. How very elegant. Arabella, now that Jake's here, stay for a while. It's a swell party."

"Swell," she said, her gaze lingering on Jake. There was something riveting about him, mesmerizing. Why, after what he had done to her, did she continue to find him so damnably attractive? And why, out of all the men in the world, did she have to fall in love with him? A love without hope.

She fastened the cape. "Thanks for the party, Jas,"

she said, still gazing at Jake. "I'm sure I'll see you soon. Good-bye, Jake."

As she made to pass him, his hand shot out in front of her, checking her exit. "It's not good-bye, Arabella."

"You're a smart man, Jake. That's what makes it all the harder for me to understand how you can consistently be so wrong."

Arabella was awake when the presents began arriving early the next morning. The first was a large heart-shaped wreath of roses, a rope of diamonds threaded among the buds. The card read, "Please be my valentine. Go out with me tonight." Beneath the message was scrawled a "J" made in one big fluid stroke.

She turned to the waiting delivery boy. "Is today St. Valentine's Day?"

"Yes, miss."

It was unlike her to forget the current date, she reflected, but then, her life hadn't exactly been normal lately. She stuffed the card into its envelope and handed it to the boy. "Take it back."

"Miss?"

"Return the wreath, the diamonds, *and* the card to Mr. Deverell." The boy's expression told her that he clearly thought she had lost her mind.

"Yes, miss."

After that, boxes of candy along with baskets and bouquets of flowers began to arrive, not from Jake, but from friends like Jas and Ed. And all the gifts came with cards beseeching her to "Be My Valentine." Her life would be so simple, she thought, if she could just choose one of these men—one of these nice, stable, predictable men. One of these men she didn't love. . . .

At noon a gold heart-shaped standing mirror for her dresser arrived. Golden cupids with outstretched hands bracketed the mirror, and each cupid held the end of a fabulous ruby necklace. Arabella stared with fascination at the sparkling red stones. And she knew before she saw the card that the mirror and the necklace were from Jake.

She opened the envelope and read. "I need to see you, Arabella. Please say you'll see me tonight." She gazed at the "J" written boldly in black ink, while pain, love, anger, and confusion ran riot inside her. But it never once occurred to her to accept either his gifts or his invitation.

"Take it back," she said to the same boy who had delivered the roses and the diamonds.

He sighed. "Yes, miss."

"Damn, Bella." Kenneth uttered the mild epithet later that afternoon as he viewed the entry hall. "This place looks like a flower shop." He grinned. "Or maybe it's a funeral parlor. I can't decide."

Arabella rested her hips against the edge of a marble table and crossed her legs in front of her. "There are too many boxes of candy, not to mention lace handkerchiefs, fans, trinkets and baubles, for it to be a funeral parlor."

His grin widened. "Oh, is that how you decide between a flower shop and a mausoleum? I've always wondered."

"They've been arriving all day."

"Another typical Valentine's Day at the Lindens, and from all the goodies here, it looks like you've had an especially fine year." He plucked a card from one of the bouquets and read it. "Marcus O'Donnell. Who's that?"

"Don't you remember? He's the young man who threw himself in front of my car at Christmastime and vowed not to get up until I said I would go out with him."

Kenneth nodded, strolling on to the next few bouquets, checking more of the cards. "That's right. And you went out with him, didn't you?"

"Sure," she said with a pronounced twinkle in her eye. "What else could I do? It was blackmail, pure and simple. My car was brand new and I couldn't risk the possibility of a dent."

With a chuckle he replaced one card and reached for another. "Of course not."

"And who did you send valentines to this year, dear brother of mine?"

"I just sent one, a bouquet, to Jennifer Cummings."

"Ah, the lovely Jennifer. I approve."

A devilish expression appeared on his face. "I live for your approval, sweet sister."

"As I do yours, darling brother."

He abandoned his investigation of the cards and sauntered over to her. "Well, as long as we're speaking of approval, I couldn't help but notice that there's nothing here from Jake."

She studied her fingernails. "He sent a couple of things, quite grand things actually, but I had the boy take them back."

He reached out an arm and patted her shoulder. "You did the best thing."

"I know."

He shot back his cuff and glanced at his watch. "Listen, kiddo, I'm on my way over to the Ritz-Carlton to meet Jennifer for tea. Want to come?"

She shook her head. "I'll stay home."

"Are you sure?" He gestured toward all the gifts and flowers. "You're not going to accept any of the invitations on those cards?"

"No." She rubbed at her temple. "If you want to know the truth, I'm a little tired."

He frowned. "Hey, are you all right? Do you want me to stay home with you?"

She looked at him fondly, happy to see him in such a good mood. Something seemed to have altered with him since they'd returned from SwanSea. There were times he seemed almost haunted. "Don't be silly. I'll be fine. You go on, and be sure to tell Jennifer hello for me."

"Okay, then. See you later."

When the door chime sounded a few minutes later,

Arabella was still propped against the table. A great feeling of lassitude had settled over her, and she was a little astonished. Listlessness was foreign to her, as was any form of illness, even minor colds. She thought about the matter for a few moments, then with grim humor realized there could be only one explanation—fighting against love must take an awful lot of energy.

Perkins closed the front door after accepting yet another large floral arrangement. "Would you like us to begin distributing these around the house, miss?"

"I think I have a better idea this year, Perkins. Send them over to Massachusetts General to the head nurses of the various sections to give to the patients who would enjoy them most. The candy might be just the thing for the children's ward, but do check with the nurses."

"Very good, miss."

The door chime sounded again, as the phone began to ring. Arabella sighed. "Go ahead and answer the door, Perkins, I'll get this." She reached around behind her, scooped the handset off the table, lifted the receiver from its hook, and spoke into the mouthpiece. "Hello?"

"It's Ed, Arabella. You said I could call today."

What she had actually said, she thought, was that she would have been disappointed if he hadn't asked if he could. "Yes, Ed, how nice to hear from you."

"Did you get my flowers?"

She stared down at the tips of her shoes, trying to

remember which flowers he had sent. "Yes, I did. Thank you so much. Violets in winter—they are truly lovely." She searched her mind to recall if he had sent her anything else. "And thank you for the candy also."

"I didn't know what type you liked, so I thought an assortment would be best."

"And you were absolutely right. Thank you again. And thank you for calling." She supposed her multiple thanks sprang from guilt. This time a year ago she would have laughed with him and flirted. But she was a changed woman. New Year's Eve had marked the beginning of her change, and a dark-haired, dark-eyed, dark-souled man was the reason. "Excuse me, Ed, what did you say?"

"I said I was hoping you would go out with me this evening. There's a party at—"

"No, I'm sorry." The last thing she wanted to do was lead him or anyone on. She opted for the truth. "You're a really nice man, Ed, and I like you a great deal—as a friend."

He groaned. "Arabella, don't call me a friend. That's the kiss of death."

Her gaze still fixed on the toes of her shoes, she chuckled. "But I want you as a friend. Friends last longer than boyfriends, Ed. Always remember that."

"You're a swell girl, Arabella. And I guess since you are, I'll give in gracefully."

"You're a smart man, Ed Forsyth. The next time we're at the same party, I'll expect a dance. See you."

She dropped the receiver onto its hook and twisted around to replace the telephone on the table.

"That was very prettily done."

Her head jerked around and her hand flew to her heart. "Jake!" She quickly searched for Perkins, but he was nowhere to be seen.

"How are you, Arabella?" he asked, walking slowly toward her. "I don't have to ask what kind of day you've had. I can see for myself. There's probably not a single flower left in all the florist shops in Boston."

His overcoat was folded neatly over one arm, and he held his hat in his hand, telling her that he had probably been in the hall the entire time she was talking to Ed. She also couldn't help but notice his clean-shaven face, his starched, pristine-white shirt, an elegantly patterned tie, and a magnificently tailored dark blue suit with vest. He looked as if he were going to church, she thought, and had to swallow the bubble of hysterical laughter that rose in her throat. Men with dark souls didn't go to church.

He stopped in front of her. "You didn't really think I'd give up, did you?"

No, she hadn't. At least not deep inside her heart she hadn't. She straightened and moved around him until she was several safe steps away. "What do you want, Jake?"

He pulled a small, slim, black velvet jewelry box from the inside pocket of his suit and held it out to her. "I thought maybe you might have a harder time refusing me than you did the delivery boy."

She eyed the box, trying to guess what might be in it. Then, disgusted at herself for her curiosity, she crossed her arms under her breasts. "Well, you were wrong. I won't accept anything from you. And if that's all, please leave."

He slipped the jewelry box back into the pocket. "No, that's not all. I also wanted to ask you to go to dinner with me tonight."

"No," she said, and thought she saw pain flash across his face. But if the expression had been pain, it disappeared as fast as it had appeared, leaving only his heart-stoppingly handsome face for her to look at.

"I didn't mean to hurt you, Arabella." His voice was soft.

"Then you were careless, because that's exactly what you did. But it's all right. I recovered very quickly." She paused. "Now, once and for all, please leave." She started for the stairs.

"My mother is going to be very disappointed."

She stopped dead still in her tracks and turned back to him. "What did you say?"

"My mother is going to be extremely disappointed. I told her I was going to bring a very nice young lady to meet her this evening."

"Your *mother*?" There were very few things that would have shocked her more than Jake Deverell inviting her to meet his mother, she thought, searching his expression. But as usual, he was keeping his thoughts and feelings to himself.

"Today is her birthday, and we're going to have a special dinner."

"Jake, I didn't even know you had a mother. Why did Edward Deverell adopt you if your mother is still living?"

His mouth quirked. "That's a good question."

"Then what's the answer?"

"The answer is Edward Deverell is a sonofabitch."

She stared at him, wondering what to think. He ran the brim of his hat through his fingers, a sign of tension in any other man.

"I'd really like you to come, Arabella. She doesn't get to meet many new people."

"Why me, Jake? Do you honestly want to introduce her to the woman whose name has been so infamously linked with yours in the newspaper?"

"She doesn't read Randolph's column. I asked her not to years ago, and she doesn't."

"Okay, but I still don't know why you want to take me to your mother's, of all places."

He gazed down at his hat. "Because I think she truly will enjoy meeting you. And because I want to be with you, and I was afraid you would say no to any other invitation."

"Did you say you were *afraid*?"

His head came up, and his eyes narrowed. "I knew with absolute certainty you would say no. But I felt you might agree to dinner at my mother's house."

He was close to being right, she thought, still dealing with her shock. He had given her an invitation almost impossible to refuse. The urge to meet his mother and perhaps learn more about him was nearly irresistible. "You've already told her I'm coming?"

He gave a quick smile, and she was shaken to realize that at that moment he reminded her of a guilty little boy.

"Yes. As I've said, I want to be with you, and I was really hopeful that you would come."

Arabella rubbed her temple. There had to be a catch somewhere. There had to be a reason why she shouldn't go. "Where does she live? New York City?"

He smiled again, and she realized with chagrin that the cause of his smile was her own thoughts. He had read them.

"No, Arabella, she lives here in Boston, the Back Bay area." His smile faded. "I wanted her to live at SwanSea, where we could be together more often, but she said she would feel more comfortable staying here. Needless to say, though, I got her out of the North End as soon as possible."

Arabella was silent for a moment. "I really don't know what to tell you, Jake."

"Say you'll go."

She hesitated. "We'll go right there and then straight back here? No detours?"

"I promise. I give you my word, and, Arabella, my word is good."

Vanessa had said the same thing last night, she thought inconsequentially. She spread out her hands. "I don't have a gift for her."

He threw a quick glance around the hall, then walked over to a table and picked up a box of chocolates. "Mother loves chocolates. Take her these. She'll be very pleased, and you didn't plan to eat them anyway."

She looked at him in surprise. "How do you know?"

"Because you like white chocolate. I haven't forgotten."

8

GWENDOLYN Conall smiled at Arabella, who was sitting a short distance away from her on the couch. "My dear, you were so sweet to come tonight."

Arabella had met Jake's mother only fifteen minutes before, but she was already completely charmed by her. "It's my great pleasure to be here," she said sincerely, and didn't notice the thoughtful look Jake cast her. They were in the front parlor of the house, a modest but stately three-story home on Commonwealth Avenue. The furnishings were elegant and feminine. And Gwendolyn was one of the most incredible women Arabella had ever met.

Her hair was pure white, and her eyes shone pale milky blue behind a pair of strong, thick glasses. Wrinkles lined her skin and arthritis had knotted and twisted her fingers, but she had a soft beauty that seemed to touch everything around her.

"How did you meet my son, Arabella?"

"I attended his New Year's house party with my brother Kenneth."

"She brought me a pair of snow-white peacocks as a gift," Jake told his mother in an amused tone. He was lounging in a big overstuffed chair a few feet away from them.

"How wonderful of you, Arabella," Gwendolyn said, her expression lighting with delight. "How did you ever come up with such an original idea for a present?"

"I visited SwanSea with my father when I was a little girl and I always remembered it, the staircase, the ballroom—everything about it." She glanced at Jake.

One black brow lifted slightly. "You didn't mention that you'd been there before."

"It wasn't really important." She looked back at Gwendolyn. "Jake told me you didn't think you would be comfortable living at SwanSea, but you've visited, haven't you?"

The expression of delight slowly faded from her face. "No, I haven't."

Even separated by a few feet of space, Arabella sensed Jake tensing. She threw him a puzzled glance, but when he didn't say anything, she continued. "You should definitely go up for a long visit, Mrs. Conall. It's a wonderful place."

For a few moments the older woman became very quiet, seeming to lose herself in her own thoughts. "Perhaps when I have grandchildren, when I can hear their laughter and their sweet voices filling those big rooms, then I will."

Surprised, Arabella quickly looked over at Jake and was even more surprised to see that his eyes were closed, as if he would not see a painful vision. Obviously, she thought, he hadn't told his mother that he didn't plan to marry.

"Thank you again for the chocolates, Arabella. As I'm sure Jacob told you, I have a bit of a sweet tooth."

"Yes, he did mention you're fond of chocolates. I hope you enjoy them and the perfume." When she had gone upstairs to change, she had found an unopened perfume bottle and on impulse had wrapped it and brought it. She was glad she had.

"Chanel No. 5 is my favorite scent."

Jake suddenly straightened and leaned forward in his chair, smiling at his mother. "You've opened Arabella's presents. I think it's time you opened mine."

A soft flush colored Gwendolyn's skin, just as if, Arabella thought, gazing at the charming sight, she were a young girl receiving a gift from her first beau.

She sighed with a playful exasperation. "Oh, Jacob, I was going to save your gift for after dinner."

"Well, you never know," he said, his tone gently teasing. "There might be something for you to open after dinner too. But I can't wait any longer for you to open this one." He pulled a large box from behind his chair and placed it in his mother's lap.

"Oh, my goodness," she exclaimed, "what have you gone and done now?"

With a grin he kneeled down in front of her and began to help her open the box, beautifully wrapped in silver paper with a big pink satin bow. "Well," he said, still with the same gently teasing tone, "let's just see what I've gone and done now."

"Now, don't break the ribbon," Gwendolyn cautioned her son.

His grin widened. "No, Mother, I won't."

Arabella realized that Jake was actually doing the unwrapping, because Gwendolyn with her arthritic hands couldn't, and furthermore, he was having a grand time.

He handed her the bow. "There you are, all in a piece."

Gwendolyn lifted the bow to within inches of her eyes. "Oh, it's so beautiful. Isn't it a beautiful bow, Arabella?"

Touched, Arabella nodded, then realized Gwendolyn wasn't looking at her. "It certainly is, Mrs. Conall."

Jake glanced at her, and for the first time since she had known him, Arabella saw a softness within the black depths of his eyes. The whole evening was worth that one look, she thought.

With a flourish Jake lifted the lid from the box and

parted the tissue paper. "There you are, Mother. What do you think?"

Gwendolyn tentatively reached her hand into the box, then gasped with excitement. "A fur, Jacob. It's a fur."

With a laugh he sat back on his heels. "Yes, I know. And it's really more than just a fur. It's a fur coat. A sable."

"Oh, Jacob." Soft wonderment scored her face and her voice as she stroked the coat. "It feels magnificent."

"That's because it is."

Her hand stilled. "But you shouldn't have bought me this. It's too expensive, and you've already bought me two other fur coats."

"Quit fussing," he chided gently. "Your other coats are mink and fox, and they're two and three years old. Now, you can't go around wearing old coats, can you?"

She laughed as he had intended. "If you say so."

"I do. And besides, we're having a really hard winter, and I want you warm." He lifted the coat from the box, tossed the box aside, and draped the coat around his mother's shoulders. "You look beautiful," he whispered, then pressed a soft kiss on her cheek. "Happy birthday for my valentine."

"Oh, darling . . ."

At that moment Arabella wished fervently for a camera so that she could capture for all time what she was seeing—Jake, kneeling at his mother's feet, his expression soft with love as he looked up at her. And Gwendolyn glowing with love as she reached out and touched his face.

Arabella turned her head away, giving the two of them a moment of privacy and was embarrassed to realize her eyes had filled with tears. But she had the satisfaction of knowing that the picture would stay in her mind forever.

Gwendolyn gave a gay laugh. "Arabella, what must you think of us? As you can see, my son spoils me terribly."

Watching Jake return to his chair, Arabella followed Gwendolyn's lead and infused her voice with lightness. "I would say, on the basis of our short acquaintance, that you are very worthy of being spoiled absolutely rotten, and that Jake gets a great deal of pleasure from doing so."

Jake smiled at Arabella, and she was struck almost dumb by the sweetness and appreciation it held.

"He bought me this lovely house and everything in it," Gwendolyn said. "And he has servants waiting on me hand and foot. He even hired a chauffeur and a car to take me out whenever I wish and a companion who does a grand job of describing to me what we're seeing."

"How thoughtful of him," Arabella said with a glance toward Jake.

He pushed out of the chair. "I think I'll go check on what's holding up dinner."

A smile on her face, Gwendolyn listened to his

footsteps as he left the room. "Now I've embarrassed him. He has so much money and power, yet he can't make me see better, and that hurts him."

"Don't worry about your son," Arabella said dryly, "he can handle a little embarrassment."

"He's a good boy," Gwendolyn said, "and I'm so glad he's found you."

Arabella started. "I beg your pardon?"

"You're the first girl he's ever brought home to meet me, and it's such a treat for me." She hesitated. "Would you mind coming a little closer so that I can see you better?"

"Of course not," she said, scooting across the cushion.

Tentatively Gwendolyn touched Arabella's face. "You are just as beautiful as Jacob said you were."

"Jake said I was beautiful?"

Gwendolyn nodded, her expression turning pensive. "He's been so lonely."

"Mrs. Conall, you're mistaken. Jake's not lonely. He's always surrounded by people, especially when he's at SwanSea. He keeps that house full."

"Don't be fooled by exteriors, Arabella." She spoke gently but firmly. "He has Lucas and Vanessa and me. That's all." She reached for her hand and took it between hers. "I'm so happy that at last he's found someone to love who is as special and as beautiful as you are."

Arabella was stunned into silence.

And Jake, who had just reached the doorway, heard what his mother said and swore silently.

Absently Arabella smoothed her hand across the crushed-leather upholstery of the front seat of Jake's car. What was the reason for his silence since they had left his mother's house? The dinner had been lovely, and he hadn't given a sign that anything was bothering him. After dinner he had presented his mother with yet another birthday gift, a beautifully colored and patterned silk nightgown and robe set. His mother had been as excited and delighted as she had been with the sable coat, and understanding had dawned on Arabella that Jake was intent on surrounding his mother with every tactile and sensory pleasure he could think of—in his own way trying to make up for her failing eyesight.

"Thank you for inviting me to your mother's tonight," she said quietly. "I really enjoyed meeting her."

In the dim glow that came from the mahogany instrument panel, she saw Jake flex his gloved fingers on the steering wheel.

"She enjoyed meeting you too."

She waited for him to continue and was disappointed when he didn't. He seemed entirely different. When he had first come to her house he had seemed to really want to be with her. Now he seemed as though he couldn't wait to be rid of her.

Tonight she had seen a side of him she hadn't

known existed, a gentle, caring side. His adoration of his mother warmed her heart. And though having been a part of the evening's birthday celebration wouldn't make her unrequited love for him any easier to bear, she felt that she had learned a little more about him, and she wouldn't have missed the opportunity for the world.

Jake pulled to a stop in front of her house but didn't turn off the motor.

She stared at him in the semi-darkness of the car. His mother had said he was lonely. Vanessa had said, 'I thought you said you saw him at SwanSea in the great hall your last night.' "

Nothing made any sense to her.

She opened the car door.

He reached across her and pulled the door closed again. "Wait a minute."

"Yes?"

"Thank you for being so nice to my mother."

"Being nice to your mother was easy, Jake. She's a lovely person."

He nodded, his expression moody. "She's been through a lot in her life. Arabella . . ."

"What?"

His words came out stilted. "I wanted to be with you tonight. I'm glad you accepted my invitation. I'd like to see you again."

"Why? So we can have an affair?"

All at once he leaned toward her and took her face between his two hands. "It's all I can offer you,

Arabella." His tone was intense, the words huskily spoken. "I know you probably don't consider that much of an offer at all, but I'd try to make sure you were never sorry."

"Jake." His name came out on a long breath of amazement. "Do you have any idea, any idea at all, what you're asking me to do?"

"Probably not. All I can think of is how much I want to be with you, all the time, in every way. . . ."

She shook her head, wishing the action could shut his heated words from her mind. "Jake, I wasn't raised that way. You would be the first man I ever made love to, and I believe with all my heart that the first man I ever make love with should be the man I'm going to love my whole life long. My husband. Jake, I'm a virgin."

He stared at her as what she said slowly soaked into him. He could hear the truth in her voice, see it in her eyes. She wasn't playing a game.

"You ask too much," she said, opening the door and getting out.

Jake watched her walk up the sidewalk to the door, furious with himself, with the circumstances. He felt disoriented, dizzy, as if the world were suddenly spinning too fast.

She was a virgin.

He had wanted like hell to be with her tonight, but he should have given more thought to the matter. It had never dawned on him that his mother would jump to the conclusion that he had found in Arabella the woman he could love. He watched grimly as Perkins opened the door for her, then closed it behind her.

In the long run his mother would be hurt to learn she wasn't right.

And Arabella had to be hurt and baffled by everything—by the visit to his mother's, by his insistent pursuit of her . . .

She was a virgin.

He had not believed her when she'd told him right off the bat, but he had sensed something was wrong the night in the conservatory, and he had stopped. Now he understood why he had.

And he knew that, given another chance, he wouldn't stop again.

Lucas unfolded the paper and dropped it in front of Jake on the breakfast table in his suite. "Read this and tell me we don't have anything to worry about. They're calling it the St. Valentine's Day Massacre."

Jake crunched on a piece of bacon as he quickly scanned the headline and the first couple of paragraphs, then looked up at Lucas, slightly puzzled. "This says they think these men were killed by some overly greedy policemen who had hijacked hooch from Bugs Moran and were afraid Bugs would tattle." He threw another glance at the paper. "Members of Detroit's Purple Gang are also suspects."

"I don't believe it for a minute, and neither does the news on our grapevine. Word is, some of Capone's gang decked themselves out in police uniforms, then went over to a garage where the seven men, five of them in Bugs Moran's gang, were waiting for a load of hijacked hooch." Lucas grimaced. "It's the last thing those poor bastards will ever wait for. They say the bodies were pretty ripped up and that there was a pool of blood you could swim in." He paused. "Only Capone's people kill like that, Jake. You know it, I know it, and everyone in the city of Chicago will know it, too, as soon as they stop to think about it. And guess who is an associate of Al Capone?"

Jake leaned back in his chair, bringing a piece of toast with him to munch on. "If our grapevine is right, our old friend, Wade Scalia."

"*Our* grapevine is always right, Jake."

He tossed the remainder of the toast back onto the plate, and with a slight grimace touched his forehead, wondering why he had expected to find pain there. "I don't want to think about this, Lucas." Arabella had a hold on all his thoughts.

"You can't close your eyes to this." Lucas stabbed at the paper with two fingers. "This is the kind of man 'our old friend' Wade Scalia has become."

With a sigh Jake straightened. "You're right, but I don't know what you expect me to do about it. We're still in the same damn dilemma we were the last time we talked about this."

"But don't you see? He's perfectly capable of having us killed if we don't do what he's asking of us and give him that damned percentage."

"Is that what you want to do, Lucas?" Jake asked quietly. "Give in to him?"

"Hell, no!"

With an inquiring look at his friend, Jake spread his hands outward. "Then?"

Lucas raked a hand through his blond hair. "I don't know."

A violent boom rattled the panes of the glass of the windows. Both men instinctively hit the floor and waited. When they heard no more explosions, they leapt up and raced to the window.

Jake jerked the curtain aside and did a quick survey of the street below. His car. His new, custom-built red Sport Phaeton had been blown up, and what remained of it was burning. His hand on the curtain slowly closed until he had the heavy velvet fabric gripped in a hard fist.

"That sonofabitch," Lucas muttered, gazing down on the scene over Jake's shoulder. "To hell with it. If the man wants a war, let's give him a war."

Jake let the curtain drop back into place and rubbed his eyes. "No."

"Jake, Wade just destroyed something you valued. His message couldn't be more clear. You could be next."

Jake shook his head, reflecting with a kind of amazement that it was morning and he already felt tired. He had been too disturbed by what had passed between him and Arabella to sleep, but lack of sleep had never bothered him so much before. "I can buy two dozen of those damned cars if I want to. I could buy two hundred. Hell, I could buy two thousand, but I'm not going to risk the lives of our men over a car."

"It's not about the car, Jake. It's about your life. Wade is obsessed with you and has been ever since we were kids. He idolized you and tried like hell to be as good as you were at things. He wanted to be like you and to be your best friend."

Jake gave an exclamation of exasperation. "Lord, Lucas, Wade was just a snot-nosed little bully who was always hanging around. I never did anything to him."

"Exactly. If you had treated him with cruelty, he might have been able to accept it better, but you barely noticed him, unless, of course, he pulled some stunt like he did with Vanessa that night."

His jaw set into a rock-hard line. "The man can blow up as many of my cars as he wants, but I'm not starting a war with him."

"Then let's get out of this damned business. It's the only way, Jake. We've had a great time, and we've made a bloody fortune. Let's retire."

He walked over to the breakfast table and poured himself a cup of coffee. "I think that's a good idea."

"Great."

His expression was thoughtful as he turned toward his old friend. "For you, Lucas. You've got the money, you've got all that land you've been buying out in California. Hell, you even have a few businesses going. And most of all, you have Vanessa. I want you to go back with her, move into that dream house you two are building on the beach, and live a long, happy life."

Lucas stared at Jake, stunned. "Are you trying to get rid of me?"

"Come on, you know better. But I see now that Wade's not going to stop these little tantrums of his, these little shows of strength. Before he gets tired of the game, more cars may get blown up, more shipments hijacked. And you and I are going to have this same argument each time something happens. No, you'll be much happier with Vanessa in California."

Sirens sounded outside as police and fire trucks arrived.

"You already have a plan, don't you?" Lucas asked intently. "What are you going to do?"

"I'm going back to SwanSea, and I'm going to double our next shipment."

Lucas exploded. "Dammit, Jake, Wade's going to kill you!"

"I'd like to see him try."

Lucas planted balled fists on his hips. "You're an arrogant, stubborn bastard, Jake, and you're not seeing this clearly."

"You're right," Jake said quietly. "I'm every one of those things."

"And it's the *bastard* part that's beneath this whole damned thing, isn't it? It's like a thorn in your skin that your father won't acknowledge you."

Lucas was the one person in the world he would let talk to him like that, so he stood and listened.

"Dammit, Jake, how long are you going to carry on this vendetta with Edward Deverell?"

"It's not a vendetta," he said, his voice low, calm, and matter-of-fact. "It's my life."

Lucas delivered a long string of colorful obscenities, then threw up his hands. "You know something? You and Wade damn well deserve each other. You're each obsessed. And you know something else? I'm not going to stick around and watch you get killed. I just decided. I'll be leaving tomorrow with Vanessa."

Jake nodded, a small smile playing around his lips. "Only promise me you'll come back and supervise my funeral. I wouldn't want Edward to put on some pompous, asinine affair."

"It would be what you deserve, you damned fool!" Lucas slammed out of the room.

Jake stared at the door, reflecting that he already missed him. But California was the best place for both Vanessa and Lucas. They'd be together and they'd be away from this mess. He sank onto the nearest chair and lay his head against its back. Dammit. He couldn't give in to Wade, and he wasn't going to join in the fray either.

A knock sounded at the door and Jake sighed. It was the police and they would be wanting to know if he had any idea who blew up his car. Even if he gave them Wade's name, they would never be able to prove anything.

He rose and slowly went to answer the door.

* * *

"I wasn't sure whether you'd agree to talk to me or not," Jake said later that day, speaking over the telephone to Arabella. "I was sure Perkins would come back on the line and inform me that you had just left on an African safari and wouldn't be back for six months."

She had had definite doubts about the wisdom of talking with him again. In the end, though, she hadn't been able not to. "No, that's next week." She had expected a light, teasing comeback, and was surprised when she didn't get one.

"I see." He paused. "I wanted to tell you, in case you saw it in the newspapers tomorrow and got worried—my car has been bombed, but I'm fine."

Her hand flew to her heart. "What?"

"I'm fine," he repeated. "It's nothing to get upset about, just a message from an old friend, that's all."

"Friend?"

"To tell the truth, we were never really friends."

"I'm not surprised to hear that. Jake, does this have anything to do with your bootlegging?"

"It has to do with exceptional greed and stupidity, Arabella. Nothing more, nothing less."

"Are you in danger? Tell me the truth."

"No. He went after the car, not me."

He sounded so convinced, she thought, but worry continued to nag at her. She started to ask him another question, but restrained herself. She had no right to ask him anything more, she realized. She had no real status in his life.

"Lucas and Vanessa are leaving tomorrow for the coast," he said unexpectedly.

He's so lonely. His mother's words came back to her.

"And I'm returning to SwanSea."

A shock ran through her, and for an instant she felt as if he were going out of her life forever. Irrational, she chided herself. Totally irrational. "You are? Why?"

"I have some business there."

"But what about your work here?" She grimaced self-consciously, realizing she sounded as if she were trying to talk him into staying.

"I can work there about as easily as I can here. One more thing." He paused. "Arabella, I'd like you to come with me."

"I can't." The answer was practically effortless on her part. She had said it to him so many times before, in so many ways.

"I've never known the kind of pain I've come to know from wanting you." The level of his voice had dropped, and his tone had gone husky and raw-edged.

She closed her eyes. Silence stretched . . .

"Good-bye, Arabella."

9

"MISS?"

Arabella's head jerked up and the book in her lap tumbled to the floor. With a rueful expression she bent to retrieve the unread book, thinking that the frayed state of her nerves was embarrassingly obvious. This evening there had been no room in her mind for anything but Jake and what he had said on the telephone. Laying the book on the table, she turned to the butler. "Yes, Perkins?"

"Miss Vanessa Martin is here to see you. Shall I show her in?"

"Vanessa Martin?" She frowned.

"Yes, miss. That was the name she gave me. Perhaps you would rather entertain her in the drawing room?"

"No, no. Please bring her back here. The fire is going nicely." She was in a small cozy parlor at the rear of the house that almost no one used but she.

"Very good, miss."

A minute later Vanessa walked in, looking stunning in a sophisticatedly simple dress of gray wool with soft loose sleeves that flared at the wrists and a bias-cut skirt. Her gray wool cloche was fashioned in the new asymmetric style that showed rather than concealed her forehead.

"Hello, Arabella, I hope I'm not interrupting you. I took the liberty of calling earlier and was told you would be at home this evening."

"Yes," she said, waving her to a chair. "I decided to have a quiet evening at home tonight."

Gazing with speculation both at the room around her and at Arabella, Vanessa sat on the chair and crossed her long legs with ladylike grace. "That was wise of you," she said, though her tone and expression clearly indicated surprise at Arabella having the good sense to stay home and read a book in front of the fire.

Arabella smiled wryly. "Yes, I thought so."

Vanessa nodded absently. "It's beastly out. Snow, with more on the way. This is a charming room, by the way."

"Thank you. I like it."

Vanessa slipped off her gloves and laid them on her lap. "Lucas and I will be leaving for the coast tomorrow. The weather will be much better out there."

Arabella barely knew Vanessa, but she was absolutely sure she was a woman who didn't waste time discussing the weather. "Jake told me you were going."

Vanessa's expression turned speculative. "Did Jake tell you why?"

"No, and I didn't ask. I assumed it has something to do with your career. Am I right?"

Vanessa smoothed her hands over her gloves with an absorption that was unnatural to the task. Without answering her question, she went on. "Did he also tell you that he is returning to SwanSea?"

"Yes."

"But you said you wouldn't go with him."

This was a very odd conversation, Arabella decided. Vanessa seemed as if she were trying to make up her mind about something. "How do you know he even asked me?"

"He did." She paused. "Jake plays only with things that don't mean anything to him. But you"—Vanessa shrugged—"I think you've gotten under his skin."

Arabella shook her head. "You're wrong. As far as I can tell, what I thought was a developing relationship was nothing more substantial than prettily colored smoke for the benefit of the public." The last word caught and broke in her throat.

Vanessa eyed her. "He took you to see his mother. Lucas and I are the only two people in the world who have ever been given that privilege, and I'm not sure we count, because we have known her for years, since we were kids."

"Taking me to see his mother is a decision I think he regrets." Arabella laughed and hoped she was the only one who heard the pain. "No, Vanessa, our private moments were only about sex. He never let me get close to the real Jake."

"Sex is a start."

Arabella shook her head again. "I don't know why I'm telling you this, but no matter what the appearances were, Jake and I never made love. I'm not sure he's capable of making love in the true sense of the words. You said it yourself—he plays only with things that don't mean anything to him. And he really was only playing with me, Vanessa, no matter what impression you may have gotten." Her eyes filled with tears, and horrified that Vanessa would see her crying, she turned her head until she could get herself under control.

Vanessa stared at Arabella for a long moment, then exhaled a deep breath. "Arabella, I'm about to give you some information that the papers would pay a pretty penny for. But I'm going on the assumption that I can trust you with it. You seem to have the same opinion as I do of the columns, plus you should be aware that I will come back and pull every hair out of your head if you reveal any of this to anyone."

Not at all intimidated, Arabella straightened in her

chair, extremely interested in whatever it was Vanessa was about to tell her. "Yes?"

"The other night you brought up the fact that Jake doesn't eat when the two of you are out together."

"As far as I could tell, he didn't eat even at SwanSea."

Vanessa nodded. "I came over here tonight to tell you why." She hesitated, but then after a moment went on. "When I was seven years old, my father died. Both my mother and my baby brother were sick and needed medicine, but we were too poor to afford it. Just about our only money came from what my older brother, who was nine, earned as a paper boy. Like all paper boys, he was given a certain number of papers each day, and he had to assume the losses for all the papers he didn't sell."

"But that's not right," Arabella said, unable to keep her indignation to herself.

Vanessa moved her shoulders, a dismissing gesture. "That was the way it was. I'm sure it still is."

The expression in Vanessa's eyes looked particularly old tonight, Arabella noted, fascinated by both the woman and her story.

"Anyway, one day my brother got sick. Suddenly. So I had to go out in his place." Vanessa's mouth twisted into a smile devoid of humor. "I didn't do well at all, and by late that afternoon a cold rain had begun to fall. Then Wade Scalia came along."

"Wade Scalia? There's a gangster named Wade Scalia who lives and operates right here in Boston.

He's getting to be quite a celebrity." Arabella gave a light laugh. "I'm sorry. I shouldn't have interrupted. It's just that for a minute there, I thought he might be the same person."

"He is," Vanessa said flatly. "And he was almost as obnoxious back then as he is now. He told me I was selling in his territory and that I had to move on. I knew I was in my brother's territory, but Wade was not only bigger than I was, he was three years older, and I had no choice but to do as he said. It started to get dark. I still had all those papers, so I moved farther and farther out of the neighborhood, trying to sell them, and soon I was downtown." She paused. "That was where Jake and Lucas found me."

"Had they been looking for you?"

Vanessa nodded. "My mother sent them to try to find me." She gave a small smile. "I don't think anyone else in the neighborhood would have gone to the trouble, but they did and it didn't take them long to figure out what had happened. They tracked me all the way downtown."

Vanessa switched her gaze to the fire. "I was soaked to the skin and colder and hungrier than I believe I'd ever been in my life. I was standing in front of a ritzy restaurant and its large plate glass window. And I was crying my heart out." Her smile broadened. "I was never so glad to see anyone as I was to see Lucas and Jake.

"The three of us stared in the window at those rich people who were eating, drinking, laughing—having such a good time without the slightest concern for the three of us standing outside—if they even noticed us. We were wet and cold and so hungry we felt like our stomachs were pushing against our backbones. Lucas was quiet. But me, well, I saw a world I hadn't known existed, where everyone wore beautiful, elegant clothes and was dry and warm and could eat all the food they wanted. And I couldn't stop crying because I wanted what I saw so badly.

"And Jake"—she looked at Arabella—"he put his arm around me and told me to stop crying. Didn't I understand? he asked. Those people in that restaurant were too self-absorbed and stupid to even look around them and see us outside staring in at them. We could even throw rocks and bricks through the window at them, and they'd probably not look up. They were no better than animals in a zoo, too busy gobbling up their food to even be aware that they looked like fools and were at the mercy of those who watched them. Don't ever cry for fools like them, he said. Laugh at them. And so we did. All three of us started pointing and laughing and banging on the window until the headwaiter came out with his big black umbrella over his head and ran us off."

Her smile faded. "Jake and Lucas took me home, then ran Wade down. They gave him my newspapers and told him not to come back to the neighborhood until he had the money to give to my family. And since that night, Jake has never eaten in front of anyone he doesn't know extremely well and trust completely. He says if he ate in front of strangers, he would feel like an animal in a zoo."

It would make him feel vulnerable, Arabella realized, deeply touched and moved by the story. She saw that Vanessa was pulling on her gloves, preparing to leave. "Why did you come here tonight? Why did you tell me this story?"

"Because I think Jake is going to need you."

Arabella was stunned into momentary silence. "Why?"

"It's just a feeling I have." Vanessa stood and Arabella followed suit. "There's one more thing—if you decide to get back in to this thing you and Jake have going, you'd better be in it for real. Because once you've crossed the line, maybe you won't be able to go back."

Vanessa's tone was challenging, while making it apparent she had said all she would. "Wade Scalia," Arabella said on impulse. "Did he ever bring you the money?"

"Oh, yes. He wouldn't have dared not to, not with Jake and Lucas on his back."

"And was it enough to buy the medicine your family needed?"

Vanessa turned and began walking out of the room. She reached the door, stopped, and looked back at Arabella. "None of this is in my official studio biography, but both my brothers died that night. My mother died two weeks later."

Arabella gasped. "I'm so sorry. You were all alone. What happened then?"

"I was sent to St. Louis to live with an aunt and an uncle. And I was still alone. Good-bye, Arabella."

For days afterward, Arabella replayed Vanessa's story over and over in her mind. In her own way, Vanessa was as enigmatic as Jake. But Arabella knew Vanessa had not told her the story to help her. She had braved the weather and put herself through the pain of reliving that time when three members of her family had died for only one reason—to help Jake.

She had said, *Jake is going to need you.*

His mother had said, *He's been so lonely.*

Arabella's head hurt as she attempted to take the few disparate pieces she had of the puzzle of Jake and put a whole picture together.

But most of all her heart hurt.

She adopted the strategy of going to parties, to laugh and be gay with her friends, to try to purge all images and memories of Jake from her body and her mind. But each time she went out, she ended up leaving conspicuously early, and she soon stopped all her social activities.

She had always found immense satisfaction in her work with the Linden Foundation, but when she went into her office, she couldn't concentrate, and only stared off into space. Since she had a number of programs already working with knowledgeable and competent people running them, she finally decided that the foundation could do without her for a while.

She couldn't work, she couldn't play.

There was only Jake left—to think about, to dream about, to ache for and to love.

And she did love him, with everything that was in her.

Time passed, shadows appeared beneath her eyes, and Kenneth began to hover worriedly around her.

Then one morning during the second week in March she woke up and realized her life had come to a standstill. Her back was against a wall, and she had retreated from Jake as far as she could.

She had to start moving her life forward again.

And Jake was the only direction in which she could go.

"Lucas is worried about you, Jake," Vanessa said over the long distance line from California.

In his study at SwanSea, Jake leaned back in his chair and propped his feet up on the desk, grinning. "Oh, yeah? Then why didn't *he* ring me instead of having you do it?"

"Because he's still mad at you and he doesn't want to talk to you because he says he'll get even madder. He's taken to calling you 'that damned stubborn jackass.' "

Jake chuckled. "Tell him there's nothing to worry about. I haven't heard a peep out of Wade."

"I don't think that's necessarily good news, Jake."

"You too, Vanessa?"

"Me too. I can't help but worry. You forget how long I've known the three of you." She paused. "Are you there alone?"

"Nope. The house is full. I've got plenty of company, and everyone is having a grand time."

"I notice you didn't say *you* were having a grand time."

His grin slowly turned rueful. "You're just looking for things to worry about, aren't you?"

"With you and Lucas I don't have to look very far." She paused. "Is Arabella there?"

His grin faded. "What made you think of her?"

"Is she?"

"No, but there are women galore here. Don't fret about me. All I've got to do is pick one."

"So why don't you?"

He sighed and rubbed his brow. "Leave me alone, Vanessa. Don't you have a movie to make or something?"

"As a matter of fact, I do. They have me scheduled to start a new one tomorrow. And"—she paused for dramatic effect—"I will be the *star*."

"Wow! I'm very impressed!"

"You better be. Starring in a Hollywood movie is a long way from the old neighborhood, and I've worked hard for it."

"I know that better than anyone, and I couldn't be more proud of you . . . and for you."

"Thanks, Jake, that means a lot. Listen, I've got to

hang up now, but I want you to think about something."

"What's that?"

"Coming out here. Our house out at the beach will be completed in a couple of weeks, and you can be our first and only guest."

He shook his head. "I can't right now, honey, but I promise I'll come out soon."

"You won't, you know."

"Yeah, I know. Tell that guy of yours to take good care of you. Good-bye, honey."

Jake dropped the receiver into its hook and frowned down at the documents he had been trying to read before Vanessa had called. But then, as now, all the letters seemed to blur and reform before his eyes until all he could see was a clear and perfect picture of Arabella. Irritated, he glanced at the phone. He had not tried to get in touch with her since he had returned to SwanSea, but the accomplishment, such as it was, had cost him a great deal.

Night and day she filled his thoughts—to the point that he sometimes felt he might go mad if he didn't see her, touch her, hear her voice and her laughter.

But he was always stopped by the knowledge that she wanted and deserved more than he could give her. Love was foreign to him; marriage was impossible. It would make Edward too happy if he married and gave him the heirs he so desperately wanted. And making Edward miserable had been a part of him for so long, that if he stopped, he might die.

Dammit. He swept his arms across the desk, sending the papers flying.

Hearing the drone of an engine overhead, he expelled a long breath. He badly needed a distraction, he decided, rising to stroll outside to see if someone might be coming in by plane for a visit.

Outside, the day was crisp and clear with only patches of snow left here and there on the ground. Looking up, he saw a golden plane bank against a golden sun, then straighten out for a long gliding descent toward the back of SwanSea.

He frowned. A plane landing at SwanSea was a rare enough occurrence, but up until now the pilots had all elected to use the meadow that lay to the north of the house. Landing at the back of the house along the cliffs would definitely be risky.

Other people were streaming out of the house now. He saw Marlon and motioned him over. "Keep everyone well back."

The older man nodded and set off, and Jake turned his attention back to the plane. At least the pilot seemed to know what he was doing, he thought as he watched the little plane descend. In moments its wheels touched down lightly and it rolled along the cliffs to a neat, safe stop.

His eyes on the cockpit, Jake walked slowly toward the plane. But a few yards short he stopped, utterly shocked. A feminine figure wrapped in a gold leather coat with a big golden fox collar and wearing high heels stepped out of the plane and climbed nimbly down from it. Arabella!

She was here.

She had to be a figment of his imagination. He blinked and looked again. It was like a manifestation of his dreams, yet there was no doubt that he was awake.

And then she was standing in front of him, golden, radiant, and smiling at him. And he finally understood that she had come to him.

Swallowing, he discovered that his throat was painfully tight. And amazingly, after all the days and nights of wanting her and not having her, there was only one thing he could think of to say. "Are you sure?"

She nodded.

Barely aware of the noisy people gathered around them, he took her hand and they walked into the house.

In the gilded brass elevator he tentatively touched her face with a hand he was surprised to see tremble. "Are you *very* sure?"

"Yes."

In the massive bedroom, after he had shut the door behind them, he steeled his nerves to ask one last time. "You're really sure?"

She shrugged out of the fox and leather coat and let it slide to the floor. "Yes, Jake, I'm sure."

He felt incapable of moving; his thoughts were in chaos. *She was here.* Her golden eyes were huge and shadowed, but there was a special luminosity about her, a radiance that made his stomach knot and unknot.

Quite simply, she was the most beautiful woman he had ever known. She could have any man in Boston, but she had come to him, knowing how little he had to offer her. He couldn't think of anything that had ever moved him as much. He was shaking, he realized, shaking with relief, with happiness, with an extraordinary passion that he seemed to have only for her.

She was here—for now that was all that was important.

He smiled. "That's a very pretty dress, but it looks as if it's going to be hard to get off. If you don't want me to rip it, you'd better take it off yourself."

So they were going to make love immediately. It was right that they should, she thought. Very right. "I have other dresses," she murmured, "but if you like, I'll take it off."

"Yes," he said huskily. "I'd like."

She lifted the dress over her head and dropped it on top of the coat. Then she sat down, unbuckled and slipped out of her high-heeled shoes, and peeled off her hose. When she stood and faced him again, she was dressed only in a gold silk and lace short slip.

He let out a long, ragged breath. "You shouldn't have come."

"I know."

"But do you know, do you understand, that now that you're here, I'm not going to let you go?"

His soft voice sent a warm shiver down her spine. Since the moment she had made her decision this morning, she had never felt more alive, more achingly happy. Standing before him in her scanty lingerie, she tilted her head back and gazed solemnly up at him. "You don't deserve me, Jake Deverell, but I've made my decision. I'm here. And I plan to stay, at least for a while, unless you do something really stupid that upsets me. Then I'll leave. And I will leave, Jake—whenever I please."

He reached out a hand and ran his finger beneath a narrow gold strap and slid it off her satiny shoulder, then repeated the action with the other strap. "I promise I will never do anything that will upset you."

The slip fell down the slope of her breasts to their stiffened tips, but she made no attempt to pull it up. "Don't make promises you can't keep, Jake."

"All right, I won't," he said, his gaze like fire, his voice rough and uneven. "But I want you to know that for you, I'll make an effort."

That was all she could ask for, she thought, and more than she had expected. He was a passionate, strangely mysterious man, full of violent emotions that raged inside him. Chances were good that he would never love her. But based on her belief that he needed her, along with her love for him, she had made a commitment that would change her world forever and that she would live with her whole life long.

She shimmied out of her undergarments, then stood proudly naked before him.

For a long moment he didn't move or breathe. In the afternoon half light streaming through a wide part in the heavy velvet curtains, he drank in the sight of her high, firm breasts with their pale pink nipples and their rigid, budlike tips. His gaze traveled to the shapely curve of her waist and hips, her flat stomach, and the enticing triangle of gold at the apex of her long, graceful legs.

"Am I the first man to see you undressed?" he finally asked.

Her throat felt strangely constricted. "Yes."

"Good." There was an intense primal satisfaction in the one word. "You're right, I don't deserve you. But that's not going to stop me."

He swept her into his arms and carried her to the bed. Arabella's heart slammed against her rib cage with wild excitement. When she had made her decision to come to him, she had thought of this moment with a certain fear, but also with a delirious kind of joy. Oddly enough, she trusted him. And from his first kiss at midnight on New Year's Eve, her desire for him had begun to grow. Until now she looked at this moment as something that had to happen before she could get on with the rest of her life.

He lowered her to a black satin spread, then with a gaze that never left her, he began to undress. First his jacket was tossed aside, then his belt was stripped free of its loops and dropped to the floor. His shirt followed.

Watching him, Arabella's mouth went dry. She had thought she had an understanding of Jake's power and virility, but seeing him undress, she realized she hadn't known the half of it. His shoulders were broad and his chest was wide and muscled with a covering of dark hair. He was all man, and his impatience showed as he dispatched the rest of his clothes with hurried movements.

And then he was naked, and Arabella sucked in her breath as heat surged through her. "I don't think I've ever seen anything as beautiful as you are."

His black eyes seemed to turn even darker. "Then you haven't looked in a mirror."

He came down beside her, and as if she had done it a thousand times before, she twined her arms around his neck and draped a leg over his. His body heat seemed to wrap around her, and she prepared for his quick entry, wanting it but at the same time tensing against the erotic invasion. It came as a surprise, then, when instead he cupped one buttock with his big hand and pulled her against him, pressing his rigid passion against her lower body. And a strange new kind of heat began to spread through her, a white-hot heat that reached down to her toes and out to her fingertips and pooled between her legs.

"How am I ever going to be able to make love to you properly?" he asked rhetorically, thickly. "There's so much I want to do to you, and I want to do everything at once."

His mouth was hovering over hers so that their breath mingled, teaching her a level of intimacy she had not considered before. She slid her fingers up into the thick vitality of his black hair and whispered, "Then do it."

Somewhat startled, he drew his head back so that he could see her lovely face. "Where did you get so much courage?"

Her love for him had given it to her, but she couldn't tell him that, and he saved her from having to answer by taking her bottom lip between his teeth and lightly tugging. At the same time, he covered her breast with his free hand. She felt, he thought, like heaven on fire.

Against her tender skin his body was rough and hard, every inch muscled, but he was the epitome of gentleness with her. He explored her body as if it were some sort of temple, slowly and reverently learning everything about her. Lying with him on the big bed, she began to writhe and whimper. But still he didn't hurry. He touched and tasted her with the thoroughness and intensity of a starving man at a banquet. He searched out every secret place on her body, caressing and kissing, nipping and licking, over and over again.

She was nearly incoherent by the time he moved over her, but she was still aware of the tangy sheen of sweat that covered his big body and of the tremors that ran beneath his smooth dark skin. And she understood the high cost he was paying for control. Blindly she wrapped her legs around his hips and arched up to him.

"No," he said, his voice sounding barely human. "Let me try to do this right." He grasped her hips and pushed them back to the bed, and then slowly and ever so carefully he began to enter her. She had such a need for him to be inside her that she could only moan with relief. He was filling her, becoming a part of her, and she had never known a greater satisfaction.

Then a sharp pain stabbed through her, and a cry escaped her lips.

His big body went motionless, and he quickly covered her face with kisses. "Lord, I'm sorry. I'm so sorry. If there was any other way . . ."

His kisses and his soft, hoarse voice slowly relaxed her tensed muscles, and gradually the pain faded. "I'm all right," she whispered.

Tenderly he stroked the damp, pale hair away from her face, looking for further reassurance. "Are you sure? I'll probably die if I have to stop, but I will. Just tell me—"

"No." His concern had an unexpected sweetness about it, making her more certain than ever that she had made the right choice. She was giving up a little to gain the world.

Faint frissons of pleasure had begun to radiate up into her stomach and down the insides of her legs, building an anxiousness within her to continue. She reached up and touched his lips with her fingertips. "Make love to me."

A hard shudder racked his body. He started to move again, and the most exquisite sensations she had ever felt flooded through her as her body slowly stretched, taking him into her.

When he had completely filled her, he stopped once more. "Am I hurting you?" he asked, his iron-corded body trembling and feverish with desire.

With an instinct and knowledge she hadn't known she possessed, she began to lift and circle her hips. "I've never felt anything so wonderful as you inside me."

The last vestiges of his control broke. With a sound that came tearing up from his chest, he surged into her.

Shocks of fire rolled through her. Jake's gentleness and concern were gone, and in their place a skill and masterfulness that had her hurtling toward ecstasy. Her wanting was now a deeply fierce thing. He thrust into her again and again, each time straining to go deeper and deeper, and she eagerly met his demands, undulating her hips in a rhythm and urgency that naturally and quite mystically matched his.

She was in flames, burning away bit by bit. Then suddenly she caught her breath and arched her back off the bed as the first climax hit her and took her into another world. She heard him say, *"My Lord,"* as if he were uttering a prayer, but still he kept plunging into her, his hips moving forcefully and furiously but with a finesse that soon had her moaning again and clawing helplessly at his back.

She was going to come apart, she thought, shuddering at the ecstasy that was once again building and building within her. And then another climax crashed hard over her, this one more powerful and electric than the last, and she cried out in utter wonderment.

He buried himself in her one last time, then his body tensed, and he made a hoarse, raw sound that before the rapture ended turned into her name.

Arabella slowly came awake and immediately felt the warm, solid strength of Jake's body next to her. She smiled, then opened her eyes to see him propped up on an elbow, staring down at her.

"Hello," he said huskily.

There was a softness to his eyes that warmed her. "Hello."

He skimmed his finger back and forth across her lips. "What made you smile before you even opened your eyes?"

"You. I felt you beside me."

His finger stilled. "You're amazing."

Her smile broadened. "Thank you for the compliment."

"It's the truth."

She stretched and looked around her. The room was dark except for the glow of light from a Tiffany lamp that sat on a bedside table. "What time is it?"

"About eight."

"Eight? How long have you been awake?"

"About an hour."

"And you've been staring at me all this time?"

He nodded. "The view was wonderful."

She grinned, then another thought struck her and she groaned. "Oh, no. Dinner will be in an hour, and all those people—your guests—they'll expect us to come down."

"No, they won't, because they should all be on their way back to Boston by then."

"Boston?" Pulling the sheet up with her, she shifted until she was propped up against a pile of pillows. "They're *all* leaving?"

He tugged the sheet down so that he could see her breasts. "A lot of them may have gone already. I woke up about an hour ago, called Marlon, and told him to tell all the guests to leave."

She stared at him, perplexed. "But why?"

He shrugged and reached out to take the weight of her breast into his hand.

A fresh warmth began to spread through her, but she had a feeling his answer could be important. "Why, Jake?"

He shrugged again and brushed his thumb over her nipple. He smiled when he heard her gasp. "I don't know. . . . Maybe I'm jealous, and I didn't want to see all the men swarming around you."

"You told me you don't get jealous—ever."

A tinge of irritation crept into his expression. "All

right, then, maybe it's because I want to be alone with you."

"You—" Words temporarily failed her. She tried again. "What are they going to think?"

He bent and pressed a kiss to her breast. "I don't care."

Fighting against the growing need to abandon herself to the feelings he was creating, she forced herself to give what he had said some thought. "Are you going to call Randolph Bruce and tell him I'm here?"

"Nope."

"You want to be all alone with me?" She had to say it aloud, to hear the words, to hear his answer.

He chuckled. "Yes. Of course the servants will be here, but they know how to make themselves scarce." He paused. "Would you rather I ask the guests to stay?"

"Are you kidding?" She gave a whoop of delight and hurled herself at him, knocking him over on his back and coming over him until she lay on top of him. "You did a very intelligent thing, Jake Deverell, getting rid of all those people."

He grinned, loving the sensuous feel and the sweet smell of her body. "Oh yeah? Why's that?"

"Because *I'm* going to keep you busy, *full-time*."

His grin spread over every inch of his face. "Sounds like a definite challenge."

She nodded in agreement. "I'm very demanding."

He skimmed his hands down the slope of her back

to her hips and moved her ever so slightly against his already-hard manhood. "Okay, Miss Linden, what's your first demand?"

"Food."

He closed his eyes and gave a mock groan. "I can't believe you want food at a time like this."

"A time like what?" she asked innocently.

He gave a growl, rolled her over onto her back, and came up on top of her. "Like right before I'm about to devour you," he said, his tone ferocious.

She gave a shriek and went into a peal of laughter, and suddenly his expression turned serious. Seeing it, her laughter slowly died, and he laid his hand along the side of her face.

"You've made me very happy, Arabella."

Her eyes grew moist with unshed tears of happiness. "So kiss me," she said softly.

"I thought you wanted food."

"Are you hungry?"

"Only for you."

"Then food can wait."

10

THE next afternoon Arabella, dressed in a white pullover sweater and a white pleated skirt, skipped down the grand staircase in search of Jake. But Marlon was the only person she saw, and he was standing in the front doorway, gazing outside.

"That's my plane," she said, coming up behind him and looking over his shoulder to see four men rolling her plane past the doorway. "What are they doing with my plane?"

"Mr. Deverell gave orders that your plane was to be tied down in the north meadow."

"Really? Why?"

"I'm sure I can't say, Miss Linden."

She smiled. "I'm sure Mr. Deverell will be able to say," she said, lightly teasing him. "Where is he?"

"In his study."

"Thank you, Marlon. And thank you for seeing to my luggage."

"I was glad to do it, Miss Linden."

A minute later Jake glanced up from the ticker tape his machine was spewing out to see Arabella peep around the door. He motioned her in.

"What a beautiful room," she said, taking in the various golden hues of the paneling, bookshelves, and desk, all made of citron wood. At Jake's side she stood on tiptoe and pressed her lips to his. To her surprise and delight, he gathered her close to him and deepened the kiss until she was nearly breathless.

Even after he ended the kiss, he held her to him a moment longer, inhaling the sensuously feminine fragrance that was uniquely hers. After a night of incredible lovemaking, he still wanted her, he realized with astonishment. "How are you?" he asked, releasing her but following an impulse to reach out and to touch the lips he had just kissed so thoroughly.

"Fine. More than fine," she said, perching on the edge of the desk. "But I'm a little angry with you. Why didn't you wake me up before you left our room this morning?"

"Don't be mad," he said huskily. "After last night, I thought you needed your rest." He hadn't been able to leave her alone, taking her again and again. And because of it, he hadn't been able to help but feel concern for her, plus being extremely bewildered at himself that his need for her should be so great.

"What about you? Aren't you tired?" She, who never blushed, nearly blushed at the implication behind her questions.

He cast an idle glance at the ticker-tape machine. "I like to be here when the market opens."

"I suppose you've already had breakfast and lunch," she said, careful to keep her tone light, and saw him nod absently. At ten o'clock the previous night, Marlon had brought dinner to the room, but Jake hadn't eaten anything. After they had made love once again, she had fallen asleep. When she had awakened later, Jake had been there, but she received the impression he had just returned to bed and had surmised that he had gone downstairs to eat.

"Jake, why did you ask the men to take my plane to the north meadow?"

He cast one last glance at the ticker-tape machine, then dropped down into his desk chair. "Because it will be safer there than on the cliffs."

"I saw the meadow," she said thoughtfully, "but I thought it would be more fun to land in back of the house along the cliffs."

"Which is just what we're going to talk about."

She looked at him in surprise. "We are?"

She had his whole attention now, and his tone and expression were serious. "Do you have any idea how dangerous what you did was? If you had misjudged, even a little—"

"But I didn't. I knew what I was doing."

He held up a stern finger. "And that's another thing. I didn't even know you flew."

"I guess the subject never came up," she said slowly, baffled by his attitude.

"Well, now it has, and I don't want you flying anymore."

"You don't—Jake, what is the matter? A lot of women fly their own planes."

"Maybe. But that doesn't mean you have to."

Suspicion crept into her mind. "Jake, have you ever flown?"

"What has that got to do with anything?"

"Have you?"

"No, and I won't either. I don't consider it safe."

She laughed. "They're talking of setting up coast-to-coast flights this summer. They wouldn't be doing that if they didn't consider flying safe."

"They'll fly only during the day. At night the passengers would have to transfer to a train."

"Still, that means someone in New York could reach Los Angeles in *two* days. Don't you think that's incredible?"

"No, I don't."

She viewed his disgruntled expression, trying to find some clue as to what was wrong, but in spite of their new intimacy, this morning he seemed more enigmatic than ever to her. She slipped down onto his lap and curled her arm around his neck. "Jake, what is it about flying that bothers you?"

"The height," he said flatly. "Planes take you too high, and I don't like falling."

"Have you ever had a bad fall?"

"No, and I don't intend to either. Promise me you won't fly anymore."

"But I love to fly. I've had the plane only a few months. My father gave it to me for Christmas, and he special-ordered the color to match my eyes."

"Promise me, Arabella."

The thought that he was concerned for her secretly thrilled her. On some level he did care for her. But at the same time, the idea of giving up something she enjoyed so much bothered her. "We'll see."

His expression told her he wasn't going to be put off by her hedging. "Arabella, promise me."

"I promise you that as long as we're together, I won't fly."

Jake frowned and looked away, wondering why her promise didn't satisfy him.

Jake sent a lazy smile down the long mahogany dining table to Arabella. "Are you happy now? We've come down to dinner just as you wanted." In spite of the great length of table that separated them and the radio that played softly, the immense dining room had perfect acoustics, and he didn't have to raise his voice to make himself heard.

Arabella saluted him with her wine glass. "Yes, I'm happy now. We've had dinner in the bedroom every night for the past week." *She* had had dinner, she mentally corrected herself. *He* had watched her, using the excuse that he wasn't hungry just then. But she knew that more often than not, around two or three in the morning, he had the habit of going down to his study to work. She also knew, because she had made friends with the cook, that the very fine gentleman was also up at that hour, ready with an elegant meal for Jake.

"I like having dinner in the bedroom. It's comfortable. Besides, in the bedroom I don't have to dress formally." With a wave of his hand he indicated his dark evening suit.

She took a succulent bite of squab, noting with growing frustration and distress that though Jake occasionally cut a new potato or a piece of squab, he didn't eat. "Now that I've spent some time here, I understand SwanSea."

"You understand SwanSea?"

"Yes, and I've decided that dressing for dinner should be required here. SwanSea deserves it."

"SwanSea deserves it. . . ." He tilted his head, and his eyes narrowed on her. "You're a fascinating woman, Arabella. And I'm fascinated by my fascination with you."

She smiled, unable to resist a little flirtation. "So you admit you find me fascinating."

"I wouldn't be here if I didn't."

In the past, other men had lavished extravagant phrases of love on her, but their words had meant nothing to her. With Jake, though, she viewed each word as a precious jewel. On the radio a man and a woman were singing a duet of the lovely Gershwin tune "He Loves and She Loves." "Jake, I've been wondering about something."

He gave up all pretense of eating and leaned back in his chair. "What's that?"

"Why do you suppose Marlon sat us at opposite ends of the table like this?"

"Because it's proper, and in spite of me and what he considers my highly improper activities, Marlon *always* tries to do what is proper."

"I find that commendable," she said, standing up and kicking off her shoes.

"Do you?" he asked, his interest heightening.

"Yes." She climbed into the chair, then stepped up onto the table. "Because I also try to do what I consider proper. And I think it very proper for me to sit near my host."

She walked down the gleaming mahogany table in her stocking feet, careful to skirt the grouping of candles in the center.

Captivated, Jake watched her come toward him. Her dress was a pale peach-gold, sleeveless with a low, draped neckline and a back that scooped to the waist. The skirt had panels that floated out and changed hues with her every movement.

She came down on the table before him, her body angled toward him, her legs to the side of her. "This is much better, don't you think?" she asked, moving his full plate from between them to by her legs.

A small smile played around his mouth. "Yes, I think you're right." Automatically warmed by her nearness, he propped his elbows on the arms of the chair and cradled the side of his face with his hand. "Actually, I think it's *much* better."

Casually, she forked a piece of squab and held it toward him.

With a barely perceptible movement, he drew his head backward. "No, thank you."

She picked the squab off the tines and lay down the fork, abandoning its use altogether. "I've been wondering something, Jake."

His slight smile broadened. "Thank you for the warning. I'm prepared now. What have you been wondering, Arabella?"

"I've been wondering if you would mind if I did a few things around the house."

His black brows arched. "What are you talking about? You haven't developed a sudden desire to scrub floors, have you?"

She brought the squab to her mouth, started to take a bite, then decided not to, but kept the small piece of meat close to her mouth. "Not exactly. But there are some things that I feel should be done."

Jake stared at her mouth. Her lips were full and colored a pale coral. Starting in his loins, heat welled up in him. "Like what?"

She absently brushed the piece of squab back and forth over her lips as if she had forgotten what she held. "Little things, nothing major. After all, this has been a bachelor residence for many years now." She took a dainty nibble from the end of the squab.

"So? he asked. She leaned toward him, revealing the fullness of her breasts. The heat reached his mind, clouding everything but her.

"Don't be so nervous," she chided him softly. "I told you I wouldn't do anything major." She held the squab to his mouth, and he took it. Suppressing the thrill of victory she felt, she reached with her fingers for a spear of asparagus and idly twirled the green stalk through its sauce. She was playing a delicate game of *watch me, want me, want this.* It might be an underhanded way to go about it, but getting him to eat with her had become extremely important. He had closed others out of their life, at least for the present, making what they had together private. Now she wanted him to go one step further and *trust* her.

"For instance," she said, nibbling on the end of the asparagus, "there are no flowers in any of the rooms, and I know for a fact that you have a greenhouse that's bursting with flowers."

"How do you know that?" he asked with a frown.

"I've talked with Harold." She held the asparagus up to his mouth, and to her secret gratification he took a bite.

"Who's Harold?" he asked chewing.

"He's your head horticulturist."

"Oh, *that* Harold." He paused to swallow several sips of wine from the crystal glass he found unexpectedly at his lips. "I thought he was in charge of the fruits and vegetables."

"He is. But he's also in charge of the greenhouse flowers. In fact, they're his special passion."

Passion. Yes, he thought. Absolutely. Totally absorbed in her, he chewed thoughtfully on yet another piece of squab she had given him. There was nothing about her he didn't like. She gratified all his senses. He loved watching her. He loved her funny little moods. And he got a tremendous kick out of her flair for life and her ability to live in the moment. He loved smelling her—when she climbed out of her bath, all fresh and dewy, or when she first awoke in the morning, drowsy and lazily sensual. But most especially he loved smelling her when her skin caught fire with passion. And he loved seeing her light up with laughter. Laughter became her . . . as did passion. "Perhaps we should take a tour of the greenhouse sometime."

She smiled. "I've already seen it several times, but I'd be glad to go again with you." She offered him a section of a new potato.

His eyes on the curve of her lips, he took it, lightly and deliberately grazing the end of her finger with the edge of his teeth. "Exactly when have you found time to take a tour of the estate?" He couldn't seem to keep the accusation from his voice. He found he wanted one hundred percent of her attention.

"I haven't toured everything, just parts of it, but I can't stay in bed *all* the time, you know, and there are portions of the day when you go to your study. . . ." She gently pushed another piece of squab into his mouth.

Forced to pause for a moment to chew, he watched her. She was sipping from his wineglass, and each time she swallowed, delicate muscles rippled beneath her smooth neck. Inexplicably, the sight made him want to lay his mouth along her neck and feel the movement. His eyes dropped lower to the delectable slope of her beautiful breasts. "Arabella—"

"What? Would you like some more wine?" She held the glass to his lips.

And suddenly he realized what had just happened. He clamped his hand hard around her wrist and guided her hand until the wineglass was back on the table.

"Jake? What's wrong?"

Slowly he released her wrist as he intently searched her face for some clue that she intended harm. But her golden eyes were completely guileless, her expression bewildered and concerned . . . and vulnerable.

His mind raced to grapple with the meaning of what had happened. She had *fed* him, and, even more boggling to him, he had allowed it. But then, if truth were known, he had been overwhelmingly captivated by her from the first.

"Jake?"

"I *never* eat in front of people."

"I know," she said softly. "But then, I never used to

awake before noon, and now I'm up with the sun." She paused, feeling the force of his wariness. Slowly so that she wouldn't startle him, she leaned forward and gently cupped his hard face between her hands. "It's all right, Jake. If you don't want to eat in front of me, it's all right."

He stared at her, stunned. Without his being aware of what she was doing, she had gotten through his guard. He didn't know how she had done it or even why. But she had dared to reach out to him and touch him with a kind of intimacy that he had never felt before. And, he realized with sudden insight, the intimacy was important to her. There was a hurting inside of him that vaguely he identified as longing—a longing to explore and have more of this exceptional and rare kind of intimacy, a longing to have more of Arabella.

Somewhere to the side of them, Marlon cleared his throat. "Dessert?"

Slowly Arabella straightened away from Jake, but she didn't move from her position in front of him. "No."

Marlon turned to go, but Jake unexpectedly raised his hand to stop him. "Yes."

"Very good, sir." The majordomo placed two goblets of chocolate mousse by Arabella's legs with an aplomb that said the etiquette books were wrong to suggest dessert should be served any other place.

His gaze fixed on Arabella, Jake said, "That will be all, Marlon."

"Yes, sir." Marlon left, taking their dinner plates with him.

Arabella eyed Jake uncertainly. "You want dessert?"

He nodded, but before she could reach for the spoon, he skimmed a finger through the mousse and reached up to brush her lips with it. Then he leaned forward and kissed it off with a thoroughness that had her gasping.

Jake couldn't remember ever tasting anything as delicious as the chocolate on her lips. He nibbled and licked, and when he could taste no more chocolate, he went after the sweetness that was Arabella's own. "There's no dessert on earth that tastes as good as you do," he muttered roughly against her mouth.

He ended the kiss moments later only because he knew he wanted more. Her lips were swollen, and in her eyes he saw the same heat he was feeling deep inside.

"Come here," he said, and pulled her to him. Then the panels of her skirt were floating upward as he brought her down onto his lap so that she straddled him. Her weight eased his ache for the moment, but the gut-wrenching desire that had so unexpectedly come up in him had made him very single-minded. "Never leave me," he whispered gruffly before he claimed her mouth once again.

Arabella's head reeled at the hunger and strength of his kiss, but she recognized that there was a fierce storm of passion rising in him, and she was in the storm's center. Even if she could break free, she wouldn't. She was exactly where she wanted to be—in his head, in his arms, in his life.

Maybe someday she might even be in his heart, but for now she was satisfied.

Because of the deep back of the dress, she hadn't worn a camisole, and the bodice of her dress easily fell off her shoulders and was soon around her waist. With a groan his hand closed around her breast.

Another ballad wafted, low and romantic, from the radio; candles flickered, sending out a soft golden light. But Arabella had lost touch with reality. Jake was her world; he always would be.

She sighed and threw back her head, exposing the vulnerable line of her throat to his incendiary kisses. Tangling her fingers through his hair, she urged his head downward, and when he closed his mouth around the rigid, aching tip of her breast, she moaned and tightened her fingers in his hair. Beneath her she could feel the hard bulge of his sex, and she moved against him, seeking escape from the excruciatingly erotic pressure building between her legs.

"Lord, you're *fire*," he said, his voice hoarse, his tone amazed.

He freed himself, then reached between her legs and with a seemingly simple pull, ripped the seam that was keeping him from her.

Holding the satin curves of her bottom in his palms, he surged upward into her until he was completely sheathed in the tight, hot velvet of her body. A primal growl rumbled deep in his throat, then his fingers tightened on her hips, and he began moving her on him, undertaking the almost superhuman responsibility of controlling both of their responses. He had an inclination of what would happen when he finally climaxed, and he wanted it to be just as fantastic for her.

But heaven help him, she was like a wild thing, twisting and undulating against him, pleading and demanding. Her sweet utterances left him scorched inside and out, and he felt as if he were going to burst apart.

Then he felt her stiffen, and her inner contractions begin. She dug her fingernails into his shoulders and arched away from him with a cry that burned into his mind. Then it was happening for him—powerful, primitive, and more magnificent than he could have ever imagined.

And he wrapped his arms around her and held tightly on to her, because at that very moment, when he felt as if he were dying, he instinctively knew that Arabella was his only hope for life.

In the days that followed, Jake stayed very close to Arabella, understanding for the first time how a person could become addicted to alcohol or drugs. She was an intoxicating experience that he couldn't seem to get enough of. And his need for her outweighed the danger of the addiction.

Edward called almost daily, trying by threat and exhortation to get him to return to Boston. Jake turned a deaf ear. When friends accustomed to being welcomed at SwanSea phoned, they were told that the doors were closed to guests. When Randolph Bruce called, he was not so politely rebuffed.

Winter was fading and spring was just around the corner. Arabella hastened spring along by throwing open the windows and bringing armloads of flowers in.

Her laughter filled the big rooms, and she danced everywhere and on everything. She danced outside in the rain and inside on top of the tables and pianos. She danced on the grand staircase and on the bed. She danced with music and without. With one part of his mind Jake realized with slight alarm that she was dancing her way into his heart. With the other part of his mind he accepted it.

By the time spring did arrive, new coats of paint decorated the walls. Chairs and couches that had been stained or had cigarette holes in their upholstery were covered with new fabric.

And a strange thing was happening. With spring drifting by, with the redecoration, with Arabella with him, SwanSea was becoming more like a haven to him, more like a home.

"I don't know what you're doing up there at SwanSea, but whatever it is, it can't be good!" Edward's voice bellowed through the telephone line from Boston.

A muscle jerked in Jake's jaw. "Your faith in me means so much, Edward."

"Yesterday an acquaintance of mine at the club asked me straight out if you were bootlegging. I denied it, of course."

"Of course you did."

"All along I've been afraid that your scandalous behavior would jeopardize the Deverell name. Now my friends are getting suspicious. Jake, I've worked too hard—"

"And hurt a lot of people."

"Now, you listen to me you, you—" Edward broke off, coughing.

"I believe the word you're looking for is bastard."

As soon as he quit coughing, Edward started again. "You think you had it hard growing up on the streets, Jake—"

"I've never once complained about how *I* grew up. My gripe has always been that you had the means to make my mother's life so much easier, but you washed your hands of her when she didn't obey you."

"You don't know *anything*. I grew up in the coal mines of the Black Mountains in Wales."

Jake rubbed his eyes. Verbally, he and Edward rarely got anywhere. The only way he could reach Edward was when he did something particularly outrageous that threatened Edward's status in society. "I know, and when you were eighteen, you shipped out to sea. You've told me this before, Edward."

"And I'll tell it to you again until you understand

the importance of what I've done. From the railing of that freighter I caught my first sight of America—the great beauty of the Maine coastline, where SwanSea now stands. That coastline symbolized something brand new to me, where all things would be possible, and I decided then to build my home there. But first I had to have money. I knew about coal. I decided I would learn about steel. I made my way to Pittsburgh, and with nothing but a strong back and a good mind I had earned a fortune by the time I was forty. But money wasn't enough to wash the coal dust off me. I had to work hard to get accepted into society."

"What in the hell difference does it make whether society accepted you or not?"

"It matters, dammit. And I've handed everything I worked so hard for on to you, and I *won't* let you ruin it!"

Jake exhaled a long breath. "What are you upset about today, Edward? It can't be the business. Things were never better."

"It's the *bootlegging,* for Lord's sake! The whole business is getting ugly. It's in the newspapers daily. The danger's increasing. You're on the road to destruction, Jake. I wouldn't give a damn except you're taking my name with you."

"I'm overwhelmed by your fatherly concern and support, Edward."

"Dammit, shut up and listen. You think because you're younger and stronger than I am you can get the best of me, but you're wrong." He coughed.

"You're smart, Jake, and you're every bit as strong-willed as I am, but I've lived longer and I've learned the answers to questions you don't even know exist yet. Life is very frail—"

Jake's fingers suddenly tightened on the receiver. "Did you just say I'm as smart and as strong-willed as you?" The admission stunned him.

"You're smart, but you're not wise, and that puts you at a distinct disadvantage. No matter how long this fight of ours goes on, you're not going to win, Jake. I will win in the end."

"We'll see about that, old man. We'll see about that."

"Arabella! Arabella!"

Hearing Jake call her name, Arabella hurried down the hall and into his office. "For heaven's sake, Jake, what's the matter? Why are you yelling?"

"Where's my desk?"

"Your desk?" She glanced at the conspicuously empty space where the big golden desk had once been and her expression lightened. "Oh, good, Bert came to get it."

"Bert? Who the hell is *Bert*?"

"He's one of your stablemen, *and*"—the smile she gave him indicated she thought he was going to be very pleased indeed with what she planned to tell him next—"the son of one of the carpenters who built SwanSea. Isn't that wonderful?"

"Why does one of my stablemen have my desk?" he asked, his voice filled with tension.

"He's going to refinish it for you. He's already done several other tables and chairs."

"Who moved my things? The papers that were in my desk?"

"I did. They're in those two boxes in the corner."

He threw a quick glance toward the corner and the boxes. "Who helped you?"

She looked at him oddly. "No one."

"Did you read anything you found?"

"No. Jake, what is this? You're interrogating me. Don't you trust me?"

"I'm sorry. It's just that I don't want you knowing too much about my activities. What you don't know can't hurt you."

"Hurt me? That sounds like you're worried about my safety."

Calmer now, he chose his words so as not to alarm her. "There's a very remote possibility that something could happen, and I don't want you too close."

"Too close to what? To you, Jake?"

"To what I am."

"Is there a difference?"

Jake paused, reflecting that she had a point. What was the difference between what he did and what he was? Probably none.

He didn't seriously believe she was in any danger. It was just that his guard had instinctively risen at the sight of his missing desk, but, dammit, he shouldn't have jumped on her like he had. With Lucas gone, though, the whole responsibility of the bootlegging operation was his, and he was having to be twice as cautious as usual. He also seemed to be working twice as hard, but he did most of it at odd hours, when she was asleep, so that she wouldn't know.

"Jake, is everything all right? I haven't read many newspapers since I've been here. . . ."

She was asking about the bootlegging, and the truth was the business had become extremely tricky. Wade's men were thick on the ground. Treasury had beefed up their patrols. Sources had dried up. Several times his men had run into roadblocks and had to turn back, causing additional problems. He couldn't tell her the truth without worrying her.

"Everything's fine." He leaned his big body back against the bookshelves and with a smile crossed his arms over his chest. "So why did you decide the desk should be refinished?"

Arabella frowned. "Because it badly needed it. I'm not sure you've noticed, but that desk is an absolutely exquisite work of art with its graceful lines and carved orchids. It's made of the same citron wood as the paneling and shelves. And you put your feet up on it every chance you get. That practice needs to stop once Bert is finished with it and you get it back."

Jake could barely keep the smile he was feeling from his face. He loved seeing Arabella involved with SwanSea. She could redo the whole place and he wouldn't care, because in some nebulous way, her interest in his house seemed to forge a connection between them—at least in his mind. Truthfully, he was scared to death she would leave him. After all, there was no commitment between them, nothing spoken or written. And he remembered when she had first come to him she had said she would leave when she pleased.

"Bert has a real feel for wood," she said, walking to the big crystal vase of roses she had placed on a table in front of a window. She studied the arrangement, then switched a couple of the roses to different spots. "Since there's very little carpentry work around here, and since he wanted to stay close to home, he decided to accept a job as a stableman here. He's very good at his work with the horses, but luckily I found out he's even better at refinishing things."

"And how did you get so lucky?" he asked, experiencing a now all too familiar pain in his gut. His belief that he could never be jealous had gone out the window shortly after Arabella had entered his life. If he thought she would sign it, he would have his lawyers draw up an iron-clad contract between them that she would never speak to another man. And even then he didn't think he would feel secure that he wouldn't eventually lose her.

"Why, I talked to him, of course."

He nodded with resignation. "Of course."

"I'll get another desk in here for you to use until Bert finishes with yours. I've already got one picked out up on the fourth floor. I found it in a bedroom that Marlon told me used to be your father's." The suddenly dark look on his face made her add, "I mean Edward Deverell's."

"Find another desk," he said.

"All right." She knew better than to pursue the subject. As close as she felt they were growing, there were still so many areas of his life that were closed to her.

The roses arranged to her satisfaction, she strolled over to the ticker-tape machine and began to idly peruse the tape. "Has anything interesting happened today on Wall Street?"

"Not really." They had been together long enough for him to realize that she had more than a conversational knowledge of business. "It's definitely still a bullish market."

"That's good. I know you were worried about the plummet stocks took last month."

"I'm still worried."

Her interest caught, she dropped the tape and went to sit on the couch. "Are you? Why?"

He shrugged. "I just believe that the faith people are placing in the market is unjustified." He paused. "Who handles your family's finances?"

"Parker Davidson."

He nodded, sitting down beside her. "He's a good man. I wonder if your father would mind if I spoke with Davidson, made some recommendations."

"Jake, my father doesn't even know I'm here with you. I've told you that before. Despite the regular arguments I have with Kenneth over the telephone about me being here, he's still helping me out by taking messages from our parents and forwarding me their mail. Then I write back to them, send it to Kenneth, and he sends it on to them from Boston."

He had always known that keeping her parents in the dark as to her relationship with him troubled Arabella. He understood; he would never do anything deliberately to hurt his mother. He had also known the fights with Kenneth put a strain on her that she tried to hide. But he wanted her with him too badly to tell her to go home. He reached out and brushed the tips of his fingers across her head. "Your parents will be coming home in a couple of months, honey."

Her lovely mouth set into a stubborn line. "I know. And when the time comes, I'll have to deal with it. But when I do, it will be face-to-face with them."

He sighed, not even wanting to think about the possible consequences of her meeting with her parents. "Arabella, I wouldn't even bring this up if I didn't think it was important. But someone needs to advise Davidson to start getting your family out of the market."

Her expression turned thoughtful. "Is that what you've been doing with the Deverell stocks?"

He nodded. "I've got us almost completely out. This prosperity is phony—and there's got to be a ceiling somewhere. There are a few other people who foresee serious problems ahead. Unfortunately, there's not enough."

"But you do? You really believe there's going to be a problem?"

"Yes, I do."

"Then I'll write my father," she said decisively, "tell him your views, but as if they were mine, and then I'll ask for permission to speak with Mr. Davidson."

He stared, slightly amazed. "Just like that? You trust my judgment?"

With a smile that warmed him, she reached over and took his hand in hers. "Of course I do."

He stared down at their joined hands for a moment, telling himself he was being silly to be so affected by her simple gesture. "And will your father listen to you?"

"Yes."

He squeezed her hand. "Then—"

"Excuse me, sir." Marlon spoke from the doorway. "Mr. Kenneth Linden is here to see Miss Linden."

Arabella made a sound of delight. "Kenneth! Show him back!"

"That won't be necessary," Kenneth said, strolling into the study. "I'm already here."

Arabella jumped up from the sofa and threw her arms around him. They might argue every time they spoke on the phone, but he was still her brother. "What a nice surprise!" She hugged him, then drew back and gazed up at him. He looked awful. He had lost weight and there were deep circles beneath his eyes. Guilt instantly surged through her. She had been so involved with Jake during the last few months, she had just assumed that Kenneth was doing well. "Have you been ill, Kenneth?"

His laugh held embarrassment. "No. I've never been one to catch things, you know that."

"Then why do you look so bad?"

Kenneth laughed, this time genuinely. "I see staying here at SwanSea hasn't improved your tact any, kiddo."

"Well?"

"It's nothing. Just too much partying." Eyeing Jake cautiously, he held out his hand to him. "It's nice to see you again, old boy. I hope you don't mind me dropping in like this."

Jake did and called himself a fool because of it. But he had grown used to having Arabella all to himself and he liked it. "Not at all. What brings you up this way?"

"The parents called yesterday." He turned back to Arabella. "They'll definitely be home September tenth."

She glanced at Jake, then back at her brother. "What else did they say?"

"They're still having a great time." He paused. "I think they're getting a little suspicious about why you're never around to talk to them when they telephone."

"I'll place a call to them tonight. I had planned to write them a letter anyway."

Kenneth twirled the brim of his hat. "I told them we were both fine and nothing else."

"Thank you," she said. "I appreciate your backing me up. Now tell me what your plans are. Can you stay for a few days?"

He grinned. "I was hoping you'd ask. I really do need a break from Boston." He cast an uncertain glance at Jake. "I just wasn't sure it would be okay."

"Applesauce! Of course it will be okay. Jake, tell him."

He couldn't refuse. Arabella was too happy to see her brother again. In addition, he also sensed her concern for Kenneth and privately felt she had cause for worry. "You can stay as long as you like, Kenneth."

Arabella smiled, but an ominous feeling came over her and she looked at Jake with a grave expression. Why, she wondered, did she suddenly feel as if their idyll was coming to an end?

11

ON the cliff top overlooking the sea and a twilight sky, Jake put his arms around Arabella and drew her back against him. He had grown to love these early evening walks with her. At times like these, with SwanSea behind them and the power of the ocean before them, he could almost believe they were the only two people in the world. He liked the idea.

Arabella felt his arms tighten around her, but her expression remained pensive as she stared without seeing toward the island that belonged to SwanSea. "Jake, I want to thank you for letting Kenneth stay on. I don't know what's wrong with him, but there is something, and I think staying here is helping him."

For Arabella's sake, knowing that she was worried, he had tried to talk to Kenneth, to offer help and support. But the more he tried, the more Kenneth stayed to himself. It had reached the point where he forgot for long periods of time that Kenneth was even in the house. But she was right—there was definitely something wrong. Kenneth was a long way from the open, easygoing young man he had known at Harvard.

He turned her around so that she faced him. "He's your brother. If it makes you happy to have him here, then that's all I need to know. You don't have to thank me." She smiled up at him, and he felt his heart turn over. If he lived to be a hundred, he would never stop marveling over the way she affected him.

He put his arm around her shoulder and they started to walk slowly along the cliff. "Did I tell you that Vanessa telephoned the other day?"

"No. What did she say? Are they coming back anytime soon?"

Shaking his head regretfully, he answered the last question first. "I don't think so. She said the studio has her scheduled to start another film as soon as she finishes the one she's doing. By the way, she told me those new movie awards went well. She said Janet Gaynor won for three films, and that the movie *Wings* was voted best picture for 1927 and *Broadway Melody* was voted best picture for 1928. She said the Academy Awards are going to become an annual event, so I guess they decided to backtrack a couple of years so they could acknowledge other films."

"I haven't seen *Broadway Melody*, but I saw *Wings*. Kenneth dragged me to it one afternoon. He raved for days afterward about the combat flying sequences." She paused. "Did Vanessa mention Lucas? What he's doing?"

His mouth twisted into a rueful grin. "You mean, beside cursing me?"

She looked at him in surprise. "Did you two have a fight?"

"You could say that. At any rate, he has businesses and property out there. I imagine he's staying busy."

"You told me once that he and you were partners in a couple of ventures—besides the bootlegging, I mean. Are you having to handle them alone now?"

"Yes, but I don't mind. They're going well. Let's sit down for a while," he said, drawing her down to the grassy bluff with him. "It's so peaceful here, I'd like to stay out for a while."

She chuckled. "It's peaceful inside the house too."

The teasing sparkle in her golden eyes drew a smile from him. "That's true. You know, I just realized that summer will be here in a few days. It doesn't seem possible."

"I know what you mean. There are days when time seems to stand still. But then there have been mornings when I have awakened and thought that time was going too fast."

He reached out and laid his hand along the side of her face, somehow feeling that if he were touching her, he had more of a chance of convincing both of them of what he was about to say. "Time is not going to affect us, Arabella. I won't let it."

Feeling a trace of sadness, she stared at the dark, hard face of the man she loved so much. He had not changed during the time they had spent together. Not really. He might have barred SwanSea's doors to his friends and the press. And he might eat with her now. But he was still the same intense, driven man he was when she had first met him. Since they had been here together, he had transferred much of the focus of his intensity to her, but his demons were still very much within him. "Not even we can stop time, Jake. Eventually something will happen with your company that you can't handle from here, and you'll have to go back to Boston. Sooner or later I'll have to go back too. My parents will be returning. And the foundation—"

His hand slid down the side of her face until he had her jaw framed between his thumb and fingers. "Arabella, you've got to tell me that things won't change when we return to Boston. *Tell* me that you'll still stay with me."

"Where? In your hotel?" With a shake of her head she freed herself of his hold.

He hadn't thought that far ahead, but an answer came quickly. "We'll get a house, anywhere you want. You can pick it out and decorate it. It will be yours."

She sighed. "Jake, I don't want to talk about this now. There's plenty of time—"

"Arabella, I have to know."

"You're asking that I live with you openly in Boston. Can you imagine how much that would hurt my parents? My friends? You're asking me to let everyone know I've become your mistress. Can you even begin to understand what that means?"

Mistress. The word struck into his heart like a cold, dull knife. Edward had made his mother his mistress.

"No. It isn't like that with us."

"What would make it different?"

"Because I would never, under any circumstances, leave you."

"No? Not even if I became pregnant? You're adamant about not having children, Jake. There've been only a couple of times when you've forgotten to use something. We've been lucky so far, but what if, during one of those times we slip up, I become pregnant?"

He was unable to give a quick answer to her question. It was too complicated, too tangled, too twisted.

He silently cursed, both for the vulnerability he saw in her eyes and because there was nothing he could do to help her. He needed her too much. He gripped her upper arms and pulled her closer to him. "I'm a selfish bastard, Arabella. There's probably nothing redeeming in me. And to answer your first question, yes, I do understand what I'm asking. And I'm still asking."

She closed her eyes for a moment. Truthfully she had made her decision that day in late February when she had climbed in her plane and flown to SwanSea. Since that day her love had only increased to the point that she didn't see how she could live without him. Her answer was already set in her heart, but the moment she agreed aloud to the life he wanted, she immediately would have a great deal of pain with which to deal, and she kept wanting to put off that final, ultimate decision. "You're giving up nothing, Jake. You're asking me to make all the sacrifices."

"I said I was a selfish bastard. But, Arabella, I'll do anything you want, be anything you want."

"Except you won't marry me, and we can never have children. And you won't explain why. I do understand that right, don't I?"

A muscle flexed along his jawline. He nodded.

Arabella eyed him with resignation. Whatever Jake's reasons were for not wanting to marry or have children, his mind couldn't be changed. All at once she realized that her head as well as her heart was hurting. "Jake, we're at an impasse on this. You're not willing to give in, and right now I'm not prepared to."

"Then when?"

"I'll make my decision when I'm ready to and not before."

With a muffled oath he drew her into his arms. "I'm sorry. I know I'm pushing you, but I can't seem to stop from trying."

All of a sudden a violent explosion out at sea sent flames shooting high into the air.

Without thought Jake pushed Arabella down and covered her with his body. Then he looked up slowly. "Dammit, he bombed the cottage!"

"Who?" she asked, bewildered. "What cottage?"

Quickly he sized up the situation. The burning alcohol had created a maelstrom of fire that no doubt could be seen for miles against the darkening sky. But the two of them were safe, thank heaven. He sat up, allowing Arabella to do the same. "There's a cottage out on the island. That's what's burning."

"I didn't know there was a cottage out there. You can't see it from here."

"I know." His tone was grim. "But it's there. My men just offloaded a shipment out there last night. It was to be picked up tonight."

"What?"

"Canadian whiskey," he said absently, still staring at the fire.

Arabella stared at him, absolutely stunned. "You're using SwanSea for your *bootlegging* operations?"

The shock in her voice finally registered with him. "Just the island, but there's nothing to worry about." He surged to his feet, reached for her hand, and pulled her up.

"Is there anyone out there?"

"None of my men are, and I'm sure the men who did it took off straight out to sea."

"What about the fire?"

"Let it burn."

"Jake—"

"Please, Arabella, let's talk about this later. For now I've got to get back to the house. There are a few local authorities I need to telephone so there won't be any panic about the fire."

From a third-story window Kenneth gazed out at the red-orange flames that burned against the mauve sky and the slate-gray sea. And he felt sick to his stomach.

If for some reason Arabella had taken it into her head to go out to the island in one of Jake's motorboats for a picnic, she would be dead now. And it would be his fault.

The fourth-floor grandfather clock struck eleven, but Arabella was concentrating so hard on Jake, she barely heard the chimes. "Prohibition may be a stupid law, Jake, but it *is* a law, and there is no justification for what you're doing. You need neither the money nor the glory. Stop it *now* before something is broken or destroyed that your money can't replace."

Jake sighed and leaned his head against the back of the chair. He had made the necessary calls, then come upstairs to find Arabella pacing the length of his private sitting room. "I don't understand what you're so upset about," he said, following her agitated movements around the room with his eyes. He was reminded of Lucas and the way he paced when he was upset, and he wished to heaven that Lucas were there. "You've known for a while now that I was involved in bootlegging."

"Yes, I've known. But it wasn't part of our lives until now. Do you know who did it?"

"Oh, yes. Wade Scalia."

"Wade Sc—my Lord!" She gazed at him in horror. "Vanessa told me that you all had known him in the North End when you were kids. Jake, he's a feared man now."

"Yeah, so I understand."

"Jake, that cottage could just as well have been *SwanSea*."

"But it wasn't. And I'm glad that damned cottage burned. I should have burned it down a long time ago."

Surprise halted Arabella. "For heaven sake, why?"

"Because, Arabella, it was where I was conceived."

"I don't understand. How could you have been conceived here at SwanSea?"

"Quite the usual way, I assure you." The words were sharp-edged and bitter. "Think about it for a minute."

Edward was Jake's real father. Another piece of the puzzle snapped into place for Arabella, and she sank to the floor in front of him.

"Edward's wife had been dead for less than a year when he met my mother. She was a young widow, poor but pretty." He smiled to himself. "When I was a little boy, I used to think there was no one prettier. Anyway, I'm not even sure how they met, perhaps by accident. Apparently"—his tone turned sarcastic—"he was instantly smitten and swept her off her feet. But he didn't consider her good enough to marry, or, I might add, good enough to bring to SwanSea. So he built the cottage, and for about a year Mother stayed out in that cottage while they carried on their affair. To this day, Mother refuses to set foot in SwanSea, and I can't say that I blame her."

"So to show your disdain for Edward and the place he used to meet with your mother, you decided to use the cottage to stash illegal booze?"

"I thought it would be both fitting and ironic, but it was also very convenient."

"And since Edward also refused to conduct an illicit affair here, you decided it would be a grand place to carry on an affair with me."

"Hey," he said softly. "You have nothing to do with what's between Edward and me."

"Don't I? I did in the beginning, though, didn't I? That was what that very public courtship was all about, wasn't it? In some way you were trying to get back at Edward."

He exhaled a long breath. "It seems like a long time ago, Arabella. I deeply regret what I did, and if I had it to do over again, I wouldn't. You've got to believe that."

She wasn't sure why, but she did. "Are you going to stop the bootlegging?"

He shook his head. "I can't now. If I did, I would be caving in to Wade's pressure."

"So what?"

He stared at her, thinking that sometimes she was the only thing in his world that made any sense at all.

A knock sounded at the door.

Jake briefly closed his eyes. He couldn't remember when he had felt so tired. "Come in."

Kenneth opened the door and walked in, looking pale and shaky. "I hope I'm not disturbing you, but there's something I have to tell you."

Alarmed, Arabella rose from the floor. "What's wrong?"

"This is really between Jake and me, honey." The movement of his mouth was meant as a smile of apology. "Would you mind giving us some privacy?"

"If this involves you and Jake, it involves me. I'm staying."

Jake nodded in agreement. "She should stay. She's been worried about you, and I hope you're going to tell us what's been bothering you. Maybe I can help."

Sadness scored Kenneth's face as he shook his head. "No, and after hearing what I have to say, you won't want to help either. Jake, I'm responsible for what happened out on the island this evening."

"But that's impossible!" Arabella exclaimed. "Jake said Wade Scalia's responsible."

"Yeah, that's right. But how do you think he knew when the shipment would be there? Jake keeps very neat notes, and he never locks his study."

She gasped, and her hand flew to her mouth.

Jake didn't move from his chair. "Is that why you came and asked to stay?"

"Yes."

"And were you also responsible for a shipment being hijacked New Year's Day?"

Ashamed, but determined to confess everything, Kenneth nodded. "Yes. While everyone was out on the terrace watching the fireworks display, I slipped into your study, found the information, and telephoned Wade. I charged the call to my private line at home."

Arabella's legs gave way, and she sank back to the floor by Jake.

Jake lay his hand on her shoulder, thinking that if Kenneth weren't Arabella's brother, he would tear him limb from limb. Instead, he felt his weariness increasing and rubbed his eyes. "You'd better tell me everything."

"As you probably know, Wade has established a headquarters of sorts in a hotel he owns in Boston."

"Yeah, I know about it."

"So does every law enforcement official in town. But he has most of the local and state officials in his pocket, and for the few he doesn't and who come nosing around from time to time, he has a system of clearing the place in sixty seconds flat. The first floor is a saloon, the second and third floors are gambling, and the fourth floor is girls for—" He broke off with a glance at Arabella. "At any rate, I lost a great deal of money there last fall."

Arabella shook her head in bewilderment. "But when we were here together over New Year's, you told me that you would be able to pay your debt off as soon as you returned to Boston."

"At the time, that's what I thought, but I hadn't counted on the surprise interest Wade would charge me." He felt like crawling into a hole, but his gaze never faltered from Jake's. "Wade told me that if I was able to get him information about your shipments while I was here New Year's, he would cancel my debt. At first I fought against the idea, and I tried all sorts of things to come up with the money."

"*I* offered you money," Arabella said, still unable to believe Kenneth would do something so contemptible.

"Pretty twisted honor, huh, Bella?" His tone was filled with self-loathing. "I wasn't willing to take money from my sister, but I was willing to betray a friend, a friend in whose home I was a guest."

His gaze returned to Jake. "There are no excuses for what I did. I'm just telling you how it came about." Jake's face was expressionless as he nodded. And Kenneth found himself wishing Jake would yell at him, hit him, *something*—anything but stare at him with those black stone eyes that hid what he was feeling. "Anyway, I thought everything was settled, but when I got back, Wade contacted me and made sure I knew he would require more 'favors' to cancel out the interest. He's an evil man, Jake. And he pushed me into a corner—he not only threatened Arabella, but Mother and Father as well. It's why I've been so wild to get Arabella away from here. I knew that sooner or later he'd come after you, and I didn't want her hurt."

There was silence in the room. Then Jake moved, standing up and walking over to a sideboard to pour himself a glass of Scotch. He took a healthy swallow and waited, letting the golden liquid slide down his throat and into his stomach with a burning that was almost cleansing. But his anger wouldn't be cleansed away—his anger at Wade, at Kenneth, at a situation that would put Arabella in danger. "What made you tell us after all this time, Kenneth?"

"I never knew if the information I gave Wade on New Year's was acted upon. I just made the call, then shut my mind to the consequences. This evening I saw with my own eyes the destruction I had caused, and I realized that no matter how much information I came up with, Wade will never let me off the hook. I can't begin to tell you how badly I felt watching the cottage burn or how sorry I am."

Jake stared down at the Scotch in his hand. "I wish you'd told me all of this sooner."

Because he wanted to hang his head, Kenneth lifted his chin a notch higher than usual. "I was too ashamed."

Arabella sprang up from the floor and went to her brother. "We'll fly back to Boston tomorrow, I'll arrange for you to have all the money you need from my accounts, and then you can pay Wade Scalia off once and for all."

"Wrong," Jake said quietly. "We'll all three drive back, and the money will come from me. But, Kenneth, you *will* pay Wade off."

The next evening in Jake's hotel suite, Arabella glanced at the diamond watch on her wrist for the tenth time in as many minutes. "Kenneth has been gone three hours."

Three hours and nine minutes, Jake thought grimly. "The amount of time he's been gone is not necessarily significant. Now, why don't you try to eat something." With a nod he indicated the dinner that had been brought up several minutes before.

"I couldn't eat a thing, but you should."

"No," he said softly. "I'll wait for you."

Tears rushed to her eyes. Those words deserved more happiness than she could give at the moment. She brushed her tears away. "I'm sorry for being such a worrier."

"You have nothing to apologize for, Arabella."

"But because of Kenneth—"

"Kenneth has less to do with this than you or

Kenneth think. This is between Wade and me, and no one else."

"Then paying off Kenneth's debt won't accomplish a thing." She nervously fingered the long rope of pearls she was wearing.

"Yes, it will. It will keep you and your family safe."

A knock sounded faintly at the door. "Good," Jake said, striding across the room, "this may be your brother now. He opened the door, and Kenneth collapsed against him, bloodied and beaten.

Arabella gasped. "Oh, my Lord!"

Jake half carried Kenneth to the sofa and laid him down, then proceeded to assess his wounds, swiftly running his hands over his body. Kenneth's nose had been broken; his face was swollen, and blood seeped from gashes. He leaned closer to him. "Do you know if anything's broken besides your nose?"

"A few ribs . . ." Kenneth tried to smile, but grimaced at the pain. "Wade didn't want the money, Jake."

Arabella came down beside the couch and reached for her brother's hand. "Wade Scalia's an abomination!" Her voice shook with her fury. "Call the police, Jake. We'll have him arrested."

"Was Wade anywhere around when you were beaten up?" Jake asked Kenneth.

"No." His breathing was labored, his words halted. "We had our little chat . . . then these two men—I had never seen them before—took me out in the alley."

"There'd be no case, then."

Arabella gently and comfortingly stroked her brother's hand, but her eyes blazed with anger as she looked at Jake. "*Why* would that man do such a thing?"

Jake's expression was grim. "It's a message for me, right, Kenneth? Wade is telling me it's my territory or nothing."

"That's right," Kenneth said, closing his eyes. "By the way . . . I came up the back way . . . no one saw me."

"Don't worry about being seen, or anything else, for that matter," Jake said, rising. "I'm going to get you help."

He made a series of phone calls to a few select employees of the Deverell Corporation, sidestepping the old-guard employees who had worked for Edward for years and going to men whom he himself had hired.

In a little over an hour Kenneth had been seen to by one of the best doctors in Boston and taken to a private hospital.

"What are you going to do about Wade Scalia, Jake?" Arabella asked when they were alone again.

Jake leaned his hand against the mantel and stared absently at the empty hearth. "I don't know. He wants me to give up the territory Lucas and I have or he wants war. I can't seem to do either."

"And it seems so simple to me. Give him the damned territory!"

Slowly he shook his head. "Besides the fact that I don't easily give up things that are mine, there's something else. Wade's power would increase tenfold if I were to hand over the operation to him. He'd have the whole of New England."

"So? At least you'd be out of it."

"I wonder," he said thoughtfully. "I wonder if he'd really ever let me out of it." He looked over at her, where she was sitting on the couch. "As soon as the doctor says Kenneth is able, I'm going to send him to a ranch I have in California. I've never even been there, but I understand it's nice. Several years ago Lucas bought it for me." He grinned, remembering. "He said it was an investment for my soul. At any rate, it will be the perfect place for Kenneth to recover, and I want you to go with him."

If she'd given the matter some thought, Arabella reflected, she could have predicted this. She eyed him calmly. "After all the times you've asked me to stay, now you're asking me to leave?"

"I don't want to, believe me, but your safety is involved."

She crossed her arms beneath her breasts. "The answer is no. I won't go."

Jake walked over to the sofa and came down beside her. "Don't be stubborn about this, Arabella. I want you somewhere I know you'll be safe."

"If you are worried about my safety, then that means you think *you're* going to be in danger. I'm staying with you. And there's no sense in trying to change my mind. I can be every bit as stubborn as you, Jake Deverell."

He stared at her. She had eyes that beguiled, a smile that enticed, skin as soft as a rose petal, and bones that seemed to him as fragile as a sparrow's. She was the most feminine woman he had ever known, yet she had steel running the length of her spine, and he wondered why he was just now realizing it. "I've met my match, haven't I?

"Yes. Now, unless you'd like to make love to me, I'm going to the hospital to make sure Kenneth is settled for the night and has—"

"Kenneth has everything he needs, but I don't." His words came out in a raspy growl. "I need *you.* In fact, I suddenly realize I may not make it if I'm not able to get inside you in the next few minutes." He jerked her to him. "I'd like very much to make love to you, Arabella."

She smiled. "What a good idea."

Sometime after midnight the telephone rang. Jake switched on the light beside the bed and reached for the receiver.

"Hello?"

He listened for a minute, then without a word hung up the phone.

"What is it?" Arabella asked, sitting up and twisting so that she could look down at him. His face was cold and without emotion, and fear gripped her heart. "Is it Kenneth? Has something happened to him?"

"No. It's Edward. He collapsed this evening. They took him to the hospital. He's in a coma."

12

A SINGLE light over the head of Edward's hospital bed cast ghostly shadows onto the surrounding white curtains. Jake stood at the foot of the bed, staring down at him, his hands knotted into fists by his side.

This wasn't right. Edward shouldn't be lying there, an oxygen tent covering him. He was *indomitable*. He couldn't die!

"Dammit, old man, you can't die now! We're not through fighting." His hand closed over the cast iron foot of the bed, and he shook it hard. "Do you hear me? Wake up and look at me! Tell me to go to hell, but *fight,* dammit, *fight.*"

A hand clamped over his shoulder. "Mr. Deverell, may I talk to you a moment?"

He swung around, ready to hit whoever had interrupted him, but his fist stayed at his side when he saw the doctor, an older man with a tired-looking face.

"What's wrong with my father?"

"As I'm sure you know, he's been ill for a long time now."

"I knew no such thing, and I'm sure Edward didn't either."

The doctor expelled a long breath. "He should have known—Lord knows, I told him often enough—but he just refused to admit it."

"Okay, then, what's wrong with him? You can cure him, can't you?"

"I'm afraid not. He has black lung, which is a chronic lung disease that occurs when carbon and silica accumulate in the lungs from breathing in large amounts of coal dust. There is no treatment, and it reached the advanced stages in your father a couple of years ago. Only his strong will has kept him going this long."

Vehemently Jake shook his head. "No, no, that's got to be a mistake. Edward left the coal mines when he was eighteen."

"Your father's black lung is the 'complicated' kind. That means it can worsen over time even if the victim is no longer exposed to coal dust."

The word "victim" grated against Jake's nerves, and he glanced back at Edward. Jake was sure that there were a great many people, including himself, who would call Edward a sonofabitch. But in all Edward's seventy-five years, no one had ever called him a victim. Edward was the kind of man who had created his life from nothing. He had *made* things happen. Even now, in a coma, he looked invincible. "You're wrong, Doctor. My father is not going to die."

"I know this must be hard for you, Mr. Deverell, but you should prepare yourself for the inevitable."

"Inevitable is not in my vocabulary, nor is it in Edward's." He looked back at the doctor. "Now tell me about this coma. How soon is he going to come out of it?"

"I really can't say. He could come out of it at any moment, or it could last indefinitely, until he dies. At this point no one can say."

Jake saw weakness and pounced. "So you admit your knowledge is limited." He jabbed a finger against the doctor's chest. "Edward Deverell is not going to die of black lung or of anything else, do you understand? Go back to your books, call in specialists, but, Doctor, *find* something to get him well."

The doctor nodded and patted Jake on his arm. "I'm sorry for your pain, Mr. Deverell. I'll give you a few more minutes with your father, but then you really must leave."

Pain? Incredulously he repeated the word in his mind. He wasn't in pain! How ridiculous to even think it.

He walked around the bed to its head and leaned down until his face was even with Edward's. "You can't die," he said, his tone low and fierce as he spoke through the oxygen tent. "You've fought all your life to get away from those damned coal mines. You can't give in to them now. Besides, there's too much left unresolved between us. If you die, I'll win. You don't want that. You'd hate that! And if you die, I'll tell everyone I'm really your son. Think about that old man, and fight, dammit. *Fight!*"

Jake saw Edward once again the next morning and was informed that there had been no change in his condition. For over an hour he stayed by Edward's side, talking, cursing, cajoling, challenging. He shocked everyone within hearing distance, except Edward. There was no doubt in his mind that Edward understood and appreciated every word. There was also no doubt in his mind that Edward would live.

The idea of going back to SwanSea returned time and again to him that day, and by the next day he and Arabella were there.

"I don't really know why it was so important to me to come back here," he said later that night as he lay in bed, holding her in his arms. "This place is nothing but a big pile of stone and mortar when you get right down to it."

"It's more than that," she said softly, her face lying against his chest. "It's your home. It's a place you can feel safe."

"Safe?" Laughter erupted from him. "What makes you think I need to feel safe?"

She tilted her head back and gazed up at him. "You're every bit as tough as you think you are, Jake.

But everyone in the world needs a place that makes them feel safe, a place where they feel they belong."

"I'm an interloper here, Arabella. I wrenched SwanSea away from Edward and I've held it hostage ever since."

"Maybe so, but SwanSea belongs to you legally and every other way. What's more, you belong to SwanSea, even if you don't know it." She paused. "The last night I was here over New Year's, I left my room to walk the halls. The house was quiet, but it was an enduring, waiting kind of quiet. I think the house was waiting for you to accept it . . . and yourself."

A slow smile spread over his face. "You're an enchanting woman, do you know that?"

She nodded, her solemn expression belied by the twinkle in her eye. "Yes."

He laid his face against her head. "I don't know what I'd do without you," he whispered. "For the first time that I can remember, I feel lost."

"Your father may pull out of this, Jake."

"Oh, Edward isn't going to die—I know that—but he *is* unconscious, and dammit, I'm mad as hell at him for doing this. It's just like him, too, to go to sleep for a few days while I fume. The last time we talked, he told me again in his own inimitable way to stop bootlegging. Said his friends at the club were getting suspicious. If you ask me, they're pretty slow."

She pushed away from him and gazed at him, her brow creased with concern. Anyone else might think he had lost his mind, but she was coming to understand the relationship he had with his father. There was hate there, but there was also need. And she heard the thread of pain that ran beneath Jake's anger.

"He can't die, Arabella. Hating him is a permanent part of me, I've done it for so long. He can't take that away from me now. *Especially* not now, when there's a very good possibility Wade and I may be sharing headline space soon." He paused. "It'll drive Edward mad."

"Have you made a decision, then? About what to do about Wade?"

"Not really."

"Jake, whether Edward dies or not, you've got to stop this insanity now. You've established a successful bootlegging operation. You've made money and you've had fun, and to top it all off, you've made Edward furious. It seems to me there's nothing more to accomplish. You've done it all. Get out now."

"But what about Wade?"

"Forget him. Sooner or later the government will be able to put him away."

He gazed down at her for a long time. "Okay," he finally said. "I'll consider it."

She was stunned into speechlessness. She had gotten through to him. He had actually listened to her and found value in what she said.

Jake watched the play of emotions on her face, then noticed the fine, faintly purple vein that lay beneath the smooth ivory skin at her temple. He didn't think he'd ever noticed it before. "I wonder if fifty years from now I'll still be discovering things about you."

Fifty years implied a long life together, and if they stayed together, it would be just the two of them, without marriage, without children. It wasn't the life she would have chosen for herself. But there Jake was, smack in the middle of her heart, and in the end there would be no choice. She leaned toward him and curled her hand around the back of his neck. "Let me tell you something, Jake Deverell—you'll go to your grave knowing absolutely that no woman you ever knew satisfied you in as many ways as I do."

"There are times, Arabella, when you steal my breath away."

"Then let me give it back to you," she whispered, and pulled his mouth to hers.

Several loud explosions shook the house and awakened everyone in it. Jake jerked upright and reached for his watch on the nightstand to check the time. It was five-thirty in the morning. He reached for his trousers, stepped into them, and was fastening them when he realized Arabella was pulling a wrapper around her.

"You'd better stay here. I don't know what's happening."

"I'm coming," she said, ignoring her trembling

limbs and stepping into her feather-trimmed heeled slippers.

"Dammit, Arabella—"

"I'm coming."

He recognized the stubbornly set expression on her face and didn't waste any more time arguing. He pulled a gun from the nightstand and checked that it was loaded. "Then stay behind me and do exactly what I say."

They took the stairway down, stopping on each floor to look for anything out of the ordinary, but saw nothing. By the time they reached the main floor, though, they could smell smoke.

Marlon, in robe and slippers, met them in the grand entry hall. "Firebombs have been thrown through several lower windows, sir. Our men are acting quickly and already two fires are out. But your study, sir. I'm afraid it's engulfed in flames. There are people already working there, trying both to put the fire out and to contain the damage. More men are on their way."

"Good. *Good.* Any sign of the people who did it?"

"None that I've seen, sir. Would you like me to form a search party?"

"No. Don't pull anyone away from fighting the fire." Wade's men had accomplished what they came to do, he thought grimly, and were probably on the road back to Boston or in a boat, heading south. He drove his hand through his uncombed hair, then tucked the gun into his belt. "Okay. Get as many people as you can to help you, and I'll be right there."

Jake waited until Marlon had hurried off, then turned to Arabella. "Wade bombed my car, then the island, now my house. Why the hell didn't I see it? Each time, he was getting closer."

Urgently she laid her hand on his arm. "Jake, last night you said you'd consider stopping this fight between the two of you. This fire just underscores the importance of making that decision."

"He's hurt my home, Arabella. He's hurt SwanSea."

"I know, but—"

He held up a hand. "I don't know how to explain to you how or what I'm feeling. And I'm not sure what I'm going to do. Except right now my house is burning, and I've got to go help the men."

Her nod acknowledged that he was right. With an effort she tried to pull herself together. "All right, then. I'll go see if I can help in the kitchen. I imagine food and coffee are going to be in great demand."

As Jake strode away, a cold feeling began to grow in her. By the time she reached the kitchen, the cold had completely encased her.

Later that afternoon Jake stood alone amid the blackened, wet ruins of what had once been his study. The destruction was total. All the beautiful, exotic citron wood was now ashes, as were the hundreds of leather-bound books.

It was like a part of himself had been destroyed, he

thought, and knew he would never be able to explain the feeling.

But one thing he did know—*he would rebuild.* The study would be completely restored, right down to the last art nouveau detail. And the cottage. He would rebuild the cottage, fresh and new and put it to a happy use.

"Looks like I got back just in time," Lucas drawled.

Jake jerked toward the tall, blond-haired man lounging in the doorway. "Great heavens, where did you come from?"

"The sky." Lucas waved his hand through the air. "Vanessa and I took the train part of the way, and flew the rest of the way. The new coast-to-coast service won't be officially inaugurated for a week or so, but I think we must have *unofficially* inaugurated it."

"Good Lord!"

A smile glimmered in Lucas's clear blue eyes. "Exactly. We prayed the whole way. Our prayers must have worked, because we're here."

Jake stared at Lucas a moment longer, then closed the distance between them and threw his arms around him. "*Lord,* I'm glad to see you!"

"I knew you would be," Lucas said, smiling broadly, "but I also knew that you were too damned dumb and stubborn to ever ask me to come back. So I decided, as usual, I needed to take matters into my own hands." He gave Jake an affectionate hit on the back as they drew apart. "So what's happened here? Was this an accident or was this Wade's work?"

"Wade, definitely Wade."

"Well?"

Jake understood the one-word question perfectly. "I've made my decision. I'm going after him."

"That's why I'm here."

Jake shook his head. "No, no. You're out of this."

"Not on your life. Jake, I got word of what happened out on the island and I started back almost immediately. I knew you'd need me."

Jake's hand was still on his friend's shoulder. "I appreciate your coming, but, Lucas, I don't know what's going to happen, and under those circumstances, the only person I'm willing to risk is me."

"You can't do it on your own, Jake, and the sooner you admit that, the sooner we can get on with things."

He exhaled a long breath. "You can help me come up with a plan, but that's *it.*"

Lucas gave him a friendly sneer. "Go intimidate someone else, because you're wasting your energy with me. I came here to help you, and that's damned well what I'm going to do."

Jake's eyes narrowed on his old friend. "There's nothing I can say to change your mind?"

"No."

"Lord, I'm glad you're back!"

"We've always taken care of each other, Jake, and together the two of us can't fail. You'll see, it'll be cream in a can."

* * *

Vanessa took a moment between bites of her dinner to examine her surroundings. "You know, I don't think I've ever been in this salon before. Arabella, you were so clever to think of it for our dinner tonight."

Arabella smiled, pleased with Vanessa's compliment. They were in a small salon on the second floor. A fire burned in the fireplace, and a mild evening breeze came in through the open French doors. The ambience was warm and cozy and cheerful. "I thought we might be more comfortable in here than in the dining room. Marlon would have had us scattered up and down that table, yards apart."

Lucas chuckled. "The old boy means well."

Jake nodded. "He does, and he's certainly put up with a lot from me over the years, but he is absolutely devoted to Arabella. And he *loves* what she's doing to the house."

Vanessa's fork halted midway to her mouth. "Everything does look wonderful, Arabella. I meant to tell you that earlier."

Happy that her efforts had been noticed, she shrugged away the compliment. "The house just needed a little love and caring, that's all, and with SwanSea, loving and caring are easy."

Jake sipped his wine. "Thank heaven Arabella had decided my desk needed refinishing. A stableman has it somewhere, and it escaped the fire."

"Bert," Arabella said. "The stableman's name is

Bert. And he and I have established a workshop for him in the back of the carriage house."

Jake looked at her with interest. "Really? I didn't know that."

"Yes, he's refinishing almost full-time now, and he really needed a place of his own. Anyway, that's where your desk is—and, as you said, thank heaven."

Jake suddenly frowned. "Vanessa, I just remembered something. You told me the studio had you scheduled for back-to-back pictures. How did you get away?"

"The first film was finished. The second one was just beginning. And"—she glanced at Lucas—"I walked out."

Arabella's eyes widened. "The studio can't be happy about that."

She shrugged an elegant shoulder. "I don't know. I didn't wait to hear their opinion, and frankly, I don't really care. It was too important for me to be here with Lucas and with Jake."

Jake reached for her hand and kissed it. "Thank you for coming."

Suddenly Vanessa laughed. "Can you believe we actually *flew*?"

Jake grinned, looking from Lucas to Vanessa. "No, I can't."

Arabella groaned good-naturedly. "I wish you understood—flying is fun and exciting. There's *nothing* to be afraid of."

Lucas reached for a cigarillo. "Only falling, I suppose."

She frowned. "That's what Jake says, but—"

Jake pushed back from the table and stood. "Would you two mind if Lucas and I go upstairs for a while? There are some things we need to discuss."

"Yes," Vanessa said in a mild tone, "we'd mind. But whether we mind or not really isn't going to make any difference, is it?"

Jake smiled at her. "I knew you'd understand. Arabella, we won't be but a couple of hours."

"All right," she said, and looked at Vanessa, who shrugged.

Marlon supervised the removal of their dinner, then placed a silver coffee service set on a pearl-inlaid table in front of Arabella, and left her and Vanessa to themselves.

She poured Vanessa a cup of coffee and handed it to her. "Vanessa, I want to ask you about something. To be more specific, I want to know about Jake's fear of flying."

"You want to know why?"

"Yes, because if I understood, maybe I could help him."

"I've just flown more than halfway across the country, Arabella, and I can tell you that flying is something that definitely takes some getting used to."

"But you did it."

"Our flying is a testament to how eager Lucas was to get back to Jake, not to any bravery on our part."

She took a sip of coffee and gazed pensively into the fire. "Maybe the concept of flying came easy to you and your friends, Arabella, but it's not so easy for us North End kids. Fear of falling was ingrained into us at an early age." She paused to take another sip of coffee. "In our neighborhood when we were growing up, innumerable men, women, and children died each summer by accidentally rolling off rooftops, out of windows, and off fire escapes because they were sleeping there, trying to escape the heat of those small, airless apartments we all lived in then. Lucas's only sister, Mary, fell off a windowsill to her death. Mary was seven years old."

Arabella's head jerked back. "Sometimes I feel so stupid."

"Don't. But do remember—patterns set in childhood carry over into adulthood. Patterns. It's why it took Jake a long time before he could eat with you. It's why Wade won't be able to rest until he has what Jake has. It's why Lucas and Jake are holed up together now, planning an attack on Wade. Patterns, Arabella. Patterns."

Dressed in a long deep-blue satin nightgown and robe set, Vanessa leaned back against the open French door and stared out at the night.

Lucas, his head against a pillow, one leg drawn up, had a gentle smile on his face as he watched her. "What's wrong, honey?"

"It's a beautiful night," she said.

"Yes, it is."

"Do you think if I keep guard here, I can keep the night from ending?"

"No, it's going to end. And tomorrow is going to come, just like tomorrow night will and the next morning. And then I'll be back."

"Then I wish we could erase the hours until day after tomorrow. I wish you were already back."

"You're wishing away a lot of time—a lot of time in which we could be together. I'm here now, and I'll be here tomorrow."

She closed the distance between them and came down beside him. "I love you, Lucas."

He looked at her for a moment, his gaze clear blue. "I love you too. You know I do. But, honey, I have to do this. I have to. But it's going to be all right. Tell me you believe that."

"I believe you," she whispered.

He reached for her and drew her down to him. And she went, eager for his kisses and caresses, knowing that only in his arms did she ever feel truly safe. And she needed above all things tonight to feel safe.

The hands of a crystal and diamond clock on the dressing table indicated it was close to midnight. Arabella gazed at Jake's reflection in the mirror as she pulled a silver-backed brush through her hair. He was quiet as he reclined on the bed, wearing only his trousers and staring out at the night. Minutes earlier she had slipped on a nightgown of pale honey-colored crepe georgine with a scalloped hem of Alençon lace and a neckline that dipped to her breasts and left her arms bare. But Jake seemed almost unaware of her, and the cause of his preoccupation had her scared to death.

Velvet curtains billowed at the French doors as she rose, walked to the opposite side of the bed from him, then sat down and shifted across the wide black satin spread until she was sitting beside his legs. "I think you'd better tell me about it," she said softly.

He looked at her. "Do you really want to know?"

"I'll worry less if I know exactly what you're doing."

"No you won't."

"Tell me anyway."

"Okay. Wade has a warehouse in Upstate New York close to the Canadian border. Lucas and I are going to drive over tomorrow evening, just he and I. We'll leave here about seven. Traveling at top speed, we figure five hours there, five hours back."

"How long will you be there?"

"An hour at the most. Our information is that there are only a couple of men guarding it at any given time. Our plan is to set the warehouse on fire. That should force the guards outside pretty quick. We'll jump them, tie them up, drag them somewhere safe, and leave before the place blows. Simple. We should be home by dawn."

She began to tremble. "Don't go." His brows drew together with concern, and he reached out for her to pull her to him, but she held up her hand, warding him off. "No. Please listen to me. I know something has to be done about Wade, but you aren't the person who should be doing it."

"I have to, Arabella. He's—"

"I know what he's done! I *saw.* And I hurt for SwanSea just like you do. But call in government agents on this. You stay home."

He shook his head, his face set with determination. "Wade has finally succeeded in making this personal for me. It's got to be me and Lucas."

"No, it doesn't!" She shifted until she was closer to him. "Jake, *listen* to me. You've asked me to give up a lot for you. You've asked me to spend the rest of my life living with you without the sanction of marriage and without ever being able to know the joy of having a child of my very own. I haven't given you an answer up to this point, but I will now."

His expression turned to one of alarm. "No, don't say—"

She drew a deep breath. "I will."

For a moment he was confused. "You will what?"

"I will do just as you want. I will never leave you, and the rest of the world can be damned. That's how much I love you, Jake Deverell. I've never told you that before, but I'm telling you now. I love you."

"Arabella—"

"Don't interrupt. I'm not through talking yet. Now, I've acquiesced to everything you wanted. And—don't get me wrong, there are no conditions—but it seems to me you could at least do this one thing for me. Go to the Treasury Department. Let them handle Wade. I know you don't love me—"

"But I do."

Now it was her turn to be confused. "You do what?"

"I love you, Arabella. I've loved you for days, weeks, months, probably since I turned around on New Year's Eve and saw you standing in the doorway with those damned peacocks."

The earth seemed to move beneath her, and definite thrills of amazement washed through her, temporarily stealing her breath and her strength. "That long?"

"Yes. But my heart is and has always been hard, and it was a long time before I realized, and even longer before I could admit that you had gotten through." He gave a light, self-deprecating laugh. "Hell, did you *ever* get through—to the point that now I can't imagine living without you. Marry me, Arabella." He gently took her face between his two hands. "Will you marry me?"

Only moments before she had been so full of words. Now she couldn't think of a single one.

He smiled softly and brushed a thumb across her cheekbone. "I've just asked you to marry me, honey. Do you think you could say something?"

"You're not playing fair," she said finally. "I asked you not to go after Wade and you hit me with a marriage proposal."

He dropped his hands from her face. "I have to go after Wade. I've fought against responding in kind to him for months, but I can't fight it any longer. That doesn't change a thing between you and me, though. What's going to happen between Wade and me is not the reason for the marriage. I love you, Arabella. Marry me. Please."

"Damn you, Jake Deverell," she whispered. "You've just offered me heaven, only you left in a part of hell."

"Only a small part," he whispered back, skimming the honey-colored crepe and lace gown from her. "And it won't affect you, only me."

Without her giving the matter any thought, she reached to help him off with his trousers. "If it affects you, it can't help but affect me. You've got to rethink—" The breath was taken from her body as he pushed her onto her back and slid on top of her.

"You haven't told me whether you'll marry me or not."

It was silly, really, she thought, somewhat bewildered. Silly and perverse. She had already told him she would stay with him without marriage. Why couldn't she tell him that she would marry him? She raised her head and briefly fastened her small teeth on his bottom lip. "I guess I haven't, have I?"

His eyes took on a dangerous gleam. "Then I'll just have to convince you, won't I?" He bent his head and gently nibbled at her bottom lip, then dropped lower to her neck, then lower still to her breast.

She didn't want to respond. She wanted to argue

with him about going after Wade, she wanted to shout at him for being blind to the fact that he was putting their future in jeopardy. But the biting kisses he was giving her quickly built a heated tide of feeling in her. The feeling was a delicate blend of a pleasurable pain that already had her mind clouding and her stomach clenching.

"How am I doing at convincing you?" he asked, his voice rough, his mouth on the tender flesh of her thigh.

She moaned softly, incapable of concentrating on anything but the rapidly growing need for relief from the tightening pressure that burned and coiled low in her body. "What?"

"Marry me, Arabella." The words were murmured deep in the folds that guarded the tiny bud of pleasure, and his tongue flicked out against it again and again. "I want you as my wife."

She barely heard him. Ecstasy had completely taken her over. The ecstasy seemed to have no beginning, no end, and no intention of ever letting her go. It held her in its grip, lifting her up and up until at last a cry tore from her and she went taut, letting the ecstasy take her wherever it wanted.

Moments later, years later, Jake again came up over her and settled himself between her legs. "You haven't said you'll marry me yet."

She felt totally exhausted, spent. Slowly she opened her eyes and looked up at him and felt a thrill race through her. His black eyes burned like coals.

Surprised to find her body still throbbed for him, she wrapped her legs around his buttocks. "And," she said, her voice barely above the sound of a breath, "you still haven't said you won't go after Wade."

He smiled. "I have more stamina than you do, Arabella. You *will* say yes."

He entered her with excruciating slowness, then began to stroke in and out of her with a torturous pace that lifted her even higher, transporting her to where there was nothing and no one but the two of them and the rapture.

Her body was his, her mind and soul were his. And sometime during it all, she cried out, "Yes, yes, yes . . . damn you, *I will marry you.*"

And still he didn't let her rest.

During the night he woke her up time and time again to make love to her. And each time he had a surprise for her.

The first time she awoke to find that instead of the black satin spread, a sea of snow-white orchids covered her. Amid the sweet, delicate scented flowers, he made love to her with a frenzy that had her believing at any moment that she would surely pass out from the pleasure.

Another time she awoke to find the flowers gone and a small mountain of pearls in their place. The strands were long, lustrous, and he wound the pearls around the two of them and made love to her gently, so gently she thought she would lose her mind before he finally entered her and gave her the peace she sought.

At dawn she awoke yet again to . . . breakfast—a huge white-chocolate ice cream sundae covered in diamond sauce. He put the diamonds on her and ate the white chocolate ice cream from her body.

She didn't know how the white orchids or the pearls or the sundae came to appear, and she didn't question.

She accepted that a crystal goblet of moonstones sat on the bedside table when she awoke at ten.

She accepted the dazzling ruby necklace he put around her neck at noon, the same one she had refused on Valentine's Day.

And she accepted his unceasing need of her, because she needed him just as much.

13

"IT doesn't look right to me," Jake said to Lucas as they knelt behind a line of shrubs and gazed toward the warehouse. "There's no sign that anyone's there. It's completely dark inside."

Lucas balanced the stock of his machine gun on one knee and spoke quietly. "The two guards probably decided to take a little nap, that's all."

"They've got to know that Wade would kill them if he caught them sleeping. No, I think they're in there, but on the alert. There's no way they could be expecting us, but they could be expecting trouble from some other quarter."

"Then let's torch the place before someone else does."

Jake shook his head. "I say we go back home and let someone else do our work."

Lucas shot Jake a look of consternation. "That wouldn't accomplish a damn thing. What's wrong with you?"

"I don't know. I just have a funny feeling. . . ."

"Dammit, we're not going back before we burn this place!"

Jake gazed at him through the eerie silvery light cast by the half moon above them. "You're determined, aren't you?"

Lucas nodded. "It'll be cream in a can, just like I told you."

"Okay, then, let's go." Lucas quickly rose, but Jake clamped his hand around his arm and pulled him back down. "First sign of trouble, head to the car. And if there's no trouble, I'll see you back there in five minutes. Right?"

Lucas gave a jaunty two-fingered salute. "See you there."

The night was still and quiet as they left their cover and ran toward the warehouse in a half crouch. Lucas reached the building first. He and Jake were both wearing backpacks that held bottles of gasoline. He propped his machine gun against the building and began lighting and tossing the bottles through the open windows.

Several yards away Jake did the same thing. The gasoline began to do its work and fires popped up. It wouldn't be long before the alcohol in the crates would catch.

He glanced at Lucas. "We've done enough," he said in a loud whisper. "Let's find the guards and get away from here."

Lucas grinned at him and stood to toss another lighted bottle through the window. "One more."

Gunfire blazed through the night, and before Jake's horrified gaze Lucas went down.

Jake's heart slammed into his throat. "Lucas?" He dropped to the ground and crawled to where Lucas was lying, on his side facing away from him. "Are you all right?" he asked, pulling him onto his back.

Blood saturated his shirt from the three bullet wounds in his chest.

Cold, hard fear crashed through Jake, but his touch was gentle and reassuring as he laid his hand against Lucas's face. "I've got you now. Don't worry about a thing. I've got you. I'm going to take care of you."

Lucas tried to grin, but choked instead. "Not this time. Not—"

Bullets hit the ground beside Jake, kicking up bits of dirt. He glanced up and saw a dark silhouette at the end of the building; simultaneously he reached for his gun and fired several times. He heard a cry and the silhouette crumpled. Another silhouette appeared. He fired again. The dark figure went down.

He slid his arms around Lucas. "I'm going to carry

you to the car now. Hang on. Do you hear me? Lucas?"

In the red glowing light of the fire, he saw Lucas gaze sightlessly back at him.

"No, no . . ." Jake lightly shook him. "Lucas?" For the first time in over a quarter of a century, Lucas didn't answer him. *"Lucas!"*

He could feel the increased heat of the fires against his back. Lord, the warehouse could explode at any second. He had to get Lucas to safety. He shrugged out of his pack and tossed it through the nearest window. Then he slung the gun over his shoulder, using its strap, and lifted Lucas into his arms. He was nearly to the car when he heard the building explode behind him. But the fact that they had accomplished what they had come to do made no impression on him.

Jake laid Lucas gently on the backseat of the car. And even though he knew it was useless, he took the time to make a pillow out of a blanket for Lucas's head and tenderly covered him with two more.

To Jake, the ride back to SwanSea seemed to last forever. The roads were long, dark, and lonely. But the memories of all the years he and Lucas had spent together came back to him and kept him busy. He talked to Lucas, asking him if he remembered them as clearly as he did. He gently laughed. He cried steadily. He asked God why, why, why. . . .

And his heart steadfastly refused to accept what his

mind tried to tell him: that there was nothing more he could do for his old friend.

Periodically he would pull the car off the road and stop so that he could check to make sure Lucas was comfortable. Time and again he tucked then re-tucked the blanket around Lucas, wanting to make sure he didn't get chilled. He'd brush his hair off his forehead and wipe specks of dirt from his face. But try as he might, there seemed to be nothing he could do about the holes in Lucas's chest.

Dawn had pearlized the summer sky with warm, glowing colors as he carried Lucas's lifeless body into the great entry hall of SwanSea. Arabella was there, wearing the simple little white wool dress she had been wearing when he had left the previous evening. She hadn't been to bed, he reflected, but at least she was safe.

Then he saw Vanessa. She stood at the base of the staircase, her hand clenched on the marble railing, her face colorless, her dark eyes stricken. "Lucas!"

"I'm sorry—" His voice broke and tears filled his eyes. "It wasn't supposed to happen this way."

Tears coursed silently down her face as she walked to him, taking slow, careful steps. "Did he suffer?"

"No. It was too fast. . . ."

Out of the corner of his eye he saw Marlon and a footman approaching. "Sir, if you'd allow us to help you?"

He shook his head and his grip on Lucas tightened, pulling him closer against his chest. How could his heart still be beating when Lucas's heart was so still? He looked at Vanessa. "The salon?" At her nod he carried Lucas into the large front salon. There he lowered him to a cushioned couch and again tucked the blankets around him. He touched Lucas's hair, then his forehead. "Marlon, light the fire, please. The room seems chilly."

"Yes, sir." Marlon put a match to already laid logs and soon had a warm blaze going. Then he discreetly withdrew.

Jake put his arm around Vanessa. "I don't want you worrying about a thing. We're going to take care of him."

"Yes," she whispered. "Yes, we need to take care of him now."

"Leave the blankets on him." He didn't want her to see the blood.

"I will," she said, sinking to the floor beside Lucas and clasping his hand with hers. "I don't want him to get cold. He's everything to me, Jake. Everything."

"I know, sweetheart."

Arabella watched from the doorway, tears blurring her vision. Jake went to her and together they left Vanessa and Lucas alone.

"I don't want to go far," he murmured tiredly. "She's going to need us."

"We can wait on the staircase, and you can tell me how I can help you."

He dropped down onto one of the marble stairs

and leaned his back against the balustrade. Arabella sat close to him.

"I wish to heaven there was something, but there's nothing you can do. There's nothing anyone can do."

"Sir? There was a telephone call just now. I took the liberty of accepting the message."

"Not now, Marlon." He didn't understand how he could feel so numb, yet at the same time feel so much pain, so much anguish.

"Sir, the call was from the hospital in Boston, and I'm sorry to have to inform you that your father, Mr. Edward Deverell, died thirty minutes ago."

Edward was buried in the large, elaborate crypt he had had prepared for himself on land he had set aside for the Deverell family cemetery. Jake and Arabella stood silently while a priest Jake didn't know read words he didn't hear.

Later in the day, he, Arabella, and Vanessa stood by Lucas's grave. Vanessa had chosen the site–a small hill with the sea in the distance and fields of wildflowers all around. Arabella had brought flowers from the greenhouse and the gardens, enough to completely cover the fresh mound of dirt under which Lucas lay and more. After the priest left, Jake and Vanessa each said a few quiet words about the man they had loved so much, yet in different ways.

After that, time blurred for Jake. He was barely aware of everyday events.

His pain never left him. It settled into his chest and

his stomach to become a part of him. He now had more power and money than most people dared to dream of. But it all meant nothing.

Edward was gone—Edward his father, Edward his enemy. And Lucas was gone, the man who had been closer to him than any brother could have been. Lucas, his partner through the bad times as well as the good. Lucas, day to his night.

He did no work, he made no decisions. He drifted in a haze of guilt and grief. The only real effort he made was to try his best to comfort Vanessa. But he knew even while he was trying that he was failing miserably. How could he offer her comfort when he had no comfort for himself?

Fortunately no one seemed to expect anything of him.

Fortunately there was Arabella.

She took care of both him and Vanessa, coming to them with whatever it was they needed even before they were aware of what it was. Whether she brought a warm sweater, a tempting meal, a quiet, comforting word, or just her presence, Jake knew he wouldn't have been able to go on living without her.

"It's time," Vanessa suddenly said one afternoon as she sat in the lawn chair next to his.

"Time for what?" Jake asked, his gaze by habit fixed on the sea before him.

"It's time I go back to California."

He looked at her in surprise. "You can't do that. It's too soon."

"It's been almost a month, Jake."

"It's the damned studio, isn't it? They've been pestering you."

"No, not at all. As a matter of fact, they've been most understanding." Her lovely mouth took on a sarcastic shape. "They think that last movie I did is going to make me a star, and they've held the next one for me." She paused. "You know, it's funny—I've worked for years to become a full-fledged star, and now that it's about to happen, I simply don't care."

He completely understood. "Then why are you going back?"

"I need to work, Jake. I need to get busy and stay busy or I'm afraid I'll go mad." She angled her body so that she could see him better. "And, Jake, so will you if you don't do the same."

"Do you honestly think work will help?" His tone was flat, tired.

"I don't know—sometimes I think nothing will ever help again, sometimes I think I'll never feel safe again—but I think we've got to at least try." When he didn't say anything, she went on. "Jake, listen to me. Lucas was miserable out in California, unable to find out anything that was happening here until after it happened. He would call you every name in the book, but then with his next breath he would say he should have stayed with you. Jake, you didn't ask him to return. He came back because he couldn't stand not being by your side when you went after Wade."

He shook his head, rejecting completely what she was saying. "I should never have decided to go after Wade in the first place. If I hadn't—"

"If you hadn't, Lucas would have. He was so sure going on the offensive was the right thing to do. Grieve for Lucas. Remember him. But don't for a minute feel guilty."

"I don't know. . . ."

"It wasn't your fault, Jake. Believe me. Lucas loved two people in the world—you and me. And he'd be mad as hell now if he knew the beating you've been giving yourself." She chuckled. "And he'd also be furious with me if he knew I'd waited so long to tell you all this. It's just that . . . I've had my own grieving to do."

He reached for her hand. "You never have to explain to me, honey."

She smiled. "I know."

His forehead creased. "I still don't like the idea of you going back. You're not eating, and you'll be out there all alone."

"I'll be all right. I'll have my work, and now I have Lucas's businesses and property to manage."

"If you need help—"

"I'll call, and I'll expect lots of telephone calls from you too."

"Will you eat?"

"I'll try. Just like I'll be trying to do everything else. And first break I get, I'll come back to visit."

"If you don't, I'll come get you myself." At that moment something made Jake look over his shoulder. In the distance he saw Arabella, coming toward them, the two peacocks following her as if they were little lambs. She was wearing a gossamer dress of white, her arms were filled with white flowers, and she seemed surrounded by light. And suddenly he was shaken by the power and force of his love for her.

Vanessa was right. It was time to turn his back on the bitterness of the past and begin again. He looked back at her. "You'll be coming back sooner than you think."

"Why's that?"

"Because Arabella and I will be getting married."

Vanessa smiled. "For that, my darling, I will even fly."

The curtains fluttered and drifted on the night's ocean breeze. Moonlight spilled like liquid through the doors and, along with the Tiffany bedside lamps, provided the room a soft illumination. Jake leaned back against the pillows, watching Arabella. It wasn't that she was doing anything special—she was picking up here, rearranging there—but to him her every move was enchanting and wonderful.

Arabella sensed his gaze on her and couldn't help but think that tonight he seemed different. He seemed to have a level of energy that he had lacked in the last month, and she prayed he was finally coming out of his depression over Lucas's death. "Are you sad because Vanessa is leaving in the morning?"

"Yes, but I understand why she has to go." He paused. "I've made a few decisions of my own."

The silk hose she had just retrieved from the back of a chair slipped from her fingers. "I'm not sure I'm going to like what you're about to say. If you're planning on going after Wade Scalia again—"

"Yes and no. Come here."

Uneasy at his answer, she went to him and perched on the edge of the bed beside him. "Yes and no?"

"There is no way this thing between Wade and me is going to end simply. I know now that he's not going to stop until he kills me. It may not be tomorrow. It may not even be next year. But one of these days, he's going to try to kill me."

"But you haven't heard anything from him in weeks."

"That's not quite true. He's been as active as ever, trying to stop my shipments and steal my customers. I simply haven't told you. But I've finally reached the point where I've got to do something. And I'm sure he'll be waiting for me. He expects me to try to seek revenge." He shook his head. "But I can't employ the tactics that he's used up to now, not again I can't. First of all because it would make me no better than he is, and secondly, because if I took one wrong step, I'd be dead."

"Then what are you going to do?"

"I'm going to take your advice and go to the government. Before dinner I placed a call to a Treasury agent I know named Noah Calloway. I told him I'll be coming to Boston tomorrow and I want to see him."

"Jake, that's wonderful."

"Don't be too happy yet, honey. Noah is going to want to use me in some way to get Wade."

"But at least you'll have government protection." She thought for a moment. "You'll also have to give up your bootlegging. Have you considered that?"

"I'll be more than happy to give it up. My men have been keeping the operation going the last month, not me. They're good men. As soon as I talk to Noah, I'll pay them off and try to find them other jobs." He paused. "After this is all over, I want us to be married." He paused again as a sudden jab of insecurity hit him. "You did say yes, didn't you?"

"Oh, yes," she said, smiling. "I did. But, Jake, you never explained. . . . For months you were adamantly opposed to marriage. What made you change your mind?"

He exhaled a long breath. "How can I tell you this without making myself sound like a fool? I really don't think there's any way. The truth is, Edward wanted grandchildren more than anything else in the world. He wanted Deverells to carry on what he had begun."

Her expression slowly changed to one of astonishment. "You mean your decisions were based on a wish to thwart your father?"

He nodded. "I was so foolish, Arabella. Edward, however grudgingly, gave me a heritage. But I was reckless—with the heritage, with SwanSea, and with myself. I used this house like a child would a playground, and in the end brought violence to it. I also put myself in danger." He reached out and touched a lock of her hair, but his dark gaze stayed on her. "If I had continued as I was going, our future would have been over before it started, and without us SwanSea would have become nothing more than a big, empty, lonely place. There would have been no one to carry on, no children or grandchildren for us to love and to teach what I've learned. But now I see SwanSea as a place where I belong, a place that is a home and where you and I can raise a family."

Her eyes filled with tears and she didn't bother to blink them away. "Jake, you're amazing."

"You're the one who's amazing, staying with me through everything. I don't think I'll ever be able to thank you enough."

"Having you is the only thank-you I need. You've fulfilled my every wish, my every secret desire."

"And I intend to continue doing that for as long as we both live." He pressed a soft, reverent kiss to her lips, a fitting seal to a vow made in love. "I have a present for you. It's the last present I tried to give you on Valentine's Day." He pulled a small, slim, black velvet jewelry box from the drawer of the nightstand.

"I remember that box. You never showed me what was in it."

He grinned crookedly. "Because you rejected it out of hand." He flipped up the top of the box and held it out to her. "I hope you'll accept it now." A large, perfect, heart-shaped, golden-hued diamond glimmered against the black velvet and hung from a delicate golden rope. "On some level even then I knew you were my heart."

Without a word she lifted the heart from the box and gave it to him.

His hands shook as he fastened the necklace around her neck, then he brought her down to the bed with him and made love to her with a tenderness that was entirely new to him and a joy he had never even dared to imagine.

14

AN early childhood bout of smallpox had left Wade Scalia's face with scars that as he had grown older gave him a vaguely sinister look women found wildly attractive—especially when he grinned as he was doing now. "Jake, how nice of you to call. I've been wanting to tell you how sorry I was to hear about Lucas. Damned shame, but my men were expecting someone else. If you'd have let us know you were coming, we would have given you a warmer reception."

"I believe you. You would have shot me instead of Lucas."

Wade laughed. "Not really. At least not yet. I don't have what I want yet, and getting your territory from anyone but you just wouldn't be the same."

"Then I'm about to make you a very happy man. I want to make a deal."

Wade kicked back in his chair and swung his feet up on the desk, prepared to enjoy the bargaining. "What kind of deal?"

"A very good one actually—for you. I'm ready to hand my territory over to you lock, stock, and barrel."

"In return for what?"

"A percentage of your business, a very small percentage for five years. But I do feel I should get *something* out of the deal. What I'll be giving you is extremely lucrative."

Wade's fingers flexed on the base of the telephone handset as his mind raced. "How much do you want?"

"Oh, say, five percent."

"No. One percent for four years."

"Three percent."

"Two percent for two years and that's my final offer."

Jake was silent for a moment. "All right, but on one condition. I want to see your books so I'll know what I'll be getting."

His grin reappeared. "What's the matter, Jake, don't you trust me?"

"I won't even bother to answer that one."

Wade paused. "Why are you doing this, Jake?"

"I'm tired of having my possessions blown up. I'm also tired of the business. With Lucas gone, it's no fun anymore. And then there's the fact that now that

Edward Deverell has died, my responsibilities within the Deverell organization will be increasing."

"You're one lucky bastard, you know that, Jake? You've got all the money in the world, plus all those society types fawning over you. I hear you even have a society babe of your own. And you got that house that everyone talks about. Tell me something, Jake. Now that we're going to be partners—and that's definitely what we'll be since I don't show my books to anyone but a partner—will I get an invite to your house for one of those swanky parties?"

"As long as you leave Ram and Barton at home," Jake drawled.

Wade laughed, pleased. "Then I guess all that's left is for us to set up a meeting. How about three o'clock this afternoon at the old Dracini warehouse down on the river. I own it now. Come alone and bring your books."

"Fine. Just make sure you do the same." Jake dropped the receiver into its hook and looked at Arabella. "I think he bought it."

"You're not sure?"

"I'm pretty sure. He would have been suspicious if I hadn't asked for a percentage in return for the territory, because it's what he would have done. And I knew the idea of being partners with me, even in a small way, would appeal to his ego, at least momentarily." He chuckled. "He evens wants an invitation to SwanSea."

"No! I wouldn't have that man in our home!"

He reached out a long arm and brought her to him. "Say those last two words again."

She smiled and went soft against him. "Our home."

"I like the way you say that," he murmured, and pressed a warm kiss to her mouth. "Now, you're not to worry about Wade. If everything goes according to plan this afternoon, he's going to be in jail by evening."

"I wish you hadn't said if."

"I thought I just told you not to worry." He tried to adopt a stern expression, failed, and instead gave her a smile. "I'll tell you what, I have to call Noah to let him in on the plans, but afterward you and I are going shopping."

"For what?" she asked surprised.

"For chairs for our home."

Arabella clapped her hands together with delight at the sight of the carved Brazilian rosewood chairs. "Elise, I'm so happy you didn't sell the chairs."

Elise arched one perfectly penciled brow. "I kept them here in the shop as conversation pieces. Their carving is so unique. I really never had any intention of selling them"—her eyes glimmered at Jake—"unless, of course, someone came along and offered me a handsome price for them."

With a wry grin Jake reached into the inside pocket of his jacket and pulled out a checkbook. "Which I am prepared to do."

"Darling, you've always been so generous to me."

Arabella gazed around the store, wondering if Elise would like a saucer of cream to go along with that purring tone she used whenever she spoke to Jake. The woman was disgusting! Still she had to admit, however grudgingly, that if the pieces of furniture Elise had for sale were anything to go by, she had good taste. Casting a surreptitious glance at Elise and Jake, she saw them laughing quietly together. "Jake, there's a woman out on the sidewalk selling flowers. I'm going out to buy some."

About to sign the check, Jake glanced over his shoulder at her. "Fine. I'll be right out." He finished the check and handed it to Elise. "I think that should take care of any heartbreak you may suffer over the loss of the chairs."

Elise stole a discreet look at the amount and beamed. "If I can ever do anything else for you, I hope you won't hesitate to ask."

He saw Arabella through the window, standing out on the sidewalk, two bouquets of daisies in her hand. She looked like a flower herself in a pale yellow frock made up of tiers of lace that floated downward to a hem slightly longer in the back than in the front. Her pumps had been dyed the same color, and a matching lace cloche covered her lovely hair. If he lived forever, he thought, he would never stop marveling over the miracle of Arabella. "Thank you, Elise, but I don't believe so."

As he started toward the door of the shop he saw a black Packard pull up with Barton at the wheel. With pounding heart Jake broke into a run, but before he could get his hand on the doorknob, Ram jumped out and pushed Arabella into the car. By the time Jake reached the curb, the black Packard had disappeared around the corner. On the sidewalk lay two bouquets of daisies.

Jake grimly shifted his account books from one arm to the other and gazed up at the warehouse. The big, run-down structure reminded him of the warehouse in Upstate New York. Only Lucas wasn't with him this time. And he was wiser now and under no illusions as to what was about to happen. Wade was going to try to kill him.

But he had had to come. Arabella was inside, and he would do whatever he had to do to save her. Even die.

He had called Noah and lied to him, telling him the meeting had been put off until the next day. He had hated the lying, but he knew that if Wade got so much as a whiff of a T-man, he would kill Arabella.

He started toward the warehouse.

Inside the door he found a note stuck to the wall. It read: *Take the stairs.* The stairs led to a railed passageway that hugged the four sides of the warehouse. And at the end of the passageway to his right, Arabella sat tied and gagged in a chair, her golden eyes full of fear and tears.

Unable to help himself, he started toward her, knowing he was playing right into Wade's hand. But the instinct to reach her was stronger than his instinct to survive.

"Stop right there," Wade said from behind him. "I've got a gun trained on you, so don't try anything fancy."

For Arabella's sake, his tone and expression were assured. "What's the problem, Wade? I thought we had a deal."

"We do. But I've known you too long not to try to tip the scales in my favor. So I nabbed your girl to make sure you'd come alone."

"I said I would."

"Yeah, but even taking into consideration everything you told me, giving in to me is just not in your nature. Never has been."

"Oh, you mean like doing all the wrong things has always been in *your* nature?" He heard Wade take a step closer to him and smiled at Arabella. The smile was a purely reflexive action. He would smile at her with his last breath.

"You think you're so damned smart, Jake, but you're wrong. You always thought you were better than me, but you were bigger, that's all. Then Deverell came along and handed you a life I would have killed for. And you didn't even have to get your hands dirty for it. And if that wasn't enough, you had the nerve to stick your fingers into *my* business. I couldn't let you get away with that."

"Don't worry about it," Jake said with deliberate casualness, trying to defuse Wade's growing wrath.

"You didn't. Here"—he gestured with his full hands—"I brought you the books. What's more, I'm all alone. I don't know what else you could ask for."

"I'll tell you what—the two percent for two years, that's what. You're not going to get it, Jake."

"Okay, okay, you've won. Just let Arabella and me walk out of here and you'll never hear from me again."

"Oh yes I will. Every morning when I open the damned newspaper. One way or the other you're always in it, reminding me of what you have and I don't."

It wasn't any use, Jake thought. Talking was only making things worse. He knew Wade planned to kill him, but he wasn't sure what he planned for Arabella. There was one question that would tell him. "Did you even bring your books?"

"Didn't have to. I keep them in a safe here, but no one knows but me and my bookkeeper."

By giving that information, Wade had unknowingly just told him he was going to kill Arabella too. Jake took one last look at Arabella and prayed she knew how much he loved her. "Where do you want me to put my books?"

"Set them down in front of you."

He moved quickly, whirling around and hurling the heavy ledgers at Wade's arm, causing the gun to fly out of his hand. Then, using every ounce of strength he had, Jake brought his closed fist against the other man's head.

Wade staggered sideways and fell against the railing. Jake was bringing his fist around for another blow when the railing cracked. Already off balance, Wade fell, plunging to the floor below with a scream.

Stunned and winded, for a moment Jake could only stare down at Wade's still, broken body. Then Noah Calloway rushed in, several men on his heels, their weapons drawn.

Jake hurried to Arabella. Kneeling in front of her, he tore the ropes and gag from her. "Did he hurt you? Are you okay?"

"Yes, but what about you. Lord, Jake, I thought he was going to kill you!"

Her hat was gone, her dress ripped, her face blotched with tears, but he had never loved her more or seen her look more beautiful. "I'm fine. Let's go home."

A smile spread slowly across her face. "Yes, let's."

He helped her to her feet; then with his arm around her, they started back down the passageway.

Noah's gaze followed their progress. "We heard and saw everything, Jake. Sorry, but I didn't feel like I should come in until he indicated where his books were." One of his men knelt beside Wade and felt for his pulse. Then with a shake of his head he got back to his feet. Noah grimaced. "Looks like I no longer have to worry about getting an indictment against Scalia. My next worry will be whoever takes over from him. And there definitely will be someone."

"What are you doing here?" Jake asked, nearly to

the stairs. "I told you the meeting had been postponed."

"Something in your voice bothered me, so I decided we should show up anyway."

"Good work, Noah."

"Likewise, Jake."

The sun warmed Jake's skin as he knelt to place flowers on Lucas's grave. "I thought you and I would always be together," he whispered. "Just goes to show how much I took things for granted. You said I was a fool, and I was. But I've learned, Lucas. I've learned. . . . I'll never forget you."

A cool, fresh breeze blew off the ocean and across a crystal-blue sky, drying his tears. Arabella waited for him not too far way, but he had one more place to go.

He stopped in front of his father's crypt. "Looks like everything you wanted has come to pass, old man. I'm going to marry the most wonderful girl in the world and hopefully have a family with her. And I've ended up loving and respecting SwanSea as much as you did, maybe even more. Lord willing, the Deverell name will continue and SwanSea will become all you dreamed." He paused. "But I won't be doing it for you, old man. I'll be doing it for Arabella and for myself."

He turned and saw Arabella standing on a nearby hill. The breeze played around her, weaving through her golden-white hair and teasing the hem of her filmy white dress. And he understood that the sun seemed brighter because of her and so did the rest of his life.

With a smile he started toward her. And his destiny.